MELISS,

FROM
·—◄ THE ►—·
ASHES

· THE COLOSSEUM SERIES ·

For Fausta's family: she just appeared,
larger than life, as I remember her.

Have you read the Moroccan Empire series? Pick up the first in series FREE from my website www.MelissaAddey.com and join my Readers Group, so you always get notified about new releases.

The city of Kairouan in Tunisia, 1020. Hela has powers too strong for a child – both to feel the pain of those around her and to heal them. But when she is given a mysterious cup by a slave woman, its powers overtake her life, forcing her into a vow she cannot hope to keep. So begins a quartet of historical novels set in Morocco as the Almoravid Dynasty sweeps across Northern Africa and Spain, creating a Muslim Empire that endured for generations.

Download your free copy at www.MelissaAddey.com

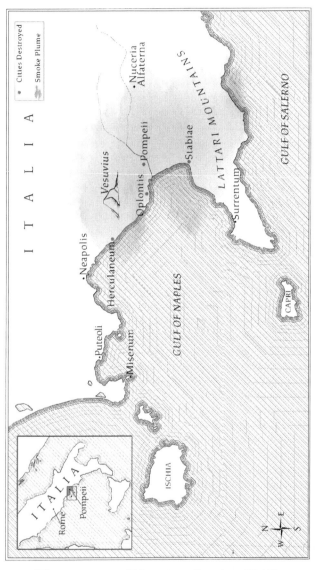

The eruption of Vesuvius, October 79AD

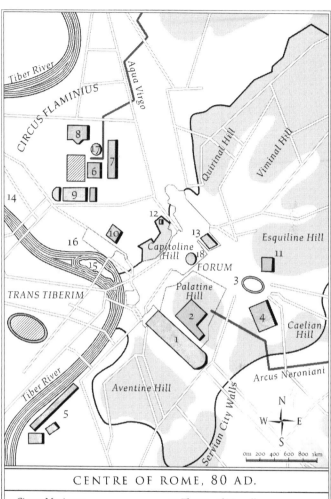

CENTRE OF ROME, 80 AD.

1. Circus Maximus
2. Imperial Palace
3. Flavian Amphitheatre (Colosseum)
4. Temple of Claudius
5. Warehouses
6. Baths of Agrippa
7. Julia Saepta
8. Baths of Nero
9. Theatre of Pompey
10. Theatre of Marcellus
11. Baths of Titus
12. Auguraculum
13. Temple of Peace
14. Stables of chariot-racing teams
15. Tiber Island
16. Virgin's Street
17. The Pantheon
18. Temple of Vesta

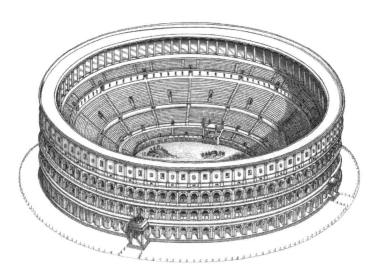

The Flavian Amphitheatre

'Roma Resurgens'

(Rome rises again)

Motto of the Emperor Vespasian, who
commissioned the Colosseum.

BRIEF HISTORICAL
BACKGROUND TO 79AD

I N 66AD THE ROMAN PROVINCE of Judea rebelled against Roman rule and drove the Romans out. Fearful that this might spark further rebellions in other provinces of the Empire, Emperor Nero recalled General Vespasian from exile (he had fallen asleep during a poetry reading by Nero) and sent Vespasian and his son Titus to quell the rebellion. This took four years, one quarter of the entire Roman army and ended in Titus' troops looting and burning the Temple of Jerusalem in 70AD. Hundreds of thousands of Jews were killed or enslaved during this period.

Emperor Nero died in 68AD, the last emperor of the Julio-Claudian dynasty. His reign was mostly associated with extravagance and cruelty, although he enjoyed some popularity among the lower classes. He had a large area of central Rome cleared to create his Golden House, a vast palace complex with a lake. Rumours said the Great Fire of 64 AD had been deliberately started by him to enable this, although he was also keen on building many cultural and public buildings.

Following Nero's death came the Year of the Four Emperors, which culminated in Vespasian taking power in 69AD and founding the Flavian dynasty, which lasted twenty-seven years.

He was the first emperor to come from the Equestrian rather than Senatorial rank and he set in motion a large number of building works, including the Flavian Amphitheatre, known to us as the Colosseum, which was located on Nero's now drained lake and largely paid for with loot from the Temple and the sale of Jewish slaves. Vespasian died in June of 79AD and was succeeded by his son Titus.

GLOSSARY

Aedile   A senator in charge of commissioning the gladiatorial games.

Atrium   Reception room in a Roman villa, often with a pool and skylight.

Bulla   Protective amulet worn by children.

Domina   Mistress

Dominus   Master

Fullery   A laundry which washed, dried and also dyed garments. Human urine was used as a cleaning and bleaching aid.

Garum   Fish sauce, a very popular condiment

Insula   Block of apartments/individual rooms, often built around a central courtyard.

Lararium   Household shrine

Lictors   Magisterial attendants/bodyguards, different ranks had differing numbers attending them, from one for a priest up to twenty-four for an emperor.

Manumission A brief ritual to set a slave free, after which they were known as a freedman/woman.

Myrmillo Type of gladiator, armed with helmet, shield, one arm-guard and an army-style sword.

Naumachia A water-based show, taking place in a lake or involving flooding the amphitheatre's arena.

Palla Large rectangular outer garment, of wool or linen, worn predominantly by married women, draped around the entire body, a fold of this could be placed over the head for protection and propriety.

Popina Streetside café (most poor city-dwelling Romans did not have cooking facilities, so street food outlets were very common and popular.)

Salutatio A morning visit from clients to show respect to their patrons.

Tablet A wooden 'book' of two or three 'pages', filled with wax, on which notes could be made using a stylus (metal pen), then erased when no longer required, while more formal, permanent writing could be done with ink and a reed/quill pen onto scrolls of papyrus, parchment or thin sheets of wood (expensive pens might be bronze or have wooden shafts and iron nibs).

Triclinium Dining room in a Roman villa

Velarium Awning for a theatre or amphitheatre

Vigiles Cohorts based in station houses in each region of Rome, acting as firefighters and police.

POMPEII, LATE OCTOBER 79AD

THE GOLDEN CUFF

"WHAT WERE YOU THINKING?"

The triclinium of my master's house looks as though it has been turned into a brothel. The wall panels, which usually depict classical scenes befitting a grand holiday villa, have been repainted entirely since this morning with images more befitting... well, a brothel. The tables are opulently laid for tonight's gathering and the couches for the guests are draped with elegant throws and plumped-up cushions, but my mistress is staring at the household slaves, who have all been stripped naked. Their newly plucked private parts have been painted in gold, the better to highlight them. They stand huddled together, faces drained with shock.

"Lucius! What were you thinking?"

My mistress is appalled. She comes from one of the best patrician families, albeit a rather impoverished and distant branch. In marrying my master, a handily wealthy import-exporter from the equestrian class, she has had to put up with many failings of etiquette over the past few years, most of which she is adept at smoothing over, but this time he has gone too far. She stands in the doorway, trying to look away from the images on the walls, which leave nothing to the imagination. Men with men, women with women, men with women, women with beasts… all in fresh, bold paint, some of it significantly larger than life. Her young daughter is coming, and she puts out an unseeing hand behind her back, seeking to push the girl away.

"To your room, Lucilla."

"But mother –"

"To your room!"

Lucilla reluctantly departs. I'd like to follow her, but my mistress is blocking the doorway and I don't want to draw attention to myself. Although I am the only slave fully clothed, I fear that my apparel might offend her even more than if I were naked. I stay still, pressed against the wall in the corner.

"Splendid, isn't it," says my master, casting a lingering glance over one of the slave boys. "It'll be a memorable evening."

"Memorable?" My mistress' eyes are bulging out of her head, her already pale skin drained white. "It looks like something organised by –" her voice drops to a hiss "– *Nero!*"

"Fit for an emperor?" he asks. Deliberately misunderstanding.

"Fit for a madman," she spits back. "I cannot be seen at such a gathering!"

"Just as well I've arranged a substitute for you then, isn't it?" he says.

My heart sinks as he gestures towards me. A look of humiliated rage grows on her face as she takes in the expensive gauzes and finely woven fabrics draped around me, my elaborately dressed hair, the gold jewellery dangling from my hair, ears, neck. A slave, dressed as though I were the rich lady of the house, about to play her part as hostess for the evening, as though it were Saturnalia when slaves become masters and masters play the fools. But this is not Saturnalia. This is an important banquet, a dinner hosted by her husband for their rich and powerful neighbours before the autumnal return to Rome, leaving their Pompeiian holiday homes behind for another year. An ingratiating attempt to be part of a class he knows secretly look down on him, and on her for marrying him, wealthy or not. And now this evening is to be staged as a debauched orgy, something from the bad old days of Nero, when anything went?

She hovers, uncertain whether she should insist on being hostess and suffer the humiliation of knowing she is being laughed at for arranging such a vulgar event, or disappear into her rooms and pretend she knew nothing about it, dismissing it with an airy laugh if anyone mentions it, "Oh *men*, they can be so crude you know, but one has to indulge their needs sometimes. Best not to enquire what goes on at their 'little dinners'!" Her face colours as she contemplates the two options and I can't help but feel sorry for her, although I know that, ultimately, she will take this humiliation out on me, since she cannot take it out on her husband. There is a final hesitation, a welling-up of tears in her eyes and then she turns her back and leaves the room, trying to keep her head high in front of the servants, although they are humiliated enough themselves at this moment. They have never been treated like this. The women and some of the younger and more attractive men have put up with occasional wandering hands from the master, as well as some of his less refined guests, but they have never been presented like this, as though they were fruits to pluck from serving platters.

"I hope you're pleased with my gift?" asks my master.

I glance down at the heavy gold cuff on my wrist. It is worth a fortune, I could live humbly for years on what it cost him. I bow my head, force the words out of my mouth. "Thank you, Dominus."

"Excellent. I must go and wash before I change, I'm sweating like a hog." He slaps the nearest girl on the behind and leaves the room.

"At least you get a gold bracelet," mutters Myrtis to me. She's the cook and my best friend. She's seething with rage. I can smell the sour reek of it coming off her in waves. Her pendulous breasts and slack belly are past their prime, she feels the gold paint as only a mockery.

I look down again at the bracelet, feel its weight.

"What in Hades was Master thinking, employing that man, anyway?" asks Myrtis.

"What man?"

"The man organising all of this. Whatever his name is…"

"Marcus," supplies Felix.

"I don't know who you mean," I say.

"The man who runs the amphitheatre."

"Runs it?"

Myrtis is losing her temper. "What are you, stupid? You think the Games happen by themselves once an editor has said what he wants? You think no-one tells the gladiators when to step out? Who to fight? Who do you think orders in the animals and advertises the shows?"

I've never really given it much thought. I rarely go to the Games. When I do, I am there under sufferance and I try to leave before midday when the criminals are executed, or at least arrive after that, if our master is intent on watching the gladiatorial shows in the afternoons. My only thought when I am at the amphitheatre is how quickly I can leave. But yes, of course, there must be a team who make the Games happen, just like at the theatre: there must be costume-makers, rehearsals for re-enacting bloody legends, that sort of thing.

"Master said he wanted a 'real show' putting on for his

4

guests," says Felix. "He said this man Marcus arranged Games with female gladiators and dwarfs last time he was at the amphitheatre."

Myrtis and I exchange glances. How vulgar. Not even proper battles, not even professional fighters fighting, and sometimes dying, like men, just speciality acts, titillation for a bored crowd who've seen it all before.

"But I was only out with the Master a few hours," I object. "How has all of this happened in one afternoon? He's repainted the *walls*."

"The *walls*? That's what's grabbing your attention in this room? Not twenty naked men and women with their tits and bits painted in gold?"

"Well, how did any of it get done?"

"The minute you and the Master went out a man arrived, with a massive team in tow. Ten painters came into this room and got to work. We were all dragged into the small baths down the road, which were empty except for us, they must have hired them out especially. There was a whole team of pluckers, and they gave us no choice about it. You should have heard Felix yell. For a big man, he's got an awfully high-pitched squeal. And an awfully tiny –"

"Shut your mouth, Myrtis," grunts Felix.

"After we'd all been plucked and washed, we were brought back to this room. And there were people waiting for us. I thought we'd be given clean robes or wear something fancier than usual, some theme, perhaps. But, oh no. Gold paint. And they had already finished the wall paintings. Though they're still wet. I've half a mind to smudge them all so the guests can't use them as instructions. Goddess Libertas, watch over us tonight, we're to be used as nothing better than whores."

There's not much I can say. It's clear that the household slaves can expect groping at the very best, or a great deal worse, tonight. I grimace. Our master, so far, has been more of a half-hearted groper than much else, and we've been grateful for it: we all know slaves who work in other houses and get a worse time of it. Looks like our time has come. "Where has this man gone who's organising all of this?"

"Oh, he dismissed the painters when they'd finished their tasks and went off to the kitchen with his own cooks. Apparently, I'm not fit to make tonight's meal, I'm just a bit of fun on the side."

"What are they serving?"

"How would I know? I told you, I'm not fit to cook a meal for his guests. After serving Domina's family for years, before she married this buffoon. I was expensive, you know. Price of three horses, they paid for me." Myrtis is clearly smarting in more ways than one.

"Should I go and see what's happening?"

"If you're allowed free rein of the house, why not? *We* were told to stay right here until the 'honoured guests' arrive."

But I am stopped by the closed door of the kitchen, guarded by a little weasel of a man, who nevertheless proves quite firm. No, I may not enter. Yes, he does know who I am. No, I may not enquire what is on the menu. Yes, his master is called Marcus. No, I may not speak with him.

"Look," he says at last, smiling as though he has been in this same situation more than once. "If I were you, I would just go back to the triclinium and wait. Everything will be taken care of. You need not worry about anything. Marcus is very experienced at this kind of thing. He will not disappoint your master."

"I'm not worried about my master," I hiss, beginning to lose my temper. "Half the slaves of this household are gathered in the triclinium, about to be groped and – and worse. I don't see *you* stripped naked and painted with gold."

He grins, showing missing teeth. "Sounds like I'm missing out." He touches my arm. "Seriously, don't worry. And tell the other slaves not to worry either. Marcus knows what he is doing, I swear on Sancus. You'll see."

AND SO, I HAVE NO choice but to wait with the others. It may be autumn, but it's warm for the time of year and there's not much of a breeze. Most of us are sweating, though whether because of the temperature or out of nerves, who knows.

There's noise from outside, the ripple of a lyre being strummed, a quick burst of chatter and then laughter. The others tense up and I find myself holding my breath. These must be the guests arriving, although they are earlier than I expected.

But when the door opens, I let out my breath in a gasp as twenty or more people stream into the room. Most are wearing light tunics, which they take off, throwing them to one of their number, who is catching them one-handed. Underneath they are naked and painted with the same gold paint our household has endured, but these newcomers seem entirely at ease in their lack of clothing. Some hold instruments: two lyres, a few flutes, various cymbals and rattles. They chatter amongst themselves and spread out across the room, arranging themselves, for the most part, closer to the dining tables. A tall, large-breasted woman, with tumbling black curly hair and olive skin bronzed from the summer, seems to be in charge, for she claps her hands together. The chatter and laughter stop, the newcomers turn to face her.

"Alright, spread yourselves out and take a partner from the

household. Remember the rules, look out for them, no funny business. Adria and Galen, hand out some rattles and castanets to anyone who doesn't get passed a serving tray. We have a little time before the guests arrive, so explain things to them, would you?" She looks around the room and her eyes narrow at the sight of me. She strides over. "Why are you dressed differently to the rest of them?"

"I'm the master's scribe," I say. "Who are you?"

"Fausta," she says, as though this explains everything. "Is it his idea of a joke to dress his slave as though she were the mistress of the house and have her host his dinner party?"

"Yes," I say.

"Seen worse," she says cheerfully. "At least you have your clothes on. That bracelet is in very poor taste, though."

This, coming from a naked woman whose vast breasts are daubed with gold, should sound absurd, but I find myself warming to her for echoing my feelings about my master's gift. "I don't really understand what is going on here," I say.

"Oh, right," she says. "Well, your master hired Marcus, so he's getting the 'Marcus treatment'."

"I don't know your master," I say.

"He runs the amphitheatre," she says. "And stages events for rich men. Like tonight. For a price."

"I gathered that," I say. "But we… this household… we have never…"

"Oh, don't worry," she says, looking around the room at her fellows, who have paired up with our household slaves, as she instructed. I notice the faces of our own staff seem to have lost their tightness. "They don't have to do much. Stand in the background mostly, making up numbers. Possibly hand out some food, shake a few rattles, that sort of thing. If they all stay well back, no harm will come to them. Any music, dancing, especially the funny business, that's all on us." She looks me over again. "Not sure about you, though," she says, doubt creeping into her voice. "I've never had a master set a slave up like you at one of these events. We'll do our best. Does he usually use you for sex? Let his friends use you?"

I shake my head vigorously.

My look of horror seems to reassure her. "Oh well," she says more confidently. "Then with any luck it won't happen tonight, either." She frowns. "Never used you at all? Unusual."

"He likes to boast that I'm Greek and can read and write better than his wife," I explain. "He likes having an educated slave, most of his household aren't, you see. So, he makes a fuss as though I'm some sort of expensive trinket. It annoys the mistress. And anyway, he prefers men, on the whole."

"She's from a family that wouldn't have thought you anything special," she says bluntly. "You get all sorts nowadays. I mean, even the Emperor isn't from a patrician family. Your master may be rich, but he must be pretty thick if he thinks he's going to impress senators just by having a Greek slave who can read and write. They're more likely to want to feel you up. But see how you go. If you get in a tight spot, look my way and I'll try to help you out."

"Thank you," I say, though I'm getting more nervous rather than less. Our household slaves position themselves behind what I'm beginning to think of as Fausta's troops, and the guests arrive.

THE EVENING IS EVERYTHING MY mistress was wary of. Nine men, no wives attending. The meal is exactly the sort of overly lavish shopping list of luxuries that only serve to give you indigestion. The fatty sweetness of roast udders, the inevitable honeyed dormice, live birds released from inside a roasted pig which create nothing but chaos as they seek to escape into the garden, fluttering madly about and shitting on the floor. Apparently, they are not enough, for the guests are also served ostrich, sea urchins and heavy wines that have not been sufficiently watered down. The guests know better than this, they will make fun of my master behind his back for his showing-off, but still they stuff their faces and belch their way through the rich cheesecake and fruit platters in ornamental designs so elaborate it must have taken the cooks all day just to lay them out. Myrtis couldn't have presented such dishes in the time, even with her assistants. The mistress is more concerned with her waistline than the master appreciates, he being something of a glutton. I wonder how many staff have been in our kitchen.

There's only one moment when my eyes dart towards Fausta. My master has me wait on him throughout the evening, expecting me to hand-feed him morsels of each dish as though he were a child. He makes a show of it, and after too much wine has been drunk, one of his guests, reclining close to where I am kneeling, puts out a hand and squeezes my breast.

"Fine girl," he slurs. "Hope you make the most of her, Lucius."

"Not as fine as me, though," comes Fausta's voice at once. She appears by the senator's side, bending over him, her gilded breasts barely a handspan from his face. "Why, she has nothing but two flatbreads under all that frippery. Not like my well-risen loaves, eh?"

The guest is distracted at once. He is allowed some caressing before Fausta adroitly moves on to fill his cup with more wine and performs a dance for him at a safe distance. I catch her eye and she grins at my grateful nod. I've already noticed more of the same going on around the room, the quickness of Fausta's troops managing to direct any unwanted attention onto themselves, then, quick as eels, extracting themselves from the worst of it, although one of the girls does disappear off with one of the distinguished guests as the evening grows late, but only after a discreet nod from Fausta.

After the dancing there's a dwarf who can juggle and then the highlight of the evening's entertainment: two well-known local gladiators who come in, oiled up and dressed in armour that looks like it's never been used in battle, all fancy details and polished to a high shine, not a scratch or dent in it. They circle the room while the men jeer or cheer, their blades fast and sharp. Blood is drawn on both sides, enough to satisfy the audience, but not, I notice, enough to cause serious injury. There's a lot of drunken arguing over who won but eventually a jokey laurel wreath and a few coins are tossed towards the victor and the two men bow out of the room, leaving the guests to be gently nudged on their way by Fausta and her team.

"Thank you," I manage to say before she leaves. She nods, adjusting the heavy folds of a toga over her tunic. The male clothing will mark her out as a prostitute on the dark streets as she makes her way home and I am worried for her, it is very late. But I see the weasel man gesture in front of him, an indication he may be about to accompany her and her troop back to wherever they live, probably in, or close to, one of the many taverns that make a profitable living selling sexual favours as a side-line.

"I told you Marcus would manage everything," says the weasel.

I look about me. "If he could manage the mistress' displeasure tomorrow when these walls remind her of this evening..." I say, grimacing.

He winks. "I think you'll find your master paid for the complete service," he says and turns away. I suppose he means that everything else has been taken care of. It is for the master to manage his own wife's response to what he ordered done. It is not the weasel or his master Marcus who will suffer for all this, so they can hardly be expected to care. At least none of our own household has suffered anything but a loss of what little pride they had. The master is happy, his guests are well fed and entertained, even if they do look down on him. Let us hope there will be no more of this kind of thing.

I'M SO EXHAUSTED I ALL but crawl onto my sleeping mat in the small room Myrtis and I share, as more senior members of the staff. Soon the birds will be singing and, not long after that, Myrtis will wake me. She has to rise early and likes someone to talk to while she prepares breakfast for the family. She's already snoring. My arm is uncomfortable, but I may not unfasten the bracelet. It has amused my master to give me an item of jewellery made in heavy gold but formed in the shape of an elaborate slave cuff, something I would be forced to wear if I were a troublemaker and standing on the slave block to be sold off. Its fastening is completed with a tiny chain and pin, which I have been warned against removing at any time, for any reason. The final detail prevents me from ever selling it to buy my freedom. On it is engraved, 'The Greek slave Althea, belonging to Lucius the garum merchant. Send her home if she has run away from me.'

JUPITER AND JUNO

THE TREMOR WAKES ME BEFORE Myrtis does. I think she is shaking me awake before I realise there is no-one there, that it is the half-dark room itself trembling. I brace in case it gets bad and I have to run, but it quickly fades away. Autumn is earthquake season in this part of the world, it's commonplace enough, although it always sparks a tiny fear that this will be the bad one, like the one that brought houses tumbling down here seventeen years ago. I was only a child in Kefalonia then but there are still plenty of buildings in Pompeii that have not yet been repaired, daily reminders of what the shaking earth can do to us, if the gods are displeased. There are cracks in the plasterwork in the servants' rooms, although those in the more important parts of the house get repaired regularly. The tremor gone, I think I should rise, but I'm so tired my eyes close again without my knowledge and when I wake the sunlight is streaming in the window. It's late.

I can barely keep my eyes open, yawning throughout dressing. My comb breaks two teeth on the tangles in my hair. I brace myself to greet my mistress, certain that she will still be offended by what has gone on in her house, readying myself to be treated spitefully in revenge. However, I cannot find her in her rooms, although her makeup is all laid out, white chalk powder for a delicate complexion dusted over her dressing table, her eyeliner and lip colour pots now closed, used applicators left out for her body slave to clean. I catch a quick glance of myself in the polished metal of her mirror, although my rippled reflection only shows how dark the shadows under my eyes are.

"Garden," says Felix when he sees me in the hallway looking for her.

I make my way back downstairs and head towards the garden, but the smell of wet plaster and paint seems even stronger this morning, which can't be right. I poke my head into the triclinium and then push the door open, amazed.

The wall panels of the room are a fresh blank white with a new coat of thin, wet plaster. There is no sign of the images that titillated our guests last night, they have vanished like a bad dream. Instead, there are two men touching up the red and gold trim that frame them, while six more and their respective assistants are busy filling the white spaces with new scenes. Two are already complete, elaborate garden scenes in the very latest intricate style, showing a variety of woodland animals and delicate flowers and plants, while the largest panel, which just a few hours ago framed a scene in which a woman was being serviced by an extremely well-endowed centaur, now features a larger-than-life image of Jupiter and Juno, gazing lovingly at one another, the very image of respectably clothed marital bliss. There is more than a hint of the mistress' lineaments to Juno's face, a suggestion of the master to Jupiter's curled locks and broad forehead. The image is everything it should be, proclaiming this household to be blessed with both high class wealth and marital wellbeing. It is almost complete. There are only another four small panels to fill up. The room will be entirely repainted by midday at the latest. The plasterers must have come the moment the guests left the room and the painters must have begun work while we were all asleep. More than that, these designs have been pre-planned to fit the space available, while Jupiter and Juno have required some prior study of our master and mistress' physiognomy. I stand gaping at the work and the painters, blinking several times in case I haven't woken up and am just dreaming.

"Help you?" asks one assistant over his shoulder.

"Who ordered this room repainted?" I ask, thinking I already know the answer.

"Marcus."

I nod and leave the room, half-tripping over Myrtis, who is all smiles. "I think I could bear to be plucked and painted from time to time, if that's the reward I get for it," she says.

"Reward?"

She fumbles in her tunic and pulls out a denarius, holding the silver coin out for my inspection. Two days' wages for a labourer, a precious sum for a slave.

"Where did you get that?"

"That little man popped in this morning, gave one to each of us. Said it was payment for our 'additional services', which luckily none of us had to provide, apart from the shame of it."

Marcus again. I know it. This invisible man has put on an extraordinary evening of spectacle and now is making all traces of it disappear, whether wall panels or the household slaves' resentment, as though it had never been.

I make my way to the garden and find my mistress sitting in the early sunshine wearing a new outfit, a long delicate woollen tunic in a pale blue. She is also sporting a new palla draped over her hair, with a trim in Tyrian purple stitched over with pearls, a level of finery I've more than once heard the master refusing to pay out for, despite his growing wealth. She's absurdly overdressed for a day at home, but she's evidently too thrilled with her new clothes not to wear them at once.

She beams when she sees me, which is not what I was expecting at all. "Althea, this is my new slave. I have named him Catulus. He is my little kitten, aren't you?" she croons to him.

"Yes, Domina," comes the obedient answer.

I look at the vast bulk of the handsome golden-haired man holding a parasol over my mistress' head. The name she has given him is ridiculous. "I did not know you had bought a new slave, Domina."

She looks up at him, still delighted. "He is a gift from your master, Lucius sent him to my rooms this morning to present me with these clothes... and himself. A little apology for his treatment of me yesterday. But that is all quite forgotten now. Have you seen the triclinium? I have been begging him for years to have it redecorated in the new style and it will be ready in time for dinner tonight. We will be able to dine elegantly at last."

I look Catulus over, wondering in what way exactly he 'presented' himself to my mistress that has left her in such a good mood. I think about the erasure of the night before and suspect that the man Marcus has had a hand in this soothing of my mistress, that he had already thought ahead and had these gifts ready to placate her: the finery and home decorations she has nagged her husband for, a handsome slave to accompany her wherever she goes, perhaps even to her bedchamber. As the weasel promised, his master has provided a complete service.

"When you're done with the master, I have letters to be written," says the mistress.

"Yes, Domina."

"I want to invite some of my friends to visit as soon as we

return home," she says. No doubt she wants to show off her new clothes as well as her new slave.

"Yes, Domina."

I make a note that I must send messages home to Rome, advising the larger household there that we will be returning in the next few days, that they should prepare the villa for our arrival. I will also let them know that we have acquired the new slave, Catulus, so that they will prepare somewhere for him to sleep.

"It will be wonderful to return to Rome," she says. "Pompeii is really quite dull at this time of year, I don't know why we have to stay till the very dregs of summer are gone, there is hardly anyone interesting left here." By interesting, of course, she means the holidaymakers, the rich senators who come here for the summer months only and leave their villas empty the rest of the year. She does not have local friends. She ignores any merchants with whom her husband does business when we are here, preferring to give little thought as to where the wealth of this household comes from, trade not being quite elegant enough for her. "I wish your master could be persuaded to have a villa in Oplontis instead," she adds petulantly. "It is so much more elegant, only the best people have villas there. Pompeii has never been the same since the earthquake. It's getting quite shabby."

"It is only a few days now, Domina," I say. She knows perfectly well why we come to Pompeii and not Oplontis; Pompeii is a trading city and one of its biggest industries is the manufacture of garum, in which my master trades. But she would like to put a greater distance between the stink of fish sauce and herself.

For myself, I will miss Pompeii a little. I like to smell the sea and live in the smaller holiday household. In Rome the household is far larger and the city, although exciting, is also exhausting, the noise and smells endlessly intruding on any peace one might hope for. And the mistress' friends are boring, rich women with nothing better to do than gossip about those less fortunate than themselves – unless they are gossiping about the new Emperor and his choice of mistress. Still, we will return here next year, as we do every summer, escaping the unbearable heat of Rome for the sea breezes and larger gardens of Pompeii, the lighter clothes and lighter way of life a relief after the constant busyness of the capital.

MY MASTER, WHEN HE EVENTUALLY rises, is greeted by a loving wife and a refurbished triclinium, as well as a household of beaming slaves. I follow him to his study after he has eaten, where I look over the bill for the evening's entertainment. It's a ridiculous sum but he seems happy enough to pay it. I know he is rising in the world, but I did not expect him to pay such a sum without blinking.

"Not every day you have a dinner like that, eh?"

"No, Dominus," I say.

"Good man that," he says, wandering off to the window, from where he can see the garden. He's silent for a while, thinking. "Send for him, will you?"

"Marcus?"

"Yes."

I send one of the slave boys to find Marcus and ask him to visit the master as part of this morning's salutatio.

"What do you want him for?" I ask.

"A thought I had." He does not say anything else, which is odd. As his scribe, I am used to hearing most of his thoughts on one subject or another, but now he is acting as though he is keeping a secret from me.

IT'S A SUNNY DAY, THOUGH the morning air holds the approaching chill of autumn. We take up our places in the receiving hall off the main atrium, the master in his chair, ensuring his toga is draped correctly, while I sit to one side on my stool, my wax tablet in hand, ready to take notes for the daily salutatio. To be honest, I rarely need to write much for these morning salutations. They are mostly only a courtesy, a respectful morning visit by the clients of my master to their patron. They enter the villa, greet him with a show of deference, perhaps ask for help or advice on a matter of business or even personal affairs. Occasionally my master will mention what favour he, in turn, might require. Then they go about their business and another client will arrive. We have fewer clients in Pompeii. In Rome the whole boring business often takes up most of the morning, not to mention the poorer clients who go from door to door with no loyalty at all, hoping for handouts. This morning I am relieved to see only three men seated in the atrium, awaiting an audience. I open my tablet and wait.

The first two men are quickly dealt with, one only offers his respects and good wishes for our safe journey home. The other asks if his son, newly sent to Rome to serve in the Praetorian Guard, might also consider my master his patron and call on him, on our return there? Lucius is all smiles, of course, of course, that would be most agreeable. I know he considers it useful to have clients in all stations of life and any who serve the Emperor are, naturally, of particular interest, for who knows what they might see or hear that might be of use? Not that a client is a spy, of course not. Yet still, a client might mention something of interest to his patron... I make a note of the young man's name. We will expect him to call on us when we arrive in Rome. I search through the pot of scrolls at my feet. There is one which lists all of my master's clients, one for here and one in Rome. I will add the name to the list in Rome when today's salutatio is done.

"Marcus!"

I let go of the scroll and look up. The man walking into the room is taller and more handsome than I had expected. I had thought he would be more like the weasel, but he looks like an army officer. Dark brown hair, olive skin burnt brown by the sun. His blue tunic is clean, but he is not wearing a toga, as though his work does not allow for such impractical clothing, and I notice that his plain leather shoes are worn at the heel. A man who walks a lot, I think, although with a noticeable limp.

"Take a seat," says Lucius. "Will you join me in a little refreshment?"

Myrtis has sent up fresh grape juice, from the very last pressing of the harvest, now completing all across the slopes of Mount Vesuvius, its rich black soil the most fertile in the area. She has also provided a platter of her own just-baked honey cakes, the recipe for which she guards with her life. Every cook makes honey cakes, but Myrtis adds some combination of spices to hers, which are often remarked on for their delicate flavour. Marcus takes the offered seat and refreshments. As he sits, I see the horizontal scar on his upper calf, a faded white with a purple tinge that speaks of a deep wound, even if a long time back. I imagine a sword slashing at him while his back was turned.

"I trust everything was to your satisfaction last night," he begins.

"It most certainly was," says Lucius, beaming at Marcus. "Most certainly. Everything you promised, and more."

Marcus smiles. "I am glad to hear it," he says. "And I remain at your service for any future occasions."

"I appreciated your attention to details," says Lucius. "In particular the way you ensured a harmonious conclusion to the festivities."

Thank you for placating my wife with pretty clothes, a redecorated dining room and a muscled personal slave, I think. Thank you for ensuring I do not get nagged to death over the next few months, nor have surly-faced slaves smarting from their treatment, dragging their feet over household chores.

Marcus makes a small gesture of dismissal. "Anyone can bring in a cook and a few entertainers. But a man such as yourself requires more forethought than that. You should not be troubled by anything; you should only enjoy yourself."

"I most certainly did," says Lucius, still beaming. "As did my guests."

There is a brief pause, in which they both sip their juice.

"The wine should be a good vintage this year," says Marcus. "The rain fell at the right time in the summer for the grapes to swell and there have been no late rains to water down the sweetness."

Lucius nods, but he seems to be mulling something over. "I have a possible job for you," he says.

"I am all ears," says Marcus.

"It is not an evening's entertainment," says Lucius. "It is perhaps the greatest job of your life, if you agree to it."

I frown. Lucius does not usually exaggerate. Even when he buys and sells, he is not as given to hyperbole as most of his competitors, leading to him having a reputation as a fairly honest man, which is perhaps why the mistress' family overlooked his lack of glorious ancestry in their search for someone to shore up their fading fortunes.

"You will have heard of the Flavian Amphitheatre," says Lucius.

"Commissioned by Vespasian," says Marcus, nodding. "Shame he did not live to see it completed."

"Yes," says Lucius. "It is nearing completion now, though. They say it will be ready next year and Emperor Titus wishes to inaugurate it with one hundred days of Games to honour his father and entertain the people of Rome. It is supposed to seat more than fifty thousand spectators. I have seen it myself; it will be the greatest amphitheatre in the empire. There is nothing like it."

I think of the vast building site in the centre of Rome that has been a nuisance to all for the past seven years. There isn't a person in Rome who doesn't know someone working on it in some capacity or other, from officials dealing with its commission to architects, traders, stonemasons and slaves. The noise and dust and the endless, endless cartloads of wood, stone and concrete being delivered have been a distinctly unwelcome addition to the Forum for years, although the muttering critics held their tongues as the building soared above them, imposing its gleaming presence above the working ants scurrying below. Now that it is close to completion there is more praise for it, a discreet jostling over how one might attend the inaugural day of Games. To be able to boast that one was there will no doubt carry some social clout for many years to come.

Marcus' eyes have narrowed slightly. "How may I be of service?" he asks.

There are many things Lucius might be about to suggest: from an inaugural dinner, perhaps even with the Emperor Titus as a guest of honour, or possibly the use of Marcus' team in creating an element of the spectacle.

My master turns up his lips in a smug smile. "I happen to know the Aedile tasked with selecting a manager for the Flavian Amphitheatre," he says and, even as he speaks, I see a slight flush on Marcus' neck, his eyes widening. "He has been racking his brains as to the choice that would best please the Emperor. It is a vast task. There is less than a year left until the opening and think of what must be put in place just for the inaugural ceremony, let alone one hundred consecutive days of Games to follow. And after those one hundred days, why, my friend tells me the Emperor will expect perhaps two hundred days of Games each year. Think of the animals, the gladiators, not to mention all the other –" he waves his hands vaguely, "– scenery and tickets and musicians and whatnot. My friend will be delighted that I have found him a suitable man for the job. It is your attention to detail they will most appreciate. We had heard that you might be the right man for the task. The dinner last night was a small test."

I know who Lucius' contact is, of course: his own patron, a senator vaguely related to the mistress. He spotted Lucius as a promising young man and has guided him through various stages of his life, not least of which was arranging a suitable match whereby Lucius would step a little closer to a patrician family, while shoring up that very family with his considerable trading prowess and growing wealth. Recently, the senator nudged Lucius in the direction of even more high-placed contacts, the guests at the dinner party. In return, as a loyal client, Lucius is about to fix the senator's problem of finding a man who can manage the monstrosity of a job that will fall to the manager of the Flavian Amphitheatre. There is a real chance of securing imperial favour if this goes well, and my master has just seen Marcus prove himself as a man with an eye for detail and a flair for spectacle. Now I know why Lucius did not blench at the bill. The money came from the imperial purse.

Marcus is very still for a moment and then he gives a half-smile. "You are more than kind to offer me the opportunity," he says. "But I had intended to retire from my work soon and move to the countryside near Puteoli. There is a farm I wish to purchase, I have been saving towards it. Another few years in my role here and I will be ready to move. My wife and I want a quieter life."

"If you can successfully deliver the inauguration and the hundred days of Games you will be richly rewarded in less than two years," says Lucius. "You will be able to purchase whatever farm you wish and live out your days in comfort."

Again, there is that slight hesitation but also a flicker of interest. "It would be a great honour," says Marcus. "But it is also a vast enterprise."

"Come now," says Lucius. He has found the right man to please his patron and he is not about to let him go easily. "I know you could handle it. Why, they gave you the amphitheatre of Pompeii to manage ten years ago when it re-opened after the ban. You must have been a mere stripling then and yet there has been no more trouble at all."

Marcus gives a rueful smile. "I was already thirty," he says. "I am past my prime. Time for me to take on a gentler life, not out all hours of the day and night, nor trying to manage gladiators and actors."

And whores, criminals and weasel-like assistants, I think. A disreputable class.

"Nonsense," says Lucius. "You're a man who has proven himself, both under command and commanding, and now you can reap the rewards of your efforts. A couple of years creating the very greatest spectacles for the Flavian Amphitheatre and you can retire to your farm. Think on it."

Marcus rises as though he's been dismissed. "I shall do so and call on you tomorrow, if I may," he says courteously.

"Of course, of course." Lucius beams as though Marcus has already agreed. "Let me walk you to the door."

I watch them go. Lucius never walks anybody to the door unless there is something he wishes me not to hear, which is very rarely. I can't imagine what he would have to say to Marcus that I shouldn't hear, unless of course he's arranging some sort of dubious tryst with Fausta, or one of the women in her team. I shrug. Not my business. I'm just grateful he doesn't use me in that way, which I'm well aware would be more likely in some other household. Instead, I make a few notes in my tablet, then store it away along with the scrolls for later.

"What did you mean, after the ban?" I ask Lucius when he returns from waving off Marcus.

"Oh, it was a while back now," says Lucius. "Must be twenty years ago. There was a gladiatorial show in Pompeii's amphitheatre and there were taunts in the crowd between the locals and the people of Nuceria, you know how they despise one another. Taunts led to stone throwing and then one sharp stone too many led to knives being drawn and things got out of hand. The locals dished out rather too much of a beating and next thing was Rome had cartloads of wounded Nucerians arriving, not to mention hearing about bereavements. Emperor Nero had an inquiry held by the consuls and when the report came back the Senate barred Pompeii from holding any games for ten years. Of course, there was the odd show here and there, but nothing substantial. When the amphitheatre re-opened, Marcus was chosen to manage it. He should have been in the army still, but he was released early after a wound to the leg. But he was used to commanding and they didn't want any funny business happening again so they thought an army man would be a good choice. Anyway, it's been ten years since then and the crowds have been perfectly behaved."

I think of the raucous nature of gladiatorial audiences, the yelling and betting and odd fistfights that go on. Hardly what I'd call perfectly behaved, but I suppose if there's been no serious breakouts of trouble Marcus can be said to have done a good job. "I can't imagine the amount of organisation that would go into running the Flavian Amphitheatre," I say. "Just to get a slave to run from one end to the other with an instruction would take longer than your meeting with Marcus this morning."

Lucius laughs. "He'll need good organisation, that's for sure. Tomorrow morning, have your writing materials to hand. There'll be a contract to write."

"You're awfully sure of him saying yes," I say.

Lucius is already walking away from me. "Who could refuse what I am offering?" he calls back.

I nod slowly to myself. Certainly, such an offer comes only once in a lifetime. The question is, whether this Marcus seeks further adventure after a dangerous life in the army, followed by managing an already-busy amphitheatre, rather than the peaceful life he claims to desire. Anyway, I have been dismissed for now, so I make myself scarce. Out of sight means out of mind, as all slaves know. Lucius doesn't really need me much. He has another scribe back in Rome for his day-to-day business. I am mostly used as an adornment and for social matters.

I AM EARLY FOR THE next morning's salutatio, curious to know what Marcus' decision will be. I lay out papyrus, ink and reed pens as well as my wax tablet and stylus. If Marcus agrees right away, there will need to be some sort of contract, or at the very least a letter of introduction, depending on whether he travels to Rome with us in eight days' time or goes ahead of us. It sounds like the role has an element of haste to it. If there is no manager already in place for a vast arena due to be inaugurated next summer, time must be running out for all the organising that will need to be done if imperial wrath is not to fall on the heads of several people. I wonder whether the weasel assistant will accompany Marcus if he takes up the role.

My master is late; four men are already waiting to see him, none of them Marcus. I tap my foot against the floor in boredom and wonder whether perhaps he has taken against the idea, whether he will come in person to turn down the role.

Eventually Lucius arrives, yawning and somewhat more ruffled than usual. Maybe the mistress welcomed him into her bedroom last night, an uncommon occurrence. He disposes of the clients in quick succession, leaving me with little to do but watch the faint autumnal drizzle in the garden. The mistress is right, it's time we were headed back to Rome. Pompeii is hardly a fashionable place to stay late into the autumn. There's a chill to the mornings, a heavy mist over Mount Vesuvius which doesn't clear till the sun is high in the sky, the frequent tremors.

"Marcus! I thought you were not coming!"

"That would be gross ingratitude," he replies, running a hand through his hair to remove the wet from it. "I was delayed by the late arrival of some new animals. I had to ensure they were safely locked up. Can't have a lion on the loose." He smiles, nods at me and sits himself down in the chair opposite Lucius. "I see Althea is ready with her papyrus."

I don't recall him being told my name.

"So is the answer yes?" asks Lucius.

Marcus hesitates, as though conscious of what he is agreeing to. "Yes," he says, and then more formally, "I will take on the role of Manager of the Flavian Amphitheatre, as you have asked of me. I am grateful for your patronage in this matter and offer you my loyal friendship."

I make a note. Marcus will now be a client of my master; I will be seeing him regularly at the daily salutatio when we return to Rome. Lucius has given him the opportunity of a lifetime; he will expect considerable gratitude in return. The term 'friendship' means a great deal more than that in this context. I hide a smile. I can tell Lucius is already envisioning front-row seats at the inauguration of the Amphitheatre, regardless of his lack of senatorial rank. And quite possibly more dinners in his own home arranged by Marcus, no detail left to chance.

"Althea?"

I look up. My master and Marcus are looking at me. "Sorry, Dominus," I say. "Just making a note."

"Draft a letter to the Aedile," says Lucius grandly. "Explain that Marcus Aquillius Scaurus will be taking on the role he asked me to fill. Ask him to have his scribes draw up a binding contract. Get it ratified by the imperial household and delivered to the Amphitheatre where Marcus can sign it. We will send the letter ahead by the Imperial Post since it is a matter that concerns the Emperor." I can tell that he is proud to be able to say such things, that his missives will use the Imperial Post, restricted to matters of importance. "Marcus will leave tomorrow," he adds. "By the time he has reached Rome, and made some preliminary plans, the contract will be ready. His family can join him later on."

I nod and set to work. It does not take me long. Most of it

is taken up with elegant forms of address and literary flourishes to make Lucius sound more important than he is, his securing Marcus a stroke of genius. I note Marcus' nickname, Scaurus, *Lame*, no doubt a reference to his past wound, and the limp it has left him with.

Lucius looks it over, affixes his seal and signs.

"I have two fine horses you can use," he says to Marcus. "They will make the journey more pleasant. You are sure you do not wish to travel with my own family? We will set off in eight days. I only have a few last trading meetings here."

"Thank you," says Marcus. "There will be so much to do, and I would prefer to travel at a faster pace than will be comfortable for your household, especially your lady wife."

He has a point. My mistress likes to travel in vast luxury, visit everyone she can think of along the way, and complain about the journey regardless. It often takes us as many as ten days to travel to Rome, although most people do it comfortably in six and it can be done in three at speed. I'm not sure why Marcus would need two horses though. Perhaps the weasel assistant will accompany him.

Lucius nods. "As you wish," he says affably. "And now about Althea."

"If you are sure," says Marcus.

I frown. What have I to do with this?

"Absolutely," says Lucius. "She is all yours."

I stare at my master in shock.

"Althea, you will need to draw up one last contract for me," says Lucius. "Write this down. 'The Greek slave Althea, scribe, formerly belonging to Lucius Hirtuleius Dives, is now bestowed upon Marcus Aquillius Scaurus and henceforth will be known as his slave. She will perform whatever services shall be required of her by her new master. She is given by Lucius Hirtuleius Dives in recognition of Marcus Aquillius Scaurus becoming the manager of the Flavian Amphitheatre and to mark the new friendship and loyalty between them.' Add whatever else is needed. Three copies."

I do not move. I stare at Lucius and then at Marcus.

"I am not sure Althea was aware of our agreement," says Marcus, his eyes steady on mine. "Are you willing, Althea? Lucius has told me he does not need two scribes, and I will most certainly need a scribe I can rely on if I am to run the Flavian Amphitheatre."

"Of course she's willing," says Lucius, waving for refreshments and moving to a less formal seating area. "Bored rigid working for me. Why, there's hardly anything to do. She'll be kept busy working for you. She's a good girl," he adds as an afterthought. "Doesn't have to be told things twice. Bought her from a very good household. Classy. Untouched, too, I can vouch for that. By the way, no offence but I will ask her to write in a *ne serva* clause. Given, you know, your line of work. Althea, add that in."

Marcus ignores him. "Are you willing?" he asks me again.

I look at Lucius, who is eating a honey cake while the wine is poured. He is oblivious to me, for I have been gifted to Marcus. I am no longer his slave, therefore I am of no further interest. I try to think what it will be like to approach my master's house in Rome as a visitor, to attend with Marcus as he pays his respects in the morning salutatio, since my master will have become his patron. I cannot imagine it at all. Will I see Myrtis again, or only watch her honey cakes being served, without being able to taste them? And as for my new master: what do I know of him? Nothing, except he is a man who will arrange for a houseful of slaves to be stripped naked and painted in gold if it pleases his clients, a man who works with beasts and gladiators and whores for a living.

I look into Marcus' eyes and all I can think is, at least he asked. At least he asked if I was willing, even though whether I am willing or not is irrelevant. I swallow.

"I am willing," I say so quietly that Marcus has to read my lips. But he nods.

"She agrees," he tells Lucius, moving over to sit beside him, accepting a glass of wine.

"Of course she does," says Lucius. "Draw up the contract, there's a good girl," he says over his shoulder. "She knows Rome like the back of her hand," he adds. "Her father was a scribe too, passed it on to her."

I start writing out the document, my startled mind wandering so that I nearly write the wrong words. I focus again, reflecting on Lucius' casual 'passed it on' as though my father's careful hours of tuition of me, his only child, were a mere trinket rather than the only legacy he could offer me, a skill he knew would elevate me above most slaves. My own diligent practise of calligraphy, shorthand, reading such books as I had access to in order that I might hold my own with an educated master... The document is complete. It includes the *ne serva* clause, so that Marcus cannot pimp me out as a whore, although it does not stop him using me for his own desires, should he so wish, of course. I make two additional copies. "I am finished, Dominus," I say, holding the first papyrus out, uncertain of which man I am addressing.

Marcus stands, takes the documents and my pen and inkpot from me, adds his own name and imprints his seal in the wax I have prepared, then passes each copy to Lucius, who does the same.

"You may go and pack," Marcus says to me. "I live in the

31

insula by the gladiator barracks. When you have your things come and find me there, anyone will know my name."

I wait for Lucius to dismiss me before I realise that he is not going to speak to me, is not going to bid me farewell. I have been given a command by my new master, and I must obey him.

"Yes, Dominus," I say, backing away from them both.

"SOLD? WHAT DO YOU MEAN, sold? Who is there to sell you to?"

"Marcus."

"Who?"

"The man who arranged the dinner."

Myrtis stares at me.

"You're burning the bread," I tell her. Acrid smoke is filling the room.

Myrtis snaps back to the flatbreads she was cooking on a griddle and flips the burning one off and onto the floor, half-charred, half-raw. "Sold? To him? What for? What have you done?"

"I need to pack," I tell her. "Can you come to our room?"

"Oy! You!" Myrtis calls to one of the slave girls podding beans. "Get through this lot." She indicates the floured board with balls of dough waiting to be shaped into flat circles and cooked. "Don't you burn any," she adds.

I fill her in as we make our way to the sleeping quarters. Once there, I look about me helplessly.

"Spare tunic," says Myrtis.

"Am I allowed to take extra clothes?" I ask her.

Myrtis shrugs. "Domina won't notice, what does she care about some old tunic?"

The chest we share for our belongings is hardly full. I pull out my leather satchel in which I keep my writing implements when we travel, and shake it out, dislodging a small scorpion which scurries away to hide in a crack in the wall. I pull out my spare tunic, identical to the one I'm wearing, a pale blue down to my ankles. I'm already wearing my shoes, my only leather belt is round my waist and a pink headwrap holds up part of my hair. I have another headwrap in brown, which I pass to Myrtis, who is folding my tunic. In Rome I had a thick brown cloak for winters, but we only have our summer clothing here.

"Don't forget your essentials," says Myrtis.

I take out a small linen bag containing a few pairs of underwear as well as the felt pads I use when I bleed and push it to the bottom of my satchel. It's not something I'd care to have fall out by accident in front of a man. Myrtis passes me my tunic and headwrap and I add my tablet, stylus and inkpot, making sure the lid is tightly closed so there are no leaks. I cannot take fresh scrolls of papyrus with me, so Marcus will need to purchase some. At the bottom of the chest is a small bundle, wrapped in a red cloth. I unroll it and look down at the reed pen. I never use it; it was a gift from my father on the day he told me he would make a scribe of me. The red cloth was my mother's headwrap. I run my fingers over them for a moment, while Myrtis watches me, then wrap them back up and put them in the satchel.

"Take this, too, yours is all broken," says Myrtis, handing me her own wooden comb. Some past suitor has carved her name into it.

"I can't take that."

"I can get another," says Myrtis grandly. "You don't want your new owners thinking you're a slattern because you don't comb your hair properly, do you?"

"Thank you," I say, and she shrugs as though it is nothing,

33

although a gift from a slave who has barely any possessions is a precious thing. I tuck it away. Everything I have fits into this tiny bag, as wide as my forearm and hand.

"At least it's light," says Myrtis, her voice too cheerful and loud. "Don't want to be dragging stuff about, do you?"

I blink.

"I suppose you can't keep a new master waiting, can you? Best be off."

I swallow and nod.

"Although I should feed you up first," she says, pulling me down the stairs and back to her kitchen. "I mean, you never know how a master will treat you, do you? Half of them practically starve their slaves, we all know that. It might be your last good meal for a while."

She forces two freshly cooked flatbreads and almost a quarter of a cheese down me, followed by her honey cakes and then dates and figs, a handful of new walnuts she gets one of the girls to shell.

"I really can't eat anymore," I say, although I want to, even though my stomach's painful with too much food. I want to stay here, in Myrtis' domain, in the too-small smoky kitchen, eating her good food.

Myrtis turns her back on me, her shoulders heaving.

I hug her from behind, my own tears falling, in sadness at leaving her and fear at the unknown future. "You'll have to come and see me at the amphitheatre," I say into her back. "When it opens."

"Oh absolutely," she says, turning to face me, wiping the tears and snot off her face with the back of her hand and trying to smile. "I like a good show in the arena. Handy with a sword, are you?"

I snort and wipe my eyes. "More of a beast-hunter, if I'm honest," I say. "Lion-killing and such."

"Oh, that will be worth a look," says Myrtis. "I hear lions like a good meal."

"Where's Felix?"

Myrtis' shoulders drop. "Got sent on an errand."

I nod. "You'll tell him I said goodbye," I manage.

"Nah, he'll only think you fancy him if I tell him that," she says and we both try to laugh.

I stand a moment too long, then nod to the kitchen slave girls, who have been watching. "Goodbye."

"Goodbye," they chorus.

"May Libertas watch over you and lead you to freedom one day," says Myrtis to me.

"And you," I say. I look about me but there is no other way to delay, no other excuse to make.

"Do I have to say goodbye to the mistress?" I ask.

"I doubt it," says Myrtis, unwilling to follow any niceties. "She never really liked you anyway. You're too pretty. Made her look old."

I shake my head at her. "I'll go out the back, then," I say.

There's a small doorway out the back of the house, rather than the grand gateway into the front. This is the route we slaves take when we nip out on errands, our lazy guard dog doing little to keep it safe. Good thing it has a bolt on it at night. I scratch Theridamas behind his ears and he rolls over, showing me his belly.

"Useless mutt," says Myrtis.

I step out onto the pavement, looking up at Myrtis.

"Now, just because you're working for that Marcus, don't let me see you with your bits painted gold," she says.

"Thought that was your line of work."

"Be off with you, you cheeky girl."

I step backwards. "Goodbye then."

"Goodbye," she says. "Go with Libertas."

I HAVE TO WIPE AWAY more tears when I get around the corner and onto the main street. I try to cheer myself thinking I will see her again. The amphitheatre is only a short walk away from Lucius' house in Rome. If Marcus will give me a little free time now and then I can easily go to see her, and I know she won't be able to resist checking up on me.

I'm so busy thinking, I almost get run over by an oxcart as I cross the street and its owner yells at me. After that I try to keep my mind on where I'm going. It feels strange to have left Lucius' house and know I will no longer live there. To be heading to a new house, one I can't yet imagine but which will surely not be as grand. Lucius' house, near the northern wall of Pompeii, may not be as grand as the villas in Oplontis are rumoured to be, but it's certainly a cut above any normal merchant, a sign he is on his way up in the world. Marcus' home is near the gladiators' barracks, down by the Stabian Gate, on the opposite side of town, just before the southern walls.

I walk past the brothel SheWolves, though not quickly enough to avoid a few lecherous comments from men nearby, and to notice some of the larger lewd graffiti scrawled on the walls, including, 'Gaius recommends Cincinnata, she's hairy but you won't be disappointed.' Further down the street are the still-decrepit Stabian Baths, as yet unrestored after the earthquake, only the women's section still in use. By now I can see the main theatre with its smaller sister next to it. Gladiators often train there; their most ardent fans watch even the training of their favourites, checking their progress, studying their form for later gambling success.

The two-storey insula opposite the barracks has seen better days and looks highly disreputable. Once a rich man's house, it was bought up by an enterprising property speculator and converted into smaller flats with partition walls so thin a man could punch a hole in them, the landlord now coining in the rent. I hesitate before entering the small courtyard, the building's former atrium when it was a single family's home. Inside is chaos. Chickens and dogs are everywhere, as are numerous poorly clad children and rough looking men. The two women I see look harassed, grabbing at a passing child to give them chores or a clip round the ear, dragging large baskets of wet laundry which they're trying to hang up without it getting dirtier than it was before they washed it.

"Help you, pretty one?"

I step back from a man who's towering over me, his arm reaching out to clasp my bum. "I'm looking for Marcus Aquillius Scaurus."

The man pulls back his hand as if I've burnt him. "Scaurus? You know him?"

"I'm his scribe."

The man takes a step back. "Oh well, no offence meant. Didn't know you was Scaurus'. No offence taken, I hope."

I shake my head. Marcus clearly has a reputation round here if a man like this is afraid of offending him. "I was trying to find him."

"Down by the barracks, love. Most likely, this time of day. You want me to take you there?"

"No thank you," I say. "I can find my own way."

"Right you are."

We both back away with relief. I had hoped to avoid the barracks for fear of meeting just such a man, but it looks as though I have little choice. I don't know which apartment might be Marcus', so I'm better off finding him first.

I can hear the loud crack of practice swords even from outside the barracks. When I mention Marcus' name to the porter sitting inside a small room watching over the entrance, he waves me through. Inside the noise is deafening. The vast courtyard is full of men and fighting equipment. Most are fighting with wooden weapons, so as to avoid unnecessary injuries or any sudden uprisings, but a few have real blades. There's a lot of cursing and shouting and I creep round the edge of the colonnade, hoping to spot Marcus somewhere. In one corner I come across a billboard painter, working on two large boards. One is an old one, the paint flaking off it after months being displayed in all weathers, which reads, 'Twenty pairs of gladiators provided by Quintus Monnius Rufus are to fight at Nola, May First, Second, and Third. There will be a hunt.' The sign is completed with a dramatic close-up painting of a gladiator lying on the ground, covered in blood, begging for mercy, while the victor leans menacingly over him with his sword, waiting to dispatch him. The new board is almost complete and proudly proclaims, 'Thirty pairs of gladiators provided by Gnaeus Alleius Nigidius Maius quinquennial duumvir, together with their substitutes, will fight at Pompeii on November 24, 25, 26. There will be a hunt. Hurrah for Maius the Quinquennial! Bravo, Paris! There will be awnings.' I'm aware that there's a local actor called Paris who's a bit of a celebrity and I assume it's his likeness that the painter is currently portraying: a handsome man being depicted with very little armour on. If he's an actor, he'll be part of some pre-fight show rather than the main event.

"The ladies like them painted with a bit less on, if you catch my drift," winks the painter, catching me watching him. "Are you looking for someone?"

"Marcus Aquillius Scaurus."

"Scaurus? Over there."

"Hello, Althea." Fausta has found me. She's in her toga, hands on her hips, looking as if she owns the place.

"Hello," I say, a little awkwardly. I don't know what status I should be giving her. As far as I know she's a prostitute, but Marcus seemed to have put her in charge at the dinner party and here she looks fully in command.

"Heard Marcus was given you as some sort of sweetener to seal the amphitheatre deal," she says.

"Yes," I say.

"You pleased about that, or pissed off?"

"I don't know," I manage.

"Not sure about the rough crowd he hangs out with?"

"I suppose."

"Including me," she grins, watching the men.

"You helped me out," I say.

"Don't worry, he isn't going to use you at events like that. He really will need a scribe, if he's going to manage that place." Her face twists. "Be sorry to lose him, though. Best manager this dump's ever had. They'll replace him with some cut-throat bribe-taker who's just in it for as much money and women as he can get."

"Is he a good master?"

"Yes," says Fausta without hesitation. "He knows what he wants and if you can do what he asks and do it well, he'll treat you with honour. Mind you," she adds, "You screw him around and he'll have you out of here so fast you won't know what happened and you'll only have scars to help you work it out."

I nod.

"Met Livia?"

"Who's Livia?"

"His wife."

"No."

"Good woman," says Fausta. "Her family were appalled she married him, think he isn't respectable. But she knows what he's really like and she knows he's headed for better things."

"Like the Flavian Amphitheatre?"

"Nah, that'll be more of the same but worse, won't it?" she says. "He wants to leave it all behind and get his family farm back."

"He mentioned that," I say.

"He mentions it all the time," says Fausta. "I think he dreams about it at night. He won't rest until he – WATCH YOURSELF, YOU IDIOT!" she suddenly bellows, startling both me and the painter, who curses under his breath at the slip of the paintbrush that's just given his handsome gladiator an extra thumb. Fausta's already picked up the spear that landed too close to comfort and hurls it back at one of the men, making him duck to avoid it.

"Throws like a man," comments the painter, now painting over his mistake. "Like to see her in an arena."

"Bet you would," says Fausta. "You wouldn't last one round against me."

The painter shrugs, unoffended. "I'm a good painter, I'd make a poor gladiator," he says.

"You're not bad, I suppose," Fausta allows, looking down at his work. "Right, Althea, let's go get Marcus."

MARCUS IS STANDING WITH HIS arms folded, watching two men fighting. Their trainer is next to him.

"Bit more flair," Marcus is saying. "He's got to learn what fighting looks like in the top tier seats. You need bigger movements. It's not about getting a quick dagger under the ribs, it's a sword heading for the throat in the biggest arc you can manage."

"Was army-trained before he got in trouble," says the trainer. "He's fighting to kill."

Marcus shakes his head. "He'd better unlearn that fast," he says. "This is about spectacle and showing off technique. I need blood here and there but neither you nor I want 'to the death' fights unless we've advertised it. Waste of good men. Still, he's got army style and height, strong arms. Might make a good myrmillo gladiator."

The trainer nods. "I'll put him with one of the more experienced ones," he says. "He'll get the hang of it."

"Better do," says Marcus. "Tell him he wants a long life in the arena, not a short one. That's for the criminals." He catches sight of Fausta and me coming towards them. "I'll leave you to it," he finishes.

"Your girl found you," says Fausta, gesturing to me.

"Well done," he says. "Did you find my house?"

"No," I say. "A man said you would be here."

"I must be too predictable in my movements," he says, then turns to Fausta. "Still here? Thought you were taking a boat to Misenum?"

"Off shortly," she says.

"And you'll be back when?"

"Only going for a few days, keep the old man happy."

"We'll be leaving tomorrow morning, so I won't see you for a while," he says.

"I'll be sure and mess things up," she says, grinning.

He claps her on the shoulder as though she were a man. "Couldn't if you tried. I've left it in too good order."

"I'll give it a try," she says.

He laughs. "I'll miss you, Fausta," he says. "Fortuna bring you luck. And may your journey be blessed by Neptune."

"I will pray to Janus that your new beginning is successful," she says. "And I will make sure Livia has everything she needs when she sets out to join you."

"Thank you," he says. "Have fun with the old codger. Show him a good time."

"He gets what he pays for," she grins back. She walks away, exchanging the odd jest with the men as she passes them.

Marcus watches her go, then turns to me. "I'll take you home to Livia," he says. "Your new mistress should at least see you before we set off for Rome."

"Yes, Dominus," I say.

"Call me Marcus," he says. "I don't stand on ceremony."

I nod, though I am not quite sure I can bring myself to call him a name normally reserved for his family and close friends. I assume his nickname annoys him as it refers to his damaged leg, though most nicknames are hardly complimentary. "Who will run the amphitheatre here when you're gone?" I ask.

"Only the gods know that. Fausta ought to, she's been my right hand all these years, but they won't let a woman run it, so whoever takes over better make a friend of her, and fast."

"Where is she going?"

"Misenum. There's a rich old general who holidays there, he's had a soft spot for her ever since he was a young officer in the army. Couldn't marry her of course, she was a slave working in a brothel and he came from a well-off family, but he set her free so she could manage her own clients and he turns a blind eye to what she does when she's not at his side. She visits him for a few days now and then, comes back with pink cheeks and a new gift of jewellery. He'd have her as a mistress, I don't doubt he does love her and she him, in her own way, but Fausta's not suited to a soft life. She really is a she-wolf."

THIS TIME IT'S EASY TO enter the courtyard, I simply follow in Marcus' wake; the crowd parts easily for him, nods and greetings on all sides. We make our way up a sturdy outer staircase to the first floor, where a small wiry mutt meets us, first with wild barks, then with bouncing enthusiasm as it recognises its master. Marcus gives it a quick pat and then pushes open the door to an apartment.

"Livia!"

A woman appears from another room. "Marcus." She is small in stature, shorter than I am and delicately built, with hazel-coloured hair, surprisingly light for a local woman. There are a few late flowers tucked into her plaited bun. Behind her follows a little boy, who waddles keenly towards Marcus, before stopping short at the sight of me and grabbing hold of his mother's tunic. Livia laughs. "Oh, not so bold after all?"

Marcus kneels to coax the child forward. "Come, boy."

The boy plucks up his courage and flings himself into Marcus' arms, narrowly avoiding falling. Marcus lifts him and turns him to look at me. "Althea," he pronounces carefully. The baby stares at me. I offer a smile and he hides his face in his father's tunic, clasping his protective bulla for courage.

"You are welcome to our home," says Livia to me, smiling.

I bow my head to her. "Domina," I say.

"Come and help Anna make supper," she says. "She will explain anything you need to know about the household."

I follow her. The apartment is not a bad size, four rooms in all, and it even has a small cooking area, which is rare in humbler apartments. The household shrine has fresh flowers on it, the same ones that are in Livia's hair, as well as the usual candles and offerings of food. There is not a lot of luxury, the furniture is plain wood with little in the way of decoration. I have grown used to houses draped everywhere with rich fabrics and bright colours, mosaics on all the floors, but there is none of that here. There is a wooden crib in one corner and a loom, which stands waiting for its mistress to return to it.

At Livia's direction I put my satchel in a corner and take up a stool next to the slave girl Anna. She passes me a knife and I start chopping carrots to add to a savoury porridge, the evening meal. Anna eyes me up curiously.

"Is it really true we're all going to go to Rome?" she asks me in an overawed whisper.

"Yes," I say. "I'm to travel there tomorrow with the master." I still can't quite bring myself to call him Marcus, especially not to another slave. "I think the rest of the household is to follow us soon. Are there other slaves?"

"Just me."

A one slave household seems unusual for someone in my new master's position, I would have expected Marcus to earn more, as manager of the amphitheatre. I've never had to cook or clean in the households I was part of, where there were plenty of slaves. Each has their own tasks to do, and a scribe wasn't expected to chop vegetables. In a smaller household a slave must do everything. I look over my shoulder, but Marcus and Livia are in the furthest room, Marcus squatting down talking to his son. I lower my voice. "Are they good masters?" It's the question every slave asks, as soon as they get a chance in a new household. You have to judge by the tone of the response how accurate it is.

But Anna's face lights up in what looks like a real smile. "They are," she says, keeping her own voice low. "The mistress is very kind; she treats me like family. Master is hardly here but when he is there's no beatings or, you know, the other. And he said that if we all go to Rome there might be other slaves and I will be set over them, might even be the mistress' body slave."

I nod. To be a body slave to a kind mistress is one of the best positions a slave woman can hope for, for they will be more of a companion than a worker. They will hear their Domina's private thoughts and care for their feelings, be treated as a confidante and occupy a position of great power over the other slaves in the household.

"You're a scribe?" asks Anna.

I nod.

"And Greek?"

I nod.

She looks impressed. She is probably a local girl, a Greek slave who can read and write is not the sort of slave she might have expected to share a bed mat with. "Did you come from a *very* grand house?"

"Lucius Hirtuleius Dives."

"The garum merchant from Rome? In the holiday villa?"

"Yes."

"So you lived in Rome mostly?"

"Yes."

"What's it like?" she asks, eyes wide.

I throw the chopped carrots into the pot. "Big. Noisy. Stinky."

She looks disappointed. "But grand? With ladies with their hair all elegant and all the men in togas and a really huge Forum, all big statues and temples?"

I smile at her vision of Rome. "Some of that," I agree. "In the rich houses. But when you go out it's just like here: traffic and slaves, horse dung and ordinary men and women wearing ordinary clothes."

She nods, stirring the porridge. "I'd like to see it," she says. "But I'm a bit scared, too. I've never been anywhere but Pompeii. My parents are slaves here too, they live a few streets down and work at the fullery of Stephanus. They thought it was better to work for just one household. You don't get worked so hard, if you have kind masters who treat you well."

I wash my hands and lay out cups, a jug of water, spoons and bread on the table. Livia comes back into the room and watches me for a few moments. "I hope you will be happy serving Marcus," she says. "I know you have come from far grander homes. Ours is a bit shabby," she says, although she is smiling rather than apologetic. "We save everything Marcus makes."

I'm surprised she would comment like this on her home and their plans. I'm a new slave and yet she is treating me as though she has known me for years. "What for?" I ask tentatively, uncertain whether I am allowed such curiosity.

"There's an old farm further up the coast, in the countryside near Puteoli," she says, her eyes dreamy. "It's shabby too, no-one lives there anymore, but we could buy it for a good sum and then work on it. It has a lovely vineyard, fertile land, a stream running nearby. We mean to buy it soon and move there. It belonged to Marcus' family once, but his grandfather was an inveterate gambler and one night he gambled the farm and lost. The family had to scrabble for a living, the grandfather died of shame. Marcus used to play there as a boy, and it broke his heart that the new owners didn't care enough to look after it. They just sold all the goods, slaves and livestock and abandoned it."

The farm again. Her sharing of future dreams makes me a little bolder. "Doesn't he enjoy what he does?"

She laughs and takes a piece of bread, crumbles it at the household shrine, bows her head for a moment, then continues. "He's good at what he does, he can make a spectacle out of just about anything. But he says it is no life, he is tired of the violence. He wants to live quietly and enjoy the sun on his face. He spent happy times on the farm as a boy, so he has it in his mind as a golden time. I tell him it will be harder work than he thinks, but he says nothing can be as hard as befriending men and women before watching them be mistreated and often die."

I'm still shocked at how honest Livia is with me, sharing comments her husband must have made in their own home, disparaging the work he does. But there is an openness to her, she speaks as though we are friends or cousins, trustworthy and understanding. I have never had such a mistress, but I am grateful for her, already like her more than I expected to.

THE PORRIDGE IS TASTY, AND we're given generous helpings. Anna and I sit on the stairwell eating, watching the to-ing and fro-ing in the courtyard below while Livia sings Amantius to sleep and then Marcus joins her in the bedroom. I can hear the sound of their lovemaking amidst the noise from the courtyard. Anna chatters on to me, perhaps grateful of company, pointing out various locals and regaling me with the latest gossip regarding them. Slowly the courtyard empties as night falls and we make our way indoors, use sand and water to clean the dishes, then lay out sleeping mats in the main living area by the table. I try to think over the events of the day but too much has gone on, my thoughts are blurred and confused. At last I whisper a prayer to Libertas to watch over me in this new place and sleep.

I'M WOKEN AGAIN BY A tremor. "Get off, Myrtis," I mutter, before realising that this time I'm being shaken by both the ground and Anna, who has grabbed my shoulder. I can hear shouts of alarm from the apartments surrounding us. I sit up but the tremor stops and, although Anna and I sit waiting tensely for a few moments in case another one comes, there is nothing.

"Stronger than the other day," says Anna, yawning and rolling up her sleeping mat. "A bird flew into the window in the night, did you hear it? Animals act funny when there's tremors. Does Rome get tremors all the time like we have?"

"Not really," I say. "Occasionally, but years apart, not every autumn like you do here."

"Spring too," says Anna. She picks up an amphora in each hand and gestures with her chin towards another two in the kitchen. "Grab those," she says. "We need to get water."

This is the sort of task I have never been called on to do and I shiver in the half-light. At this time of morning I am used to being awake, but usually I'd be sitting in Myrtis' kitchen, petting the lazy dog and eating the first of the pancakes she cooks for the masters, cracking a few nuts and maybe drinking some of the grape juice that's so plentiful around harvest time, its rich sweetness a treat I associate with the last days of the holidays here. I'm already missing Myrtis and Felix, they've been my only friends for the past few years and I will only see them briefly from now on. I wait patiently behind Anna and other women at the nearest public fountain, then struggle back to the apartment with the load. I never realised how heavy two full amphorae were.

When we get back a dishevelled Livia is feeding Amantius but Marcus is nowhere to be seen. Anna lays out bread, wine and cheese, along with nuts and olives. Livia yawns, nods and eats while coaxing Amantius to pay more attention to his food and less to playing with the dog.

"Marcus will be back soon, he is fetching the horses," she tells me. "Are you ready to leave?"

I nod, fastening the strap of my satchel a little tighter.

Livia gives up on Amantius and stands. She takes a basin Anna has filled into her bedroom, where I can hear her washing.

Amantius stares at me. I hide my face behind my hands and then pop out and he giggles.

"Again," he says, and I do it again, to more giggles. He tries it himself, one eye unable to resist peeping out even while he should be hiding his face, then throwing his arms wide for the big reveal. I can't help giggling myself.

Livia is back, her hair now combed and twisted into a bun, her palla wrapped around her to keep her warm. "It's chilly," she says. "Take this, Althea." She is holding out a woollen cloak in a dark blue. "When we get to Rome, I will see to everyone's clothing, but you will need something for travelling. It needs mending but it will do for now."

"Thank you, Domina," I say gratefully, putting it on. The cloak is thick and very warm, I feel the morning chill leave me. She's right, it has a worn-out patch with a hole in it but it's nothing a little darning won't take care of.

"The horses are ready." Marcus stands in the doorway. He, too, has a cloak on.

"I will ask a blessing on your journey," Livia says.

Marcus nods and follows her to the household shrine, bowing his head. Anna and I stand behind them, while Amantius watches with interest, holding onto the dog for extra balance, as Livia lights a candle.

Livia raises her hands, palms upturned, and bows her head. "Gods of this household and of the world beyond our doors, it is I, Livia, mistress of this home, who asks for your blessing," she begins. "Look after my husband, Marcus Aquillius Scaurus, father of our son Amantius, on his journey to Rome. May his journey be worthwhile, and may this new endeavour be blessed by Janus, bear fruit and take our family closer to the day when we will return to the countryside and the ancestral farm, where we can restore the Aquillius family's honour and legacy." She looks briefly up at Marcus and then over her shoulder at me. "And may our new slave Althea be watched over also, now that she is part of our household. May her skills as a scribe be useful to Marcus. May he protect her body and honour as a good man should."

Perhaps this is a warning to Marcus not to try any funny business with me while we travel alone together, but there is something heartfelt in her words, an almost-innocent trust in Marcus and genuine care for me as a fellow woman that is touching. I have never worked in such a small household with so few slaves. Perhaps it is this that makes Livia treat me as though I were part of the family rather than an unimportant object to be bought and sold, commanded and punished on a whim.

Livia has finished her requests to the family gods and now she lifts Amantius up for Marcus to kiss. He stoops over the two of them, holding them both in a tight embrace.

"I won't be long," he says. "I'll send for you in a matter of days, once I have seen the amphitheatre for myself and found somewhere for us all to live. Then we will all be together again. It will be a great new adventure."

"All the hubbub of the capital," she murmurs.

"Only for two years," he reminds her. "Then we will be done with all of this and go to the farm. You will be as brown as a country girl in no time."

She laughs, although her eyes have filled up a little. "Stay safe," she says. "Don't go down dark streets at night. You don't know Rome like you do Pompeii."

"I will be the most cautious man in Rome," he assures her. "Now we must leave. Juno watch over you both." A last tightening of his embrace, then he kisses her upturned lips and ruffles Amantius' golden curls, before striding out of the house so quickly I turn in a fluster to follow him, but Livia has caught my hand in hers.

"Keep Marcus safe, Althea," she says, her large eyes still anxious. "Look after him for me." She jiggles Amantius on her hip as he starts to cry.

I nod and pull away, half-running towards the door. "Don't worry," I call back to her, trying not to trip over the threshold as I step out into the street. "I will keep him safe. I promise!"

STRAWBERRY GRAPES

MARCUS IS WAITING AT THE end of the still-dark street with the two horses, a boy holding the reins of the first while Marcus attaches the reins of the second to the harness so that it will follow his lead. The horses are both tall, the second seems skittish and I stand well back from them.

"Have you ridden before?"

I shake my head.

"Not much to it," he says. "You'll ride pillion with me, we'll swap the horses over from time to time to give them a rest."

I am clumsy at climbing up from the mounting block. I try to pull myself up in one move, but I slip twice, and Marcus has to half drag me up the third time, his hand gripping my arm so hard that I have to rub the pain away once I am seated. The horse shifts beneath our combined weight and I am unsure of where to hold onto Marcus, trying to hold my body rigidly away from him. It seems too intimate a position, but if I do not hold onto him I will most certainly fall off the horse, since I am riding pillion, both legs to the left rather than astride, which would not be seemly.

"Hold on," he advises me.

I put both hands lightly on his waist, trying to touch him as little as possible.

"Can barely feel you," he says. "Don't fall off just for modesty's sake."

I don't reply, but I'm not about to encourage a new master to consider what he might do with a new female slave, far away from his wife.

AFTER A FEW HOURS' TRAVEL boredom overtakes my anxiety and I simply keep one arm or the other around his waist, allowing my body to lean against his back. He seems entirely comfortable, the reins held in one hand, his body swaying with the movement of the horse.

We swap horses twice, each time taking the opportunity to drink some water. On one of these breaks, we eat bread and cheese Livia has sent with us, sitting in the shade of a tree. Marcus wanders away behind some bushes to relieve himself and I do the same. By the third time we mount I have grown better at the fast, hard push off required from the milestone mounting blocks.

"Were you born a slave?" he asks.

"No," I say.

"Want to tell me your story?"

"I was born in Kefalonia."

"I don't know it."

"A Greek island," I say. "My father was a labourer, but he could read and write. I was his only child. He had family in Athens. My mother and I were to accompany him there. But pirates took the ship we boarded."

He nods without speaking.

"We were taken as slaves and sold in Rome," I say.

"All three of you?"

I swallow. *Screams and blood, her hand losing its grasp on me.* "My mother was killed."

"I'm sorry," he says.

We are quiet for a little while.

"How old were you?"

"Ten," I say.

"And your father could not prove his freeborn status?"

"He had no connections," I say. "The slave trader was crooked."

My father sought ways to regain his freeborn status, year after year, the bitterness of failure eating away at him.

"Were you and your father sold to the same household?"

"Yes." *Crying on the slave block, my father on his knees, begging his new master to buy me too so that we would not be separated. Literate Greeks are desirable slaves. Classy.* "My father swore to the man who bought him that he would serve him with great loyalty if he would only keep us together. I could read and write a little already and speak Latin, so I could be useful. My father managed our new master's accounts. I became a body slave to his daughter Cornelia, as we were the same age. I kept her company and studied with her."

"Do you remember much of Kefalonia?"

"No." *The waves on the beach, the chickens in our yard, my mother humming as she hung out washing.*

"How did you end up with Lucius?"

"Cornelia married and her new husband had plenty of slaves. Lucius knew my master and was in need of a scribe."

"And your father?"

The bitterness claiming him, his hand, too, loosening its grip. No-one left to hold my hand. "He died a year before."

"And now you're to help me inaugurate the greatest

amphitheatre there's ever been, and little enough time to do it. A different kind of business altogether."

"Can it be done in the time?"

"I doubt we have much choice," he says. "The contract I'm about to undertake will have me in the arena instead of under it, if I don't deliver what Titus wants."

"You don't sound very worried," I say.

"You can't worry," he says. "You can only work hard and think fast."

"I'll try and remember that," I say.

AS NIGHT FALLS, HE STOPS outside an inn, and asks for stabling, a room and a meal.

"Can I offer you the use of a girl?" asks the innkeeper.

"No, thanks," says Marcus, patting the horses as he hands over the reins to a stable hand.

"You have your own slave, of course," says the innkeeper. "Very pretty too," he adds, leering.

"She is," agrees Marcus without smiling and my stomach drops. I should have known I was too lucky with Lucius. Marcus will use me tonight and there is precious little I can do about it. I offer a quick prayer to Libertas, that he will be gentle, it is all I can hope for.

But once in our room Marcus only takes a rough blanket from the bed and indicates that I should use it to sleep on the floor.

"Thank you," I say, surprised and unsure whether I am thanking him or Libertas, whether this is a one-off kindness or what I can expect always.

HE WAKES ME VERY EARLY. We have eaten some stale bread and a handful of olives and mounted before the sun has risen. It is cold and I am glad of his warm back. I press against him a little, emboldened by his courteous treatment of me last night.

"So was Lucius a good master?"

"Yes," I say.

"You didn't look like you had much to do," he observes.

"No," I say. "I mostly did the social engagements and salutatios; he had another scribe for the business side. His wife said a man of means should have a Greek scribe for his social life, someone who looked elegant. She said his usual scribe was too coarse for the sort of society he was moving into."

"Like her family?"

"Yes."

"I don't know what you'll think of the kind of people I do business with, then," he says. I can't see his face, but he sounds amused. "Gladiators, actors, prostitutes. The disreputable class."

I'm not sure what to say, so I say nothing. It is not my place as a slave to comment on my master's business.

"Still," he says, "I do know some of the better classes. When we arrive in Rome we'll stay with a Vestal Virgin."

"A Vestal Virgin?"

He laughs at my tone. "I should say she *was* a Vestal Virgin. Chosen when she was six years old. Served her time and then got married after the thirty years were over."

"Really?"

"I know, not many do. But she fell in love with a carpenter and married him. A nobody. Her family had nothing to do with her after that. But she's a good woman and he was a good man."

"Was?"

"He died after only a few years of marriage. Left her a crumbling insula. She filled it with all the down and outs who couldn't afford rent elsewhere. I had a room there for a while when I left the army, before I made my way to Pompeii."

"Is that where your family is from?"

"No. We're originally from the countryside near Puteoli, we'll pass it this morning. But after my grandfather lost the family farm we moved away, down the coast to Pompeii, so no-one would know us, not that it matters now. Plenty of work in Pompeii for my father. I joined the army and was stationed in Alexandria in Egypt, until Vespasian was declared Emperor. Got wounded in a skirmish and was discharged. Came back to Pompeii just as they were about to reopen the amphitheatre and they liked the idea of an ex-centurion keeping the plebs in order."

WE PASS PUTEOLI WITHOUT ENTERING the city, but only a little further down the northern road towards Rome, Marcus turns off the main road and onto a country track.

"Where are we going?" I ask.

"I want to see something," he says.

We pass a couple of farms, one close, one further away in the fields, before turning off again, this time down a track that looks like it barely gets any use, with tall grasses brushing against our legs. We pass through a little scrub of young trees, forcing us to duck our heads, and then emerge into a wider clearing.

"There it is," Marcus says.

Nearby is an abandoned farm and its buildings, set in an overgrown meadow, above olive groves and a stream that winds its way through the shallow valley. Marcus jumps down from the horse and I follow him, the horses left behind to munch on bushes while we wade through the long grass.

The outer gateway, set into a surrounding wall the height of Marcus' head, is open to anyone who wishes to enter, its wooden gate long gone. We pass through and find ourselves in the main courtyard, an olive mill to one side of us with cracked amphorae buried to one side of it, fallen beehives in a far corner, a dovecote beyond it, still standing. A sudden fluttering greets our arrival. One wall is a stable block, the stalls standing empty. I look back at the horses, but they are happy enough. In front of us is the main house, two storeys high, its shutters and door closed up. Low outbuildings complete the square of the outer wall, pigsties and chicken sheds now bereft of their former occupants. A pergola runs the length of the house, heavy with an unpruned vine and the remnants of its fruits. Marcus is walking the perimeter of the courtyard. I make my way to the pergola and find a few last bunches of grapes, the rest, no doubt, eaten by the doves. The grapes are a dark purple and very sweet with a fresh fragrance to them.

"Strawberry grapes," says Marcus from behind me.

He is right, the fragrance is of fresh berries rather than grapes. "I've never had this variety before," I say.

"I loved them as a child," he says, reaching up to pluck a bunch of his own and dropping a few grapes on the ground for the gods. "You never find them in the markets. Make a good wine, too. Might not be the best Falernian but it's very drinkable and doesn't give you the headaches you get from the local Vesuvinum and Pompeianum wines. There's a small vineyard on the other side," he adds, pointing beyond the back of the house.

We stand eating for a few moments, spitting the pips to the ground. "Is this the family farm Domina mentioned?" I ask.

He nods. "Did she tell you the story?"

"Your grandfather gambled it."

"Foolish old bastard. Yes. He couldn't help himself, he

gambled everything he had and then he went too far. He ruined our family."

"Can you buy it back?"

"That was my plan when I came back from the army but at the time the man who won it was still alive and he set the price too high. Now he's dead and his heirs would sell, but I need more money, they're a greedy bunch. It doesn't look like much, but it has a lot of good land. If I can get the amphitheatre inaugurated successfully, I'll be able to buy it outright and my family will be able to hold their heads high again." He spits more seeds. "Besides, it's not just that. I liked this place, I grew up here. I enjoyed the life. I'd be a happy farmer."

"You wouldn't miss what you do now?"

He laughs out loud. "Oh, it has its fun moments. I have the best team a man could wish for, all of them mad, all of them fiercely loyal to me. We put on the best shows Pompeii has ever seen. But…" He puts more grapes in his mouth.

"But?"

He sighs before answering. "The gladiators are my friends and it hurts when one of them dies. The women we use for the shows are prostitutes and they get badly treated by clients from time to time and there's little that can be done about it. The animals are mostly terrified, we have to goad them to fight. The criminals we put to death: I have no quarrel with their sentence, but it would be kinder to cut their throats than make them re-enact some bloody myth."

"Why did you choose it then?"

"I didn't have much choice at the time." He spits some more seeds and half-laughs. "It turned out I was good at it. I kept the peace in the audience, I put on shows everyone remembered. I find ways to manage things that I think are right. Mostly."

I think back to the dinner at Lucius'. "Like keeping household slaves out of the way of being groped at your events?"

He grins. "Spotted that, did you? Fausta is my best woman. She should have my job. No-one lays hands on her without her permission, whether they know it or not." He looks around the courtyard. "We'd better go. I couldn't resist seeing it, since we were passing."

I follow him towards the gateway.

"So now you know my dream," he says over his shoulder. "What I work for. What's yours?"

"I'm a slave," I remind him.

"Everyone has a dream," he says, pulling the lead horse away from its meal. "What's yours?"

I don't answer.

He pulls himself up, reaches out a hand to me. There's no mounting block here, I'm going to struggle. I do my best and after a failed attempt he pulls hard enough that I only just avoid falling, grabbing hold of his waist for balance. Once we're settled, he turns the horse's head back into the thicket. "Your freedom, I suppose?" he says, ducking his head.

I duck my own head just in time to avoid getting a branch in my face. "I am loyal to you, Dominus," I say awkwardly. The friendliness I had felt between us evaporates. It is unthinkable for a slave to tell their master to their face that they want to be set free, it makes them sound like a troublemaker.

He snorts. "Every slave wants to be free," he says, as we emerge back onto the track that will bring us back to the main road. "Besides, I think you have already tried and failed for your freedom."

My stomach turns over and a hot flush rises to my cheeks. I'm glad he can't see my face. "Dominus?"

"Not all slaves wear a slave collar," he says calmly. "Mostly just the ones who have tried to run away. And yours may not be a cheap metal collar, but a fancy gold cuff that tells people to whom you should be returned if you're caught is as good as a slave collar."

I say nothing.

"We will make a deal," he says, after a pause. "You will be utterly loyal to me. You will work hard and think fast. And when the hundred days of the inaugural Games are over and I have been rewarded, I will leave with my family to buy the farm and I will set you free with a purse of money, to live as you wish, a freedwoman. We will both achieve our dreams in the arena."

I swallow. "As you say, Dominus." I fight not to feel a thrill of excitement. I still don't know if I can trust him to keep his word, but if there is a chance to be set free...

"Call me Marcus," he says. "But you must be more than my slave. You will work harder than you have ever worked before, but you are working for your freedom, so it is worth it. You will be my right-hand woman, as Fausta has been in Pompeii. Is it a deal?"

I think of tall, bare-breasted Fausta and her quick eyes, her broad shoulders, her loud voice. I am not sure being compared to a prostitute would be a compliment from anyone but Marcus, but there is something about the way he speaks of her, a real respect as though he were speaking of a man, that makes me feel differently about the comparison. "I will do my best, Domin-Marcus."

"Good," he says with satisfaction. "Then we will do well together. And if you're still wondering, I am not about to bed you, this evening or any other night. I have Livia and she is enough for me."

My shoulders slump in relief.

He laughs at the movement of my body. "I'm glad you are so relieved," he says. "I will tell my wife I am far uglier than she seems to think I am."

I give a small gasp of a laugh, unsure of whether I have just offended my strange new master.

"You'll get used to my ways and the work," he says. "But it will be a different kind of life for a dainty scribe slave from the fancy villas of the Caelian Hill. Prepare to rough it."

We have rejoined the main road. Soon we will join the Appian Way, which will lead us to the very gates of Rome. An ox cart rumbles past us, its noisy wheels all but obscuring my reply. "I am ready."

ON THE FOURTH DAY I sit a little straighter. We have made excellent time, even though my behind is aching from days of riding. The tall umbrella pines of the last stretch of the Appian Way make me feel at home. I forget how vast the city is every time I leave Rome and return to her. This last part of the journey is a mess of noise and traffic, the rumble of wheels, shouting and curses all around us. The evening will bring the carters and traders, only permitted to enter the city at night to drop off their wares, in an effort to leave the streets passable in the daytime, and so we find ourselves swept up in a rush towards the city gates.

There are shouts behind us and the sound of a horse at full gallop. I twist in my seat in time to see an imperial messenger on a sweating horse, who thunders past and on to the city gate, other traffic scattering before them.

"Feathers," says Marcus.

"What?"

"He was carrying feathers. Bad news."

"From where?"

"Who knows," says Marcus with a shrug, caught up in trying to guide our two horses through the city gate, fighting for a place in the throng. "May Roma bless and protect us in her city," he adds as we enter. I murmur an echo, anxious. Coming back to Rome should mean heading towards the Forum and then east to the wealthy region of the Caelian Hill and Lucius' home, which in turn is close to my first master's home. But Marcus turns the horse's head towards the river, and we make our way along it until we come to the bridge by the island.

"We are going to cross the Tiber?" I ask. The Trans Tiberim is a rough district, known for the stench of its tanneries and its overcrowded backstreets filled with the lower classes and Jews. No one of high class would willingly head there. I cannot imagine a Vestal Virgin residing there and I'm not sure I am brave enough to live there myself. Lucius may have said I knew Rome like the back of my hand but in truth a female slave to two rich households knows little more of Rome than the Forum and the shops and houses of her masters' own district.

Marcus chuckles. "Not quite. We're in the Ninth Region, the Circus Flaminius. Just off Sand Street."

"Sand Street?"

"Sand builds up in that area when the Tiber floods. It's a nuisance in winter. The locals call the side street we're on Virgin's Street because of Julia."

I'm relieved we aren't actually going to cross the Tiber, a step too far away from the areas I've known all my life. But I know nothing of the Ninth Region except it has a Circus barely worthy of the name, just a big oval of land without a proper racetrack, nor any seating. It's spoken of disparagingly by the higher classes, as a place less for entertainment and more of a vegetable market for plebs. Still, if Marcus knows the area, I can only hope I will be in safe hands. My days on the Caelian Hill feel like a long time ago.

Sand Street is broad and full of traffic, the first carters of the evening arriving with their slow ox-pulled carts, ponderously making their way with little heed for those trying to adopt a brisker pace. Many of the deliveries are of tanned skins, to be dropped off at leather workers and cobblers around the city. I catch an acrid whiff of the tanneries from the other side of the river. There's grumpy shouting up ahead and I'm glad when we turn off to the left, into a small street. A large four-storey insula towers above us. There's a broad green wooden gate that's barely hanging on to its hinges. On the ground floor of the insula, further up the street to our left, is a bakery, although it's closed for now, its shutters pulled to. To the right of the door, taking advantage of the corner of the building to give it two possible streams of customers, is a popina. There's a girl inside lighting lanterns while an older man is laying out big covered dishes of food to keep warm, but no evening customers as yet.

"It looks like a breath of wind would knock it down," I say, looking up at the insula. "It wouldn't last one morning in Pompeii with all the tremors we've been having lately."

Marcus laughs and slips down from the horse in one smooth moment, leaving me to drop less graciously to the ground. "You'd think so, but it's still standing ten years since I thought the very same. Vesta must continue to bless her handmaiden." He ties the horses up to a metal ring set into the wall and whistles loudly, attracting the attention of two little boys playing on the kerb. "If these two get stolen I'll give you a thrashing," he says, pointing at the horses with a cheerful grin.

"If they don't get stolen, do we get a coin?" asks the older boy.

Marcus winks. "You never know."

The boys jump up and stand by the horses, adopting fierce poses for nobody's benefit. Marcus pulls down the saddlebags and gives me one to carry. I follow him to the green gate, which he shoulders open, ignoring the rusty creaking.

The courtyard paving inside is as run-down as the building around it, cracked and uneven, weeds growing through the mortar. But all around the edges and dangling from every balcony all the way up to the third floor are tubs of flowers and plants, tumbling down or creeping upwards, spilling colour and greenery all over the faded and cracked walls, which must once have been painted the usual white with a dark red band on the ground floor. The white is now more of a memory, the red a blotched orange.

"Julia! JULIA! Visitors!"

The deafening bellow echoes round the courtyard. I'm surprised to match it to a large woman on the second floor who is sitting on her balcony, arms settled around a cushion balanced on the railing, there to support ample breasts. She is clad in a bold blue tunic, her palla tightly wrapped about her against the cool of twilight.

Marcus is laughing out loud. "Maria! You're still here! And better than any guard dog, as ever."

The woman peers over the balcony edge at us and then smiles broadly. "Marcus? Has Roma brought you back to us? And still just as handsome."

Marcus laughs. "How could I stay away from you? My wife is sick of hearing your name."

"Married? About time! Is that her?"

"This is my slave, Althea. Livia is at home in Pompeii, she will join me soon."

"And children?"

"One, a boy."

"May the Great Mother Cybele bless him."

Marcus nods his head in thanks.

"Marcus!"

Marcus turns and smiles, opens up his arms. "Julia!"

A woman is walking down the rickety wooden stairwell leading to the upper floors. She is perhaps fifty, of average height and beauty, nothing that anyone would remark on. But she carries herself in a way that only the Vestal Virgins do, I would know her for one at once, even without the white robes and red-bound hair. There is a practised grace to her, a certainty that people will step back and bow their heads, the knowing one is always, always observed. Even in a plain violet tunic and an unadorned green palla, she makes me want to take a step backwards from her presence. I can feel my head bowing without having thought about it. Marcus, however, steps forward and greets her at the foot of the staircase, the two of them relaxed with one another, a warm embrace between old friends. Marcus turns back towards me, waving an arm in my direction.

"This is Althea," he says.

"His slave girl," supplies Maria from above, keen to pass on the new gossip. "He has a wife now, though, and a son."

Julia looks in my direction. Her expression is solemn, but her eyes stay very steady on me for far longer than a slave would merit. I blink under her gaze.

"Welcome, Althea," she says at last. "May Roma welcome you to her city and protect you while you are here."

She speaks the words like a priestess, a formal prayer, not a casual blessing like most people throw into conversations. I feel I ought to be kneeling. I can't think of how to reply but she has turned back to Marcus.

"Still so brown," she says, patting him on the arm. "You look as though you never left the army. The amphitheatre is not a place for a soft life, I see."

"It is not," says Marcus. "And my life is not about to get easier. I have been tasked with something beyond my expectations. Hence my return to Rome after all this time."

"Come and tell me all about it," she says. "I will make a meal. Althea, you can take the bags to the roof. There is a little building there where you can both sleep. It is the larger of the two up there. I am sorry, Marcus," she adds to him. "If I had known you were coming, I would have offered you better sleeping quarters, but the insula is full at present. There are some soldiers staying who will be leaving soon, you will have a better lodging as soon as they depart."

"We are happy to lay down our heads wherever there is space," says Marcus. "I came in haste, there was no time to let you know we were on our way."

"Return to us afterwards," says Julia to me. "We will be in my apartment, it is just through there." She indicates a doorway on the first floor, at the far end of the courtyard. "Take the lamp with you," she adds, nodding up at a lamp burning on the first-floor balcony.

I take the two sets of saddlebags and make my way up the stairway, then add the lamp to my burden, staggering slightly to get my balance, my satchel bumping awkwardly against the arm carrying the lamp. I am being watched intently by Maria; I can feel her gaze on me. I'm glad to reach the rooftop and feel less scrutinised.

67

The rooftop is large, encircling the courtyard below, edged only with a thin wooden railing that I would not care to trust with my safety, old amphorae stacked here and there, some of them broken. In the corner nearby is a ramshackle little wooden hut, opposite, on the far side of the building is another, even smaller, with three beehives next to it. I edge my way into the closest hut, disturbing a flock of doves that take off from the rooftop with a wild fluttering of startled wings. Inside the hut the flickering lamp shows me an empty space, dusty with neglect. There is a man's chamber pot in the corner, but it has such a deep crack down one side that I am not sure it will survive even one night's service, and there is nothing for a woman. There are no beds, I can only hope Julia has some sleeping mats or we'll be on the bare floor. I gladly drop the saddlebags before removing my own satchel and placing it in the corner furthest from the chamber pot, hoping to avoid any unwary night-time accidents. There's a rough wooden ledge on one wall, which will be handy for placing a lamp.

Bags dropped, there's nothing to keep me here and I need the toilet, I hope the insula has one somewhere. Julia will be able to direct me, although it will feel strange to ask a Vestal Virgin where I can relieve myself. I pull the decrepit door open again and step outside, almost shoving my lamp into a face. I step back with a yelp.

"Who are you, girl?" In front of me is an old woman, shoulders hunched, neck twisted forward. Her dark clothes are faded, ragged here and there. Her face is deeply wrinkled. She is wearing a sort of cap over her head.

I try and gather myself. "Althea."

"Greek," she says.

"Yes."

"What are you doing here, a young woman alone? You're not a prostitute, are you? I won't live near a whore."

I blink, still confused by her sudden appearance. "I'm a scribe," I say. "A slave. My master is a friend of Julia's. We have come to Rome to work."

"Work as what?"

"Managing the Amphitheatre."

"What amphitheatre?"

"The Flavian Amphitheatre being built near the Forum. Emperor Titus is to inaugurate it next year –"

But at the name, the old woman draws back from me, her face crumples into a grimace of anger. "Titus? *Yimakh shemo!*" she says, and spits.

"What?"

"May his name be erased."

"I don't understand."

"He defiled and plundered the Holy Temple of Jerusalem, then burnt it to the ground. That place you mentioned, I will not speak its name, neither now nor ever. It is built from the blood and the gold of my people. And their sweat too," she adds as an afterthought. "Half the prisoners of war brought back to Rome are being used as slaves to work on it."

"You are a Jewess?" I ask.

She nods, peering up at me from her twisted shoulders. I think of the triumphal procession Titus received on his return, the endless treasures and prisoners of war from Jerusalem, paraded through the streets. In the vast crowd Cornelia and I waved palms and branches of laurels and shouted till we grew hoarse, excited by the floats and falling flower petals, the endless heavy marching feet of victorious soldiers bearing their standards thudding in our stomachs, giddy with twirling dancers and trumpets. Later we danced until Cornelia's mother said it wasn't proper for a girl from a good family to be dancing in the streets, making a spectacle of herself. It was a day of fun and celebrations, of Rome's triumph over some distant nation; I hadn't thought till now that it was a temple that was plundered.

"I am sorry," I say. "It was wrong of them to dishonour the god of your country."

She shakes her head. "What would you know? You are nothing but a child," she says. Her rage seems to have left her, she shrinks in height to a weary huddle, wrapping her shawl more tightly about her from the cold. "Go back to your master."

"Where do you live?" I ask.

She points into the growing gloom, over at the other hut. "There."

"Alone?"

"Who else is there?"

"Are you warm enough?"

She blinks at me. "What would you care?"

"I wouldn't want anyone to be cold."

Her face softens a little. "Good child," she mutters as though to herself. "A good child. I do well enough."

"I'll bid you goodnight, then," I say awkwardly, but she is already shuffling away from me, back to her hut. I make a mental note to warn Marcus of her existence, in case she startles him, too.

I make my way back down the staircase. It sways alarmingly and I wonder how firmly it is secured to the wall. I grip the bannister tightly and hope for the best.

"Met Adah, did you?"

I've reached the second floor and Maria has been watching me. Now that I'm level with her I can see she's shorter than she

70

seems from the courtyard, although her breadth makes up for her lack of height.

"Is that the Jewess?"

"Yes."

"She didn't like me mentioning Titus."

"She says he will be punished for what he did to her people, now that he's Emperor."

"Do you believe her?"

"She's a mad old woman," says Maria. "Although," she adds, thinking it over, "they did defile a temple and that's not a thing to do, is it, whoever your gods are? What if their god is still able to punish Titus for desecrating their holy place? Look at what happened to Nero after he looted half the temples in Rome and the Empire to pay for his grandiose building plans."

I shake my head. "How does she live?"

"She sells the honey from her bees, it keeps her going. Heading back down? Can you find your way?"

"I think so," I say. "But I need the toilet. Is there one?"

"There is. Ground floor, just off the courtyard that way," she says, leaning perilously over the edge of the balcony to indicate a small door.

"Thank you," I say.

THE TOILETS ARE SHABBY, FIVE seats, not many for an insula this size and there's a smell that indicates the drains here are less than adequate. I think of my previous masters' houses, where there were ten seats just for the slaves and servants and running water was something we took for granted. There's no fountain in the courtyard here, I notice, so I can see it'll be me on daily trips to the nearest public fountain for water to drink and wash with.

At least there are old amphorae all over the rooftop, I'll be able to find one or two that aren't cracked.

WHEN I FIND JULIA AND Marcus they are sat at a table, eating a thick bean stew with bread and olives. Julia passes me a generous plateful and I nod in thanks without interrupting their conversation, then take a seat on a stool to one side in the room. I'm tired, but the food is good and I'm grateful to be somewhere peaceful after the long journey.

"And Livia is happy to move here?" asks Julia, continuing their conversation.

"She will miss her family," says Marcus, ripping a piece of bread. "But it is only for a couple of years and then we will be able to go to the farm. She will like that, and it will be good for the boy."

"She will be welcome. I'm sure an apartment will be available soon."

"Thank you," says Marcus. "Livia will need a friend here, she's never even been to Rome. She will find it a little overwhelming."

"She will have Althea?"

"No, Althea will be too busy working with me. But we have a good girl at home, Anna. She's cheerful and works hard, we'll bring her along."

I think of Myrtis. Perhaps I'll be able to see her one day when we are settled. Lucius' house is not far from the amphitheatre. She will feed me her honey cakes and I'll tell her all about the new work and what Marcus has promised me. She'll probably be disbelieving, Myrtis always was a pessimist, but Felix will grunt and say that freedom is worth trying for, that perhaps the gods are smiling on me.

"Althea?"

"Sorry," I say. "I was thinking."

"Your eyes are tired," says Julia. "Time to sleep. As I recall, Marcus wakes horribly early. By the time the sun rose he was always gone. And tomorrow is the big day?"

He nods. "I'll be signing the contract and seeing the amphitheatre for the first time."

"Then take the sleeping mats from the corner and get some sleep. Althea, there are two blankets on the chair."

Sleeping mats are heavy, but Marcus lifts them as though they were nothing. "Carry up the lamp," he tells me and so I walk ahead of him up the dark internal staircase. On the whole, I prefer the rickety wooden contraption outside.

We don't speak. Marcus throws down the two mats in the hut, I lay out the blankets and we both lie down. Marcus is snoring by the time I have even thought through everything that has happened today. I relax. We have made it this far. We are back in Rome, if not quite in the sort of house I have been used to. Tomorrow we will visit the amphitheatre, I think sleepily. It must have changed since I last saw it, several months ago.

THE ASHEN SKY

I WAKE EARLY, THE SKY STILL dim. Pompeii's morning noise is nothing to Rome. Endless carts trundling by, hurrying to get out of the city early, for they are only permitted to make deliveries until a certain hour. Curses involving just about every deity float up to the rooftops. I creep out of the hut and make my way over to the outer edge of the roof, peering cautiously over the wall. I wonder if there will be space for us to walk safely, so narrow and busy is Virgin's Street. Sand Street may be wider, but it will be even busier. At the opposite corner of the rooftop the bees are already coming and going from their hives. There is the smell of woodsmoke as thousands of fires are lit across the capital, in homes and businesses.

I tiptoe back to the hut to get my shoes. If I can find an uncracked amphora, I can fetch washing water from the nearest public fountain.

"Take my purse."

I startle.

Marcus has woken. He has one arm over his eyes but gestures vaguely with the other hand. "I'll be downstairs in a moment."

"I was going to fetch washing water."

"We'll go to the baths later. Right now, we need food and then we'll go straight to the amphitheatre, I want to get there early. Go to the popina downstairs and order breakfast. I'll be there shortly."

I pack our clothes and pick up his purse, worn old leather, but heavy enough. He is taking a risk, letting a new slave walk out of a lodging house with a purse of money in a city the size of Rome. But where would I go? With a gold cuff on my arm that on closer inspection marks me as a slave? I make my way downstairs, use the toilet, then step cautiously out onto the street, glancing left and right and keeping well back against the wall out of the way of too-fast carts. To my right is the bakery, from where the good smell of fresh bread is coming. I turn left to the popina. The shutters are up and there's a wide counter against which bleary-eyed customers are half-leaning, munching bread and cheese. Two men who look the worse for wear are dipping their bread in wine as though to continue last night's fun.

The insula above us may look as if a good puff of wind would bring it tumbling down, but the bread smells good, no doubt from the bakery next door, and the girl at the counter has a cheerful smile under tumbling black curls, escaping her attempts to tie them back.

"Morning, love, what'll it be?"

I find a space that will fit two of us at the counter and lean an elbow on it for comfort. "Bread and cheese for one and…" I look behind her and see a jug of what I was hoping for. "Pancake with date syrup?"

She nods and pours batter out of the jug onto a hot griddle, then flips it over expertly while laying out bread and cheese. Scribbled on the wall at the edge of the popina is graffiti which declares, 'Hands off Cassia, she's mine,' next to which someone else has retorted 'Use your hands on yourself, Cassia is too good for you.' I wonder if the serving girl is Cassia and whether she

75

manages to fend off her admirers if they get a bit too amorous of an evening.

"Marry me, Cassia!" calls a trader from the street as his cart rumbles by.

"Don't let my father hear you!" she calls back with a grin. "You don't want to feel the end of his stick!"

"You really don't," mutters one of the men eating wine-dipped bread. "Made me see stars."

Cassia brings the two dishes just as Marcus joins me. "Ah, I thought you were going to eat double helpings," she laughs at me.

Marcus nods to her and grimaces as I bite into the pancake. "Oh, a sweet tooth?" he comments. "Never really took to sweet foods first thing in the morning." He bites hungrily into the bread and cheese. "Good bread. Hate the stale stuff."

"That's the advantage of being next door to a bakery," Cassia says with a smile.

"I really don't know how this building is still standing," says Marcus. He leans back to look upwards at the crumbling insula.

"Perhaps Vesta looks out for it, since it belongs to her handmaiden," says Cassia over her shoulder, now frying another pancake for an elderly man who has taken the place of the two hungover customers.

"Bad luck to marry a Vestal Virgin," mumbles the old man. "Vesta does not share her handmaidens."

Cassia shrugs. "Julia is a kind woman," she says. "She was devastated when her husband died. I heard her crying like a child for months afterwards."

"And now?" I ask.

"She hasn't got a lot, but she keeps the rents low and looks out for others. The insula may be crumbling, but everyone gets by."

"We need to go," says Marcus.

"See you later," I say to Cassia. "We're staying for a few days." She nods and smiles as we leave.

It takes all our concentration to cross Sand Street safely.

"I've never met a retired Vestal Virgin before," I start to say, but get distracted by Marcus leading us down a street so tiny I could touch the walls on either side with my arms outstretched. It stinks of piss and I fear, given the early hour, that someone will empty a chamber pot over our heads from above, rather than bothering to empty it in their building's toilets. I keep my clothes and satchel pulled close to me in case they touch anything and try not to breathe through my nose. "How do you know the way?" I ask.

"We need to head south-east," he says, which I know, although in this mess of tiny back streets I can't understand how he's keeping track of what direction we are headed in. I'm hopelessly lost. I don't have much choice but to follow him, so I offer a quick prayer to Mercury. The messenger of the gods must at least know how to find his way about Rome. No doubt, having been in the army, Marcus can look out for us if there's any trouble, but I still think I'd have preferred the main roads, however busy they are. A few people give us odd glances, knowing we aren't locals, and I catch one or two men leering at me. I keep close to Marcus.

When we emerge from the tangle of backstreets though, I glimpse the Forum in the distance and my shoulders relax. From here I know my way and at least we've left the worst of the stink behind. Plus, there's more room to walk here and less chance of chamber pots.

The Forum is already busy. Smoke drifts from the domed roof of Vesta's temple, assuring everyone that her fire still burns, tended by the Vestal Virgins within, ensuring that Rome will not fall. Street vendors are setting up little stands here and there, soothsayers and astrologers prepare for their day's work. The streetcleaners rest on their brooms, chatting rather than finishing their work. Beneath the basilica's colonnade the lawyers gather, ready to do business or take on new clients.

"Tell your fortune, Dominus, Domina?" calls out a woman as I pass. Her wrinkled eyes are thickly rimmed with soot, her hair is an unlikely jet-black and adorned with little gold beads in the Egyptian fashion. A mangy leopard skin has been spread out before her, on which are laid out her talismans and other tools of her trade. My half-decent tunic, leather satchel and especially the gold cuff I am wearing must make her think I am Marcus' wife rather than his slave. "I see great things for you both!" she adds as Marcus strides by with me trotting to keep up with his longer legs. "But warnings also, oh yes, you would do well to heed my warnings," she delivers to my back. My past mistress used to spend a fortune on these people, having her chart or palm read, listening with bated breath to their revelations, while Lucius scoffed and forbade her from inviting them to peddle their wares in the house.

Now that we are out in an open space, I can look about me. The morning is crisp and clear, one of those beautiful autumn days where one would swear it was the end of summer rather than close to the start of winter. The sky is a sharp blue, the rising sun still has some warmth to it. Ahead, and far above us, the Colossus glitters, the golden body of Nero now topped with the sun god's head so as not to waste such a fine statue. And next to it is the Flavian Amphitheatre, hundreds of workers already gathered around it, coming in and out of the great arches with tools, materials and carts. I can't help but feel a thrill. It is a vast undertaking and the spectacles that will be put on here will be the greatest in the Empire, that much I can be sure of. The closer we get, the further back my head has to tilt to take in its full height.

I nearly bump into the back of Marcus, who has stopped abruptly in front of me.

"Something wrong?" I ask, coming round to his side and seeing a frown on his face.

"No velarium?" he says, shading his eyes.

I follow his glance. At the top of any theatre or amphitheatre there should be a set of high wooden poles, forming the anchoring points of the awning which will stretch out across rigging, bringing shade to most of the seats on the blisteringly hot summer days. No audience can sit for long on the hottest days without an awning.

"Doesn't look like it's been built yet," I say.

"Make a note," he says. "Velarium."

I fumble in my satchel, pull out my tablet and stylus and jot down the word. Marcus is still standing, head turning from one side to the other, taking in the surrounding area. He nods to himself and straightens his shoulders, lifting his chin as though going into battle. I follow him through the largest entrance and onto a half-built wooden arena floor in the centre of the amphitheatre.

I can't help staring around me. I've been in a few amphitheatres, but this is on a different scale. It's still being built, but the main structure is in place and it is truly vast. Even the arena floor is double the size of any I've ever seen. I look upwards, at the rows upon rows of seating, mostly complete. The very top section is still being constructed, white stone slabs being fitted into place by sweating stonemasons and their teams who have had to carry them to the highest areas.

A distinguished looking man in an immaculate toga is standing a little way off. He is surrounded by five assistants, two of whom at least are scribes, I can see their own tablets at the ready. We make our way over to him.

"I am Marcus Aquillius Scaurus, I have been appointed as Manager for the Games. Are you the head architect?"

"I am," says the man, preening a little.

"Excellent," says Marcus. "I have a number of points to cover with you this morning."

The architect looks down his long nose. "I am sure you will find that everything has been designed on a more than magnificent scale and with every attention to detail," he says.

Marcus doesn't look impressed by this statement. "Why don't you tell me about it, and I'll ask questions as you go along," he suggests.

The architect nods as though he is doing Marcus a favour and takes up a pose, opening with a broad sweep of his arm as though he is acting a part in a play. "It is the largest amphitheatre in the Empire. It will seat fifty thousand people at the very least, although you know how slaves and the rougher sort cram themselves in," he adds with distaste. He waits for a nod, but Marcus only raises his eyebrows, and the architect continues. "There will be four seating areas. The first is the podium, that's for the patricians, senators and their guests, our most distinguished patrons. Best view in the amphitheatre, close to all the action. There are four terraces, but they are very broad, so you will be able to provide chairs for each performance. They'll have their own cloakrooms and latrines on this level. The podium level includes the Emperor's box and the box for the Vestal Virgins, facing him on the other side of the arena, a similar design but a little smaller. The next tier has a larger capacity, that's nine marble terraces for the equestrian class, but sitting on the terrace itself. They can bring cushions, as one does at the theatre. Then two more tiers, which hold thirty terraces between them, they seat everyone else. Slaves and women in the very top tiers at the back." He points at the work currently underway. "We're doing those in white travertine stone. You can't tell the difference too much from a distance, but the equestrian class will appreciate knowing their tier is more refined. It's these sorts of details that matter." He looks upwards, shielding his eyes against the sun's glare. "There's the possibility of adding wooden seating into the very top tier in due course, behind those columns, if it proves popular, but right now we have our work cut out getting this lot done in time, so it'll be standing space only. Toilets on every tier, over one hundred drinking fountains across the building. We haven't even finished the main building works and there's still all the decorative touches: a specially commissioned sculpture of Emperor Vespasian driving a chariot at the imperial entrance leading to the Emperor's box, statues in the second and third tiers of arches outside. On the inside, stone carvings up all the balustrades and, of course, family names will be carved into the podium terraces. Not to mention the paintings: fighting and hunting scenes in all the corridors on the way to each terrace." He pauses for Marcus' appreciation of the vast task before them.

Marcus doesn't seem to be paying much attention. He is looking into the darkness below the half-built wooden arena floor. It's just wooden scaffolding, set into a plain brick floor below. "Can we flood it?"

"What?"

Marcus gestures downwards. "If the Emperor wants a naval battle, we'd have to flood the arena floor, to a depth of at least a man's head to allow for large enough vessels. So, it'll need waterproofing."

"To the depth of a man? It'll flood the service corridors!"

Marcus shrugs. "Watertight doors."

The architect looks flustered. "How would you fill it fast enough? And drain it?"

"I thought you'd already installed drainage in the plan."

"For rain, yes. Not for deliberately filling up the arena floor with water!"

"Isn't this built over what used to be Nero's lake?"

"Yes?"

"I should imagine it's marshy underfoot, it'll probably half-flood itself."

"We've gone to a great deal of trouble *not* to let it flood," protests the architect weakly.

"I suggest you build in the capacity for naval battles," says Marcus, as though the suggestion is only a minor alteration to the plans. "I will not be the one to tell the Emperor he can't have naval battles put on, if it turns out he wants them. Will you?"

The architect's shoulders slump. His scribe is already making notes, having quickly understood that this is not an argument his master will win. I can see '*waterproofing/flooding/drainage*' appear on the tablet, in a very poorly formed shorthand. I'm surprised he can read it all back later on.

"It needs to both flood and drain in less than half an hour either way," Marcus adds.

"That's hardly any time at all!"

"It's not impressive if takes any longer."

"It might not be possible!"

Marcus looks around him at the hundreds of slaves, the dozens of surveyors, draughtsmen, engineers, masons, everyone already sweating in the warming sun. "It's your job to make it possible. Mine to make it impressive."

"Anything else?" asks the architect sullenly.

"I need lifts installed around the edges of the arena with trapdoors above, to release animals and gladiators."

"Oh yes," says the architect, relieved to be back in control. "We've planned all of that in."

"How many?"

"Thirty-six trap doors, twenty-eight lifts will be placed underneath."

"Pens for the animals?"

"Space for thirty-two, around the edges. Can't fit elephants though," he adds defiantly. "If you want those, they'll have to come in via one of the main entrances and you must stable them elsewhere."

"How many entrances?"

"There are seventy-six public entrances. Your ticket will tell you where you're seated and which entrance to use. They'll look something like this." He hands Marcus a small clay tablet, with numbers marked on it. It's very plain.

Marcus turns it over in his hands. "That'll be easy to copy then, won't it?"

"Copy?"

"Forgers," says Marcus, handing it back. "You'll have ticket touts all around the building, claiming to offer better tickets: in the shade, closer to the Emperor, closer to the action…"

"But they use these at all the theatres!"

"None of them seat fifty thousand people. By the time everyone's in and discovered there's sixty thousand tickets, it'll be too late, you won't see the touts for dust."

The architect looks as though he is about to cry, I almost feel sorry for him.

Marcus evidently doesn't. "What are the other four entrances for?"

"Four entrances have their own special uses. The Emperor has his own entrance leading to the imperial box. That's on the south side. Opposite is the magistrates' entrance and the Vestal Virgins' box. To the east is the Gate of Triumph, where the gladiatorial processions will enter. The west gate is the Gate of Death. That's the exit for the dead bodies and so on."

Marcus gestures to me. "Make a note: the criminals must arrive at least the day before they're to be executed, we'll keep them under the arena floor in a pen."

"Why?"

"I'm not having a cartload of criminals bump into the Vestal Virgins as they arrive."

I make a note. He's right. Any criminal who crosses the path of a Vestal Virgin can be pardoned and set free. It's a very rare occurrence and tolerated, but if cartloads of them are going to arrive for execution just as the Virgins arrive to see a show, I can see the authorities eventually getting annoyed.

Marcus has wandered away, back through one passageway and out into the connecting corridors. He leans out of one exterior arch, looking down at the area outside the amphitheatre, at the endless labourers and materials moving like ants through the dust. We follow him. Peering down makes my stomach turn over.

"There will be a wide pavement surrounding the amphitheatre," says the architect reassuringly. "We will complete it at the end of the building programme, and it will give a very smart impression as one approaches the arena."

"How are we supposed to manage the crowds into the right entrances?"

"I told you, they have their tickets, which have the right entrance number."

"So they'll all just mill around outside trying to find their entrance numbers? Fifty thousand people?"

"What would you suggest?"

Marcus looks back down. "Stone columns surrounding the building, about chest height, with holes so we can pass ropes through them."

"Ropes?"

"The ropes will create pathways leading to each entrance, so that people begin to move into the right entranceway as soon as they arrive near the building."

"Nowhere else –" begins the architect.

"This building has no equal," Marcus cuts him off. "So, it must have features that no other theatre or amphitheatre has. Now: how high is the wall surrounding the arena? Before the first row of seating?"

"Almost twice the height of a man."

"Are you fitting it with rollers?"

"What?"

"Rollers. You make them out of ivory from elephant tusks, it works very well. Marble's too heavy. Wood gets damaged too easily."

"I meant what for?"

Marcus looks weary. "Do you not attend Games, yourself?"

"Occasionally."

"Have you never noticed the rollers? Set around the arena walls just below the spectator walls? Columns about this high set against the wall, with the ability to roll on an axle, like a wheel but staying in one place?"

"I thought they were decorative."

"They're to stop animals leaping the wall into the spectators' seating."

The architect looks at the wall. He looks back at Marcus.

"Trust me, they can jump that," says Marcus. "And a senator does not want a lion in his lap."

"Marcus Aquillius Scaurus?"

We all turn. There's a senator standing behind us, with an entourage of bodyguards, scribes and various hangers-on.

"Aedile." The architect practically disappears into a deep bow. "We are honoured with your presence."

A lot of flourishing and bowing and elaborate introductions go on. We scribes step behind our masters and take notes for future reference. The senator does not, of course, recognise me, even though it was he who suggested Lucius employ me. The senator is in good humour, pleased that someone has been appointed to the role the Emperor has asked him to fill and which he promptly entrusted Lucius with sourcing.

The contract they go through, and which Marcus signs and adds his seal to, is binding in the extreme. He may not leave Rome without permission. He may not resign until at least the inauguration and one hundred days of Games have been completed to the Emperor's satisfaction. If the Emperor should in any way be displeased with his work, it will go very badly with him. Throughout it all, Marcus remains smiling and relaxed, although perhaps it's just for show. At last the senator is satisfied and leaves.

"I've seen enough for today," Marcus tells the architect. "I'll be back tomorrow."

"Surely we've covered everything?" protests the architect.

"Barely even started," says Marcus with a grin. "But I'm in urgent need of a good bath. Till tomorrow."

WE MAKE OUR WAY BACK to the Circus Flaminius. Marcus points upstream as we pass near the river. "One day we'll go and visit the stables."

"The racing stables?"

"The very ones. Might borrow charioteers for some of the Games, it adds to the spectacle. We can re-enact some exciting battles with them."

"Do you know people there?"

"Where do you think our horses are staying?"

"Your horses are in the racing stables?"

Marcus winks. "I know some people there. Have you met Celer?"

"No, who is he?"

"Lives at Julia's, in one of the little rooms on the top floor. Retired charioteer. Did well in his day, drove for the Blues. Spent it all on women and wine," he adds. "But he can tell you some wild stories of the stables."

Close to the Pantheon are the Baths of Agrippa, which are free to all. I make my way to the women's section. It's been a good while since I was given leave to go to the baths, before the dinner party even. I put my belongings in one of the cubbyholes in the changing rooms, making a show of how grubby my tunic is and wrapping it round my satchel, to make it less likely anyone will steal it. The hot water is bliss and afterwards I approach another slave girl and offer to help her wash if she will do the same for me. Having been rubbed down with, and then stripped of oil, my skin feels better than it has in days. I rub my hair with oil, then give it a vinegar rinse. At least now it will be easier to comb. I pull on my clean tunic and wrap up my hair to be combed out later.

Marcus looks refreshed too, in clean clothes, his beard trimmed short and his hair cut. "Food," he says as a greeting. "We'll buy what's needed so Julia does not have to cook for us every day."

We return to Julia's with late grapes and melons, olives and cheese as well as still-warm breads picked up at the bakery. Marcus has added pickles and roasted spiced chickpeas to the bounty. I lay the table and pass them both plates of food, then take my own dish to the balcony, where I eat while watching the inhabitants come and go. Maria keeps up a running commentary for my benefit, mostly focused on the shops, complete with workshops, on the ground floor of the building.

"That's the baker's family: the parents are looking after the children while their son and daughter-in-law work, though on busy days it's all hands needed, even the little ones. That's Balbus the toymaker and his wife Floriana. He stutters, you know. Can't get five words out together. But they make beautiful toys, even sell them up on the Palantine Hill, the best households call them in for their spoiled brats. Rest of the workshop space on the ground floor is the cobbler's shop. He does a lot of work for the army. Good work that, never run out of business. Even supplies the Praetorian Guard. Could have a fancier place, but he says Julia brings him luck. Whole of this insula pays a lot of respect to Vesta."

Given that Maria seems to know everything about everyone, I venture the question I've been asking myself.

"I thought Vestal Virgins were rich when they retired. How did Julia end up with a crumbling insula and not much else?"

"The Vestal Virgins end up rich because some people leave them money in their wills. Julia gave away almost everything she had when she got married. She told me once she'd rather offer a real hearth and home to the people of Rome than stand guard for thirty years over a make-believe hearth." Maria frowns slightly, evidently viewing this statement as borderline heresy, but unable to argue with the charitable intention behind it. "That's why this insula is full of waifs and strays as well as respectable people," she adds, straightening her shoulders to indicate her own position as firmly in the respectable camp.

ON OUR SECOND DAY I at least recognise a couple of the streets on our way to the amphitheatre. When we arrive, Marcus announces his intention to walk all the way round it.

"Meet me inside," he says.

I walk through the arches, skirting round cartloads of gleaming white stone and already-sweating men. Inside, standing on the half-built arena floor, I am struck again by the size. I look upwards to the most complete side, and decide to climb up to the highest seats, to see what the view is like. My thigh muscles are aching within a few steps. By the time I get to the top seats I'm panting. I turn, thrilled at the height, the perilous swoop down to the arena floor. The view is still excellent, although not quite what the Emperor and his cronies will see: their seats are such that they will hear the gasps of dying men and smell their blood. From up here, it will be more like a play, a pretence of death rather than the reality of it. This is where the women sit, and they are less likely to desire the intimacy of death. The Games are mostly a man's world, although one hears whispers about wealthy women who pay good money to be taken to a gladiator's bedchamber the night before he must fight to the death, the tragic romance of it titillating them, not to mention the simple fact that a dead man is a lot more discreet than a live lover. I shade my eyes from the bright sun and wonder when Marcus will arrive.

"Enjoying the view?"

I twist to look up at Marcus. "How did you get behind me? I never saw you climb up."

He jerks his thumb over his shoulder to a treadmill at the very top of the building site. "Got myself hoisted over the wall like a block of marble," he says, as though this is an everyday way to arrive in an amphitheatre. He sits beside me and looks down at the arena floor, then takes out a pocket sundial. He looks at it, then puts it away again. "It's going to be dark down there," he says.

"Down where?"

"Under the arena. It's where you and I are going to be spending a good deal of our time. Make a note: we need to buy several water clocks for timekeeping. Sundials aren't going to be of much use in the dark."

"Is timekeeping very important?"

He grins at my ignorance. "If I release a lion at the wrong moment it'll be very important for the man who has to fight it. Timekeeping is everything in this line of work. Part of your job will be making plans of what has to happen and when during a given performance. We'll hold rehearsals for every part of the show. Then we give signals according to that plan. We spend shows above the arena, sending signals to those below as agreed.

Before and after shows, we'll be down there in the dark. We use the water clocks, as well as sundials and our own eyes, although of course we may have to adjust events according to how it's going in the arena. If there's a really good battle happening, you can't interrupt it with some other distraction. But if the battle's getting dull you have to move quickly. No one wants a boring show. The audience gets restless and then you're in trouble."

I nod and make a note. "What do we need to discuss today?"

But Marcus is not listening to me. He is frowning at the southern sky, which is turning grey, vast clouds rolling in from that direction.

"I thought it would be sunny today," I say.

"So did I," he says. "Right, let's find the architect again before it starts to rain."

"I don't think he likes you," I say.

Marcus laughs out loud. "No, he doesn't," he agrees. "But he has to put up with me. He only has to build the place, then he can walk away. I have to run it. I'm not having stupid mistakes made. I barely covered anything yesterday."

I CAN ALMOST SEE THE architect sigh at the sight of Marcus and me. His toga is immaculately clean and pressed again, I wonder whether he wears a fresh one every day, a very expensive habit. He frowns down at an imaginary speck on his tunic sleeve, picking it away with disdain.

"So: a velarium," begins Marcus, with barely any niceties.

"It simply can't be done in time," huffs the architect. "We have to progress to the decorative stage as soon as possible."

"The audience will faint if they have to sit in the sun," says Marcus.

"Oh, they'll be fine," says the architect.

"The rich will," agrees Marcus. "They'll have slaves to carry a shade for them and fan them."

"Look, the Emperor and Vestal Virgins will have awnings," says the architect. "Then you can rig up smaller awnings for the senators and any extremely fussy or rich equestrians. That will have to suffice. There isn't time to have a full velarium erected and you'd need a lot of slaves to rig it each time."

"Sailors," says Marcus. "Two hundred, by my calculation. No-one else will have the knowledge and teamwork for it."

"There you are then. That's not happening in time for the inaugural Games."

Marcus sighs. "You may be right," he admits. It's the first time I've seen him not insist on having things his way. "It will have to be for after the inauguration. Althea: make a note, we will need awnings within the amphitheatre for the senators at least, or we'll never hear the end of it."

I jot down 'awnings, senators.'

The dark clouds keep coming. At least we will be able to shelter within the arches and continue our conversation. Drops of grey rain are beginning to fall, the storm coming closer. There are specks of dirt on the sleeve of my clean tunic. I brush them away but they only smudge, leaving marks. I look back at Marcus and the architect. Strange. The architect was so particular about his pristine toga, and yet it is now speckled all over with dirt. How has that happened? Marcus is not listening to the architect anymore. His face is tilted upwards, eyes narrowed. I follow his gaze.

The sky is raining grey. Tiny fragments float downwards from the dark clouds, slower than rain, silently landing all around us, on us. I hold out a hand and at once my skin is dotted all over, the grey landing so softly I barely feel it. I rub my fingers together, smell my hand. It must be ash; I can think of nothing else that looks and feels like this. I have had ashes fall on me when I was close to a funeral pyre, but where would a sky full of ash be coming from? The Temple of Vesta is nearby, but no temple fire is big enough to darken the sky. I look at Marcus and he glances at me. I shrug and he shrugs back, shakes his head.

All around us, silence falls. I look over my shoulder and see that the treadmill wheel is no longer turning, the men have stopped working. A few make discreet gestures against evil spirits.

"What is it?" I ask Marcus.

"Ash," he says.

I nod, wait for more, wait for his theory on what it can be from.

He says nothing, looks down at his hand again, rubs his fingers together.

The architect looks around. "Keep working," he says loudly. "It is nothing."

The men do not move. I hear one of them mutter something about the Great Fire. It's fifteen years' back, but most of these men would remember it. There would have been ash floating across the city for many days.

Marcus calls up to the men working on the highest points of the amphitheatre. "Is there a fire? What can you see?"

The workers lean over the edges, scanning the city. They should be able to see a long way from their vantage points, but one after another calls back, "Nothing," from all around the great oval.

"Work will stop for today," calls Marcus.

"You can't stop the work!" protests the architect, horrified. "We can't afford to lose a day's work."

"They're not going to do anything while this goes on," says Marcus.

"It is not your place to…" trails off the architect, but he can see for himself that there is nothing to be done about it. The men are already moving swiftly away from their places, heading downwards towards the exits, no doubt hurrying to find news about what is happening.

"Come on," says Marcus to me, turning to the nearest exit.

I follow him.

"What do I…" begins the architect, waiting for someone to tell him what to do.

"Whatever you think best," says Marcus over his shoulder.

We leave him hovering, alone in the vast space.

THE FORUM IS ALREADY BUSY, stalls everywhere, priests on their way to their respective temples. Someone is adjusting the public calendar, marking the day and which gods should be honoured, what activities avoided or undertaken, depending on their auspiciousness. But more and more people are stopping in the street, looking upwards and around, holding their palms out, as I did, inspecting the ashes as though expecting an answer. Marcus is looking for a herald and spots one further down the Forum, close to the Temple of Vesta, a crowd beginning to gather round him. We walk briskly that way, Marcus striding so fast that I am trotting by the time we reach the crowd.

"… we can presume the god Vulcan has been in some way displeased and shown his wrath, further messengers expected today with details of what has occurred. The great Admiral Pliny feared dead…"

Admiral Pliny is based in Misenum. "What's happened?" I ask, tugging at a woman's sleeve.

"A mountain has poured out fire and killed everyone in the region of Campania," says the woman, her eyes wide at the horror and the vast potential for gossip.

"What mountain?"

The woman shrugs. "I didn't catch it," she says vaguely, already extracting herself from the crowd so she can go and spread the news.

Marcus has pushed his way to the front of the throng and grabs hold of the herald's arm. The two bodyguards shove him back. "I need to know what has happened!" Marcus says.

The herald looks affronted at the loss of dignity. "You cannot assault an imperial herald," he says, adjusting his clothing.

"I beg your forgiveness," says Marcus quickly, raising his hands in the air. "I am from the region of Campania, what has happened?"

The crowd murmurs. This is making the news even more interesting.

The herald, enjoying their renewed interest, nods graciously and the two assistants retreat back to his sides. "*As* I was saying," he says and then lifts his voice to the right volume for a public announcement, "The mountain Vesuvius has opened up and poured out fire and ash across most of Campania. We have reports from Misenum, Puteoli and Neapolis, where it seems there was much fear and earth tremors as well as a falling of ash." He gestures grandly at the still-falling ash around us and gets a few frightened cries from women and many signs against evil spirits from the men. "We believe, from first reports, that the great Admiral Pliny may have died. Also reports, as yet unverified, that Herculaneum, Oplontis, Pompeii and Stabiae have disappeared."

"Disappeared?" says Marcus. "What do you mean, disappeared? A city cannot disappear."

"Sir," says the herald, drawing himself up, "I am announcing what I have been told to announce. Messengers have been arriving at the imperial palace both day and night since the occurrence, but we do not yet have all the details."

Marcus turns and walks away, his stride now so fast I have to run to keep up.

"What do you think has happened?" I ask, panting.

"I don't know," he says. "But we have to return. At once."

I try to nod while running and almost trip. "Will it be safe?"

"I don't know," he says. "Shall I leave you with Julia?"

"No," I say. "Take me with you." There is something about the silent falling ash that frightens me, that makes me want to be close to Marcus, who seems so commanding, as though he will keep me safe and know what to do, whatever strange and terrible thing has happened. I think of Mount Vesuvius, so green and peaceful, its slopes thick with vines and orchards and I cannot imagine what the herald means when he says that it opened up and poured out fire. I have heard of such mountains, but surely such a thing would be known about a mountain, it would give off smoke and tremble… "The tremors," I gasp. "Were they an omen? A warning?"

"I don't know," he says, his face tight. "Run back to Julia's, pack our bags. Tell her what we know. I will fetch the horses."

Julia does not gasp, she does not repeat back what I have said and question me. She picks up a cloth bag and puts a loaf and half a cheese from her cupboard in it, fills two metal water bottles, the kind they use in the army.

"Where is Marcus?"

96

"Gone to get the horses."

"You can't travel at that speed," she says. "It'll take at least four days, like it did when you came here. You can't have the horses gallop continuously without changing them."

"Wouldn't a ship be faster?"

She's already out the door, making her way along the walkway and up the stairs to one of the small rooms on the top floor. I stand in the doorway clutching our supplies and when she emerges it is with a slight-framed man.

"It's the only way," Julia is saying and he nods and hurries past me.

"What is?" I ask.

"Chariot," she says.

"Racing chariot? We can't travel in those!"

"Whatever has happened," says Julia, her face very pale, "it is something serious. You need to get there fast. The horses cannot gallop endlessly with both of you. A chariot will be faster. Marcus can change the horses as you go."

"But a ship –"

"Marcus is afraid Livia will be headed on the roads towards Rome to find him if something bad has happened. He cannot risk missing her. And arranging passage on a boat may take time. He will not wait."

"They said Pompeii disappeared," I say, following her down the stairs. "What does that mean? Is it a thick fog, do you think? Or smoke from the fire? So they could not see it well?"

"I don't know," she says, but her tone makes me more afraid rather than less. "Would you rather stay here with me?"

"No," I say again. "I promised his wife I would look after him," I add, as though I had made a binding oath instead of uttered a hurried platitude. A sudden thought occurs to me.

"Marcus is not allowed to leave Rome," I say. "The contract he signed forbids it."

Julia nods. "Pray you get there and back fast," she says. "I will send a message to say he is busy in other parts of Rome, making plans for his family. If all is well, make him return quickly. Livia and the boy can follow, as was planned before."

"Do you think all will be well?" I ask her, wanting reassurance.

She looks away. "I have heard of mountains with fire in them," she says slowly. "They can be dangerous. It is possible Pompeii has been badly damaged, but that does not mean Livia could not have found a way to escape. Marcus' friends would have looked out for her, for certain."

MARCUS HAS TO BE RESTRAINED by Julia, but when she convinces him it is worth waiting for the chariot he reluctantly agrees. When it arrives, pulled through the streets by two stable hands, Celer oversees the harnessing.

"I picked a training chariot, sturdier than we use for the city races, but you will have to change horses as often as possible if you want a fast speed," he warns Marcus, who only nods, his mouth set in a tight line.

I hover, nervous. The chariot is tiny, it is made for one man to stand in, for maximum lightness and speed. It barely reaches our waists. I think of the rough roads more suited to lumbering wagons and slow walking horses. The only chariots that go really fast on the main roads are the imperial mail. I know they could reach Pompeii in under two days if it was a matter of urgency and that Marcus will want to do the same.

Half the building's inhabitants have gathered in the street to wave us off. Julia stops Marcus before he climbs into the chariot. "May Jupiter bless you," she says, one hand on his chest, invoking the greatest of the gods, her voice serious. "May you return safely to us, with your wife and son."

Marcus stares back into Julia's face as though he can't hear her, then turns to me. "Up," he says, as though to a dog, and I climb quickly into the chariot. We are pressed together, hip to hip, my satchel at our feet by his own small bag. I feel Julia's hand on mine and then we are moving.

WE STRUGGLE TO GET OUT of Rome; the chariot with two people in it draws stares and the roads are not made for speed, full of traffic and pedestrians. I wonder whether the chariot is the best choice. They are made for smooth racetracks and quick laps to glory, not for a three-day journey on a main road. At last we reach the Appian Way where there is a little more space.

"Ha! Ha!" Marcus urges the horses into a fast gallop. His hands are tight on the reins, his face is set, his eyes darting across the road ahead, judging the best place to guide the horses to avoid other traffic and deep ruts in the road that would have us flung out of the chariot if the wheels were to unbalance. The speed is terrifying, I have never gone so fast before. I clutch the edge of the chariot below my waist, certain I will be thrown out at any moment, whimpering to myself when the chariot hits bumps in the road and jerks one way or another. I want to talk to Marcus because I want to hear him speak, want the reassurance I never got from Julia, but I can't think what to say and I am afraid of distracting him, am afraid of what he might reply. So we ride on and on, no words between us, the world rushing past, the endless hoofbeats and wheels against stone creating such a din in my head that after a while I can barely even think. I have never spent this long in abject terror. *Once, on a ship, the waves rocking, my mother gone, my father beside me in silent agony.* I am still afraid of our speed and the likelihood of an accident, but also afraid of what we are heading towards. Is it something very bad, but from which those we know have escaped? Or is it something so bad, something I cannot even imagine, is there news to come which will break the grim, silent man next to me? I try not to think of Myrtis. Try to imagine a horror not too great. I imagine fire emerging, somehow, from Vesuvius, perhaps setting fire to houses, people running and screaming, but, and this is what I spend my time imagining, running and screaming to safety, making their way to a safe place while many brave people fight the fires. The crowds will be bewailing possessions lost and perhaps even houses but nothing worse. Nothing worse. My imagination hones to perfection an image of Livia, carrying Amantius. Smudged with ashes, weeping at the sight of Marcus. But safe. And Myrtis. Somehow the two of them together, Anna trailing behind. All safe. I add Fausta, I add Felix. I even add the weasel as well as Lucius, his wife and their daughter Lucilla, because I need as many people as possible to be safe.

And yet the sky above me is still dark and ashes continue to fall on us. It coats my hands and I brush it away as though it were eating me alive.

We change horses twice that first day, each time I step shaking from the jolting chariot and run to relieve myself, then step back in because we must ride on, the fresh horses picking up pace as my fingers tighten on the chariot rim again. Marcus speaks only briefly to the innkeepers and it is his money that does the talking, the clink of coins bringing fresh horses, nervous at their new owners and new harness, no time to accustom them to us or to this mode of transport before they must gallop onwards as fast as Marcus can make them.

The dark sky above us makes nightfall come faster than it

should do. Marcus slows the horses as we approach another inn and when the stable hand comes out, he steps out of the chariot.

"Change of horses," he says.

"We can't ride at night," I say, clutching at his arm, my legs unsteady. "We can't see anything, there'll be an accident. We can't ride for three days with no sleep."

"I can't sleep," says Marcus.

"You have to," I say. "Please. We'll ride on as soon as there is light. Please."

"We have to ride on," he says.

"If we have an accident in the dark, we won't get there at all," I say.

The stable hand waits for a decision.

"We will stay the night," says Marcus. "A room and care for the horses. We will keep them for tomorrow morning."

"Yes, Dominus," says the man.

"We need to eat," I say.

"I can't eat."

"We have to," I say. "You have to be strong for when we arrive, it may be that we have to…" I'm not sure what we may have to do. "Perhaps there have been more tremors," I say, alighting on the only thing I can think of that is likely. "Perhaps we will have to carry all your family possessions somewhere, or help others. You cannot be tired and hungry; you have to be strong."

HE EATS BECAUSE I MAKE him, and he lies down on the bed in our cramped room because I make him. But I am not sure he sleeps. I sleep at last, when my legs have stopped trembling and the exhaustion of hours of fear suddenly washes over me. I wake over and over in the night, startled from the poor sleep by dreams of fires, of ashes raining down on me, the shaking of the chariot reverberating through me even though I am lying on the floor. When dawn comes, we are on the road again, my face no doubt as pale as Marcus'. The first burst of speed frightens me again but after a while the exhaustion takes over from the fear as I cling tightly to the rim of the chariot and keep my eyes on the road ahead. I try to stop thinking, repeating to myself over and over prayers to various gods. I am not really sure to whom I should be praying. Perhaps to motherly Juno, to keep Livia and Amantius safe? Or Vulcan, god of fire, who has somehow been angered and opened up a mountain of fire, which I still cannot imagine? Or Jupiter, greatest of the gods, since this is clearly an event of vast proportions? Twice in the morning we see imperial messengers heading for Rome, their horses sweating, and I dread seeing any more, for each additional one suggests worse news and when Marcus sees them, he urges the horses on ever faster.

The silence between us is louder than the noise of the horses galloping and our wheels, it hovers over the two of us. Marcus' voice is hoarse when he speaks to the stable hands at the two inns where we stop briefly. I offer him food, but he waves it away and I have to press the bread into his hands. He eats a few bites but then shakes his head. Come nightfall I have to insist, again, that we must stop.

"We will reach Puteoli tomorrow, we are making good progress," I say. "They will have more news there. But we must be rested."

Marcus looks at me as if he does not understand what I am saying. He must be dizzy with tiredness, as I am. He looks down at his bare arm and the ashes that have fallen on it, his skin turned grey. "It is still falling," he says, and it comes out as a guttural whisper. "How can it still be falling?"

I look down as though I am unaware of being covered in

ashes myself, as though it is a surprise to me rather than the growing dread I have been holding in me, a question I have not dared to ask. "We are closer to the source," I say. "By now it will no longer be falling in Rome."

"But it is still falling," he says, one hand loosening its grip on the reins so that the stable hand can take the horses away. "What kind of fire is it, that is still burning after so many days?"

I think of the Great Fire, which lasted six days and destroyed half of Rome and swallow. "I don't know," I say, and my voice starts too high, I have to lower it before tears start to fall. "I don't know, but we must eat and sleep now, come."

He allows himself to be led, as though a child, the grim determination from when he was driving gone. He sits, I order food, insisting on a thick vegetable porridge to warm us, pushing bread towards him as he eats in silence. I pour him more than one glass of wine and refill his plate against his refusal. He spoons food into his mouth as though it has no taste. Halfway through the second plate he pushes the bowl away and walks up the stairs to the small room we will stay the night in.

He does sleep, but fitfully, as do I. We are too tired not to sleep at all, but I wake regularly and when I do Marcus is often awake too. By dawn we are both lying, eyes wide open, waiting for enough light to depart.

AT FIRST THE DAY BEGINS like yesterday. Soft ash still blows through the cold air and the grey-yellow sky does not fully lighten, despite the sun rising. The road is fairly empty, as one would expect first thing in the morning. But soon we see a family come towards us, in a donkey cart. Behind them, only a few moments later, another family, this time on foot, with one pack mule between them, laden with possessions. When a third family come into sight I pull at Marcus' arm and he slows the chariot. When we are almost abreast, he stops. This family have two horses, pulling a large cart. On the cart are a man and woman, three children and various possessions: a few pieces of furniture, a chest that might hold clothes. The children are asleep, the man and woman look drained. Everything is coated with the fine ash that will not stop falling.

"Where are you from?" I ask.

"Herculaneum," says the man.

I feel my shoulders relax. The cities have not 'disappeared' then, as those gossips in Rome would have it. Clearly what I imagined was true: there has been a bad fire and some people, like these, may have lost their homes but here they are, a family together at least, still with some possessions. "How bad is the damage to the city?" I ask.

The couple stare at me. At last the woman speaks. "It is gone," she says.

"Gone?"

"Gone," says the man. "Vesuvius opened up, there was a vast black cloud, so vast, it…" He looks about him, as though to find something to compare it with, to explain it to me.

I nod, pointing up at the ashen sky. "It is very bad, it came as far as Rome."

The man shakes his head. "This is nothing," he says. "This would not harm anyone."

"Have many people been harmed?" I ask.

They look at me as though I am a fool. They shake their heads a little, open their mouths to explain and then close them again, unsure of how to begin. It is the man who finally manages to speak. "The cloud was black and filled with fire," he says. "It rose up and up and then burning stones and ash began to fall.

My brother is a fisherman, he said we could sail to Misenum. We left with him and his own family, sailed away. There was a wave of heat that came across the bay…"

"Like opening an oven door," says his wife as he trails off. "Then the ash fell and fell. We barely made it to Misenum. There were tremors and a great darkness in the daytime as if it were night. A great wave rose up and then the sea withdrew, pulled back from the shore, further than it has ever been. By then we had reached the town but, when the sky grew light again, my brother-in-law went back. The shoreline was full of animals from the depths of the sea, some he had never seen before, thrown onto the land, dying. Many of the boats were gone but he found his. We slept there one night. In the morning he said he would go back to Herculaneum to see what had happened and if he might help others, or if it were safe to return."

"And?" Marcus has spoken at last; he is leaning forward.

The man shakes his head. "He said it was gone. That there was no trace that a city had ever stood there."

"How can that be?"

"He said all of the land was grey with ashes and that he could not make out any part of the port nor the city or land beyond, that everything had disappeared. He has fished from that port for his whole life and he no longer knew its shape. He –"

I yelp. Marcus has suddenly used the whip and the horses leap forward. I clutch at the chariot as we race away down the road.

WE DRIVE SO FAST THAT the ever-falling ashes are driven into our faces. I have to keep my eyes narrowed so that I will not be blinded, wiping and wiping again, the other hand clutching at the side of the chariot.

We are very close to Puteoli when Marcus veers left, away from the main road and down a smaller one. The chariot rocks at the sudden change of direction and I can feel the right wheel lift entirely off the ground. I cry out, certain that we are about to be thrown to our deaths. But the wheel slams back down onto the road and we are safe. I want to ask Marcus what he is doing, but when I wipe my eyes again, I see what he has seen.

Ahead of us is an encampment. To the left, a mess of ramshackle shelters, tiny and misshapen. To the right, a detachment of marines is working to create a far more organised area. There are men digging latrines and trenches, others putting up brown army tents, which range in size, some of them truly vast, the full floor span of Lucius' holiday villa. These are arranged immaculately, row by row, bringing order to the scene of chaos before us. An entranceway has been created, a wall of posts with a gate, to which Marcus drives without hesitation.

At the gate stands a centurion accompanied by a scribe.

"We are not yet ready to house refugees," says the centurion as soon as he sees us. "You have to make your way over to the other encampment and wait. We should have the first tents ready by tonight for those with children."

"We're not refugees," says Marcus. "We've just arrived from Rome."

The centurion looks us over with a frown. Clearly, we are not messengers from the Emperor, or from anyone else. "What are you doing here?" he asks.

"I've come back to look for my wife and son in Pompeii."

Something passes over the centurion's face, but he doesn't answer right away. He glances at the scribe, then back at Marcus. "Pompeii got hit pretty bad," he says at last. "You'll need to search the refugee camps here and below Stabiae."

"How bad?" Marcus asks. "What happened, exactly?"

The centurion shakes his head. "Can't go into that," he says. "You need to go into the other encampment," he repeats. "Some of my men are there, taking names of everyone who is missing and the people who are looking for them. Tell them your name and who you are searching for. The tents here will mostly be ready tonight, everyone should be housed by tomorrow evening. Orders direct from the Emperor. Detachments of the Praetorian Guard will be arriving tomorrow. We've been promised whatever is needed, he's even going to send two senators to manage the region in person."

For a moment I think Marcus is going to argue, perhaps tell the centurion that he, too, was once an army man, try to claim some kind of bond between them so that he can have more information, but he only nods and pulls at the reins, directing the horses back towards the makeshift shelters that stretch out across the fields, into the distance.

THERE ARE NO WOODEN POSTS here to form a barricade, only individual soldiers, spaced out along the edge of the field where shelters begin. This must be some farmer's land, I think, perhaps willingly given over to this crisis, perhaps simply commandeered. This camp is like nothing I have ever seen before, worse than the rougher backstreets of Rome, where at least there are insulae, however dirty and crumbling. These are fields full of people, covered by the ever-falling grey ash, kneeling to crawl into tiny shelters made of whatever came to hand, sticks, cloaks, upturned carts, even branches from nearby trees, still thick with red and yellow leaves from the changing days of autumn. I stand in the chariot, gazing out over the fields, almost unaware that Marcus has now jumped down and is fastening the reins of the horses to a tree. He nods to the nearest soldier.

"Keep an eye on them, will you?"

The marine nods, and Marcus strides out into the camp.

It takes me a moment to gather my thoughts, my satchel and his bag, and hurry after him, almost falling into a rainwater ditch before finding my footing and joining him in the field.

For a moment Marcus hesitates, looking to one side and then the other, before turning around and addressing the soldier again. "Who's in charge?"

"Marinus. Over by the red tent."

He's right, there is indeed an army tent set up in the middle of the camp, and Marcus is already heading towards it. I stumble after him, the already harvested field's last remaining stalks of barley scratching at my ankles.

Inside the tent is an older man with dark brown skin and short tightly curled hair, who looks exhausted. He has two scribes sitting with him, each with many rolls of papyrus at their feet in large containers. Clearly they have been doing this work for many hours.

"Name?"

"Marcus Aquillius Scaurus."

"And the woman?"

"My slave, Althea."

They don't note down my name. A slave who is looking for someone is hardly worth registering in this situation unless someone is looking for them. I can imagine there are plenty of slaves who will use the disaster to escape.

"Looking for?"

"My wife Livia and son Amantius."

"Age of child?"

"Not yet two."

There is a pause, while the two scribes check through their current lists, hesitating here and there when they find another woman named Livia, only to shake their heads when there is no mention of a child. I daren't look at Marcus' face. At last there is a final shake of the head and Marcus lets out the breath he has been holding.

"If we come across them, where are they to find you? We're crosschecking the refugees from all the camps we find, copying lists of names and sending them to the other camps."

"They should stay here in the military camp until I come for them. I will seek them myself in Pompeii first of all."

The scribes continue making notes, but the man in charge looks up at Marcus and the same look crosses over his face that I saw on the centurion. "Pompeii is gone," he says. He says it with a measure of gentleness, but also with absolute certainty.

"What do you mean, gone?" asks Marcus and there is nothing gentle in his tone. "A city cannot disappear."

"It has been covered in ashes," says the man.

"Of course," agrees Marcus. He holds out his own arm, still lightly covered in ash from our journey. "It's still falling. Of course it is covered in ashes."

The man stands up. He is tall, his gaze is level with Marcus. "Most of the roofs of the houses have caved in under the weight of ashes and stones," he says slowly. "When seen from the sea, in a ship we took to carry out a reconnaissance, there is nothing left. Only ashes."

Marcus says nothing. His face shows no emotion. My own face must have gone very pale, because the man glances at me and indicates a stool I may sit on if I wish. I shake my head but have to swallow more than once to calm the desire to vomit.

If what this man is saying is true, then how can anyone have escaped? I cannot imagine what he's saying, I cannot imagine a city disappearing under ashes, as though it were a child's toy house made of little blocks of wood rather than a city of brick and stone. And people. The man has not mentioned the people. It is not my place to speak, as a slave, but I can't help myself.

"How many survived?"

The man's eyes flicker towards Marcus but then come to rest on me. "We don't know," he says honestly, and I see again the exhaustion in his eyes and the slump of his shoulders. "There are hundreds arriving in makeshift camps every day since it happened, but…" He pauses. "There should be more," he says at last. "There should be far, far more people arriving. We now know Stabiae is still standing, although it is severely damaged, there is a huge refugee camp nearby. But the camps on this side, we've had hardly anyone from Pompeii, Herculaneum and Oplontis. There should be a lot more."

"Perhaps the people from Pompeii went to Stabiae," I say.

"Perhaps," says the man, but he drops his gaze from me as he says it. I think of what he said before, that Pompeii has gone.

I'm about to ask for more details, I want to know more from this man, I want him to describe Pompeii in more detail, I want to know exactly what he saw, and from what distance, whether perhaps he was mistaken, if there was mist or fog even, mixed with the ashes, making it hard to see from the ship. I want to challenge him, to suggest that, if he was on a ship, he cannot have been that close to the shore and perhaps he was mistaken.

"Your master has gone," points out one of the scribes and I turn to see Marcus ducking out of the tent flaps, striding away. I have no choice but to hurry after him.

OUTSIDE THE TENT ARE THREE more people, two women and one man, waiting to register their names and the names of their loved ones. The women are weeping, the man looks like Marcus, his face set in grim disbelief. One of the women has a child, who is clinging to her knees, grey face streaked with tears.

I catch up with Marcus, who turns to me when he becomes aware of my presence and takes his bag from me, slinging it over one shoulder.

"We will work the field together," he says. "Line by line. Do not miss a single shelter. Start on this line and make your way to the end of the field. Then work your way back along the next line and so on. I will work from the bottom up and meet you when we have both finished."

"We have registered our names and theirs," I start. "They said they weren't here. Yet," I add hastily.

"They've only just started registering people, they could easily have missed some," says Marcus. "Start."

THE SEARCH IS EXHAUSTING, AND not just because it stretches over more than three fields over the scratching, scraping barley stalks. My ankles are bleeding by the time I have covered three rows. At each tiny shelter I must call out, ask to see the inhabitants, all of them shaken, ashen, afraid. Children cry, women too. The men do not know what to do, everything has been taken away from them, even the ability to provide for their families. They have been told to wait. They have been told they will be fed by the army this evening and housed in military tents as soon as possible. There is nowhere else to go. Most of the people I meet have already travelled further from their homes than they have ever done before, and they are lost, bewildered. They believe they have incurred the wrath of the gods and yet escaped with their lives and they do not know whether to be grateful or guilt-ridden. They ask me questions to which I do not have answers. Is Rome sending more soldiers to help? Will there be money to rebuild their houses, replace livestock, fishing boats? How long will they be able to live in tents, with winter coming? They are afraid and their fear builds in me, as I make my way from shelter to shelter and person to person. I ask for Livia and Amantius, but also for Fausta, Myrtis and Felix. I even ask for Lucius and his wife, certain that a wealthy man like my past master must surely have had the means to escape this disaster. I want to ask these people for more details of what happened, but I know that Marcus will want me to complete my checks as quickly as possible.

I finish my allotted part and find Marcus already waiting, shifting from foot to foot, nervous and fretful.

"Nothing?"

I shake my head. "I'm sorry."

"And you asked for them by name? In case they had been seen elsewhere?"

"Yes."

He takes a deep breath, looks one way and another, then stiffens, narrows his eyes. "Fausta?" He raises his voice. "Fausta!"

A woman, hesitating at the entrance to the military encampment, turns, then makes her way at speed across the uneven field.

"Marcus!" Her black curls are in disarray, her tunic and toga filthy. "I give thanks you are already here, and I have found you," she says, clasping her hands and looking upwards as she covers the last few steps between us, then embracing Marcus. "I will sacrifice as I vowed," she adds. "Althea! The two of you must have travelled at such speed! I am glad to see you."

"Where are Livia and Amantius?" asks Marcus.

"You haven't found them?"

He shakes his head.

Tears start from her eyes and she claps a hand over her mouth. "I have looked everywhere."

"Where?"

"Puteoli and the camps here both yesterday and today, I have combed them."

"She may have gone south," he says. "Perhaps to her family in Stabiae, she would have known I would seek her there if she had not already headed to Rome."

"Yes, of course," says Fausta quickly, although there is doubt in her eyes. I know she is thinking what I am thinking: how could a woman and small child have made their way to Stabiae so fast after such a disaster? They would have had to ride on horseback at speed and no-one is travelling at speed. The families we have seen have been on foot or with slow carts. And besides, the rumours said Stabiae had disappeared too, would she have headed there?

"I will search this camp once more, the far field where the new people are arriving, then we will head to Pompeii," says Marcus. He is already striding away.

I sink to the ground, exhausted. Fausta squats near me. "I have already searched," she says, and tears trickle down her face. "They are lost, all of them."

"Have you found no-one you knew?" I ask.

"No," she says. "Most of the people in this camp come from the villages or farms at a greater distance from Pompeii, not from the city itself."

"Were you still in Misenum when it happened?"

She nods, wiping her eyes.

"What did you see?"

She shakes her head. "Nothing on the first day, the morning was clear, a blue sky. I was with the old man in his bedchamber till late morning. The sun was just past its highest point, he was dozing, but I heard shouts down by the bay. I looked out from the balcony and there was a strange dark cloud over the mountains. I know now it was Vesuvius, but I couldn't tell from that distance. The cloud was vast, like nothing I've ever seen before. It went straight up, like a tree trunk or a mast and then it started fanning out, it looked like an umbrella pine. It was black at first and then it started flaring out, first dark, then bright with fire, red and yellow flashes, then it would go black again and then the fire would show again, over and over."

I stare at her, trying to imagine what she is describing.

"The old man sent a slave running to a friend of his and so we heard that word had come. They said it was Mount Vesuvius and they were afraid Pompeii was in grave danger."

"They said Admiral Pliny died trying to rescue people?"

"That's what I've heard. Certainly, he set out, we saw the galleys setting sail. But later we heard they couldn't land at Pompeii. There were burning rocks falling into their boats and giant boulders which rolled down and blocked the shoreline. I spoke to one of the surviving sailors yesterday, not all the galleys returned. They tried further down the coast and made land at Stabiae. The sailor said there were noxious fumes, tremors, one after another, burning stones and ashes falling everywhere, people running in the streets with pillows held over their heads to protect themselves from being struck."

Myrtis and Felix, did they run with pillows or were they forced to obey Lucius' orders, maybe told to go to their rooms?

Fausta runs a hand through her hair, her fingers shaking. "He said even though it was still daytime, you couldn't see anything. Pitch black. The waves were so strong it was hard to make a landing and almost impossible to bring anyone to safety."

"And in Misenum?"

"Constant tremors. We realised by then they weren't just the usual tremors you get at this time of year. They were a warning, an ill omen, but none of us knew that." She tries and fails to pin her hair back, eventually giving up. "We stood on the balcony all day, watching the cloud spreading. We tried to sleep that night, but the tremors grew worse and worse, we were almost flung out of our bed. We didn't dare stay indoors after that, we went to the garden and waited for the dawn, the old man, me, all his slaves, even his daughters were there. Everyone praying and sobbing for Misenum to be spared and me thinking, what's happening in Pompeii? I knew it had to be worse than where we were. We waited for the dawn and there was only a yellowish half-light. The sea suddenly rolled back on itself, as if it was being pulled back from the shoreline against its will. That's when the old man said we should get out of the city, the countryside would be safer. He called for carts and horses but none of the stable hands could manage the horses, five of them bolted, none of them would be harnessed. In the end we managed to get a couple of carts lined up and let the rest of the horses go, they were unrideable, rearing up and trying to run, kicking out, they'd have broken someone's leg if they'd caught them. The old man's stupid daughters were trying to grab all the valuables, running in and out of the house with armfuls of clothes and boxes of jewels. The old man shouted at them in the end saying they'd be dead if they didn't hurry up. I kept watching Pompeii and the cloud was growing all the time, flames still flashing inside it, like sheet lightning in August when the summer heat breaks. Then it started lowering, losing the pine shape, moving low down and across the whole coastline. The Island of Capri disappeared first, then the cloud was creeping across the sea towards us like some beast out of a nightmare, everyone screaming at the sight of it, great crowds trying to follow anyone who looked like they knew what they were doing. We had more than four hundred trying to follow us. In the end we couldn't even see the promontory of Misenum, the cloud had reached it." Her voice cracks, hoarse with the telling and the fear.

I offer water and Fausta gulps it loudly, wipes her chin. She takes a deep breath and puffs the air out, as though trying to get rid of something inside her.

"Then what?" I ask.

"We set out on the high road, although we couldn't go fast, there were too many people and everyone shouting at those ahead to walk faster. When we looked back the cloud was low over the ground, following us like a dark mist. We tried to run, but the old man couldn't go that fast and I was afraid we'd be trampled, people were pushing and shoving from behind to go faster. There were ashes falling everywhere, clouds of them, it made it hard to breathe. We were holding up our clothes over our mouths, but it hardly helped. In the end I told the old man we had to step away from the main road, we'd die underfoot if he fell. He ordered the daughters and his slaves off the road, though some of the servants refused and carried on ahead. We'd barely got off the main road, found ourselves a little area we could stand in a field and then the mist caught up with us."

She breathes again, a shuddering breath. It's making me uncomfortable seeing Fausta so shaken.

"It was like being shut up in a dark room, no moon or stars, no lamp, just black night and screaming all around, children crying, women shrieking, men shouting, angry in their fear, cursing the gods while the women prayed to them. Then there was a sudden burst of heat and flames, I thought we would die for sure if more came, but there were only ashes after that. They fell so thickly we had to shake them off every few moments or we would have been buried under them." She stops again, then speaks quickly. "The old man died," she says. "Maybe he couldn't breathe, I don't know, he clutched at his chest, he was gasping and then he was gone, even in the dark and with all the screaming, I felt him go limp, I knew he was gone. I held him till the light came back," she adds, her chin held too high, tears trembling in her eyes as she fights not to let them fall.

"I'm sorry," I say. I remember Marcus talking about Fausta's lover, how he would have made her his mistress and given her a soft life, how they had been lovers since she was a young woman. I touch her hand and she gives a quick nod that makes a couple of tears fall.

"The light came back eventually," she says. "But it was strange, a half-light like an eclipse. When his daughters saw their father was dead, they started screaming and wailing, then they turned on me. They've always wanted to," she adds. "He wouldn't let them speak ill of me or be rude to my face, but they hated me, didn't like that he favoured me over their mother even when she was alive. The moment they saw he was dead they were screaming insults at me."

"What did you do?"

"Got up and walked away," she says and I see her lips tighten in an effort not to cry at the thought of walking away from the old man she had loved and been loved by for years, the pain of being chased away from his side. "Walked back to Misenum, found a fisherman the next day who'd take me to Puteoli at least. No-one would sail to Pompeii. I kept checking the city and then the camps as the refugees started arriving. I knew Marcus would arrive eventually, but I was afraid I'd miss him. I've done nothing but search for our team, but I've found none of them. They would have sheltered in the amphitheatre or the gladiator's barracks until it was too late."

"And his wife and child?"

Fausta puts her face down on her knees, her voice comes out muffled. "They would have gone to the amphitheatre, they would have known our team would protect them from anything, anything at all. But how were they to protect them from what happened? Who can stand against the wrath of the gods?"

"They might have escaped," I try.

Fausta looks up and rubs at her already-red eyes. "He won't find them," she says, and it is only now I see how much she has held back, what a brave face she has put on for Marcus' benefit. "Vulcan has taken them. There are so few who have survived and most of them only through luck: living a little way out of town so they had a head start, or fishermen who took to their boats and made it further down the coast, the people who were out of the city on business, as we were. A woman with a small child would have sought shelter, not struck out on her own. Livia was no adventurer." She gulps back a sob. "They are all gone," she repeats. "All of them. I know it."

"But Pompeii…"

She shakes her head. "The ashes were falling so thickly," she says. "And that was in Misenum, we were far away. Puteoli's ankle deep in ashes as it is, Pompeii…" her voice trails away.

"They said it had disappeared," I say, hoping she will disagree, but she nods.

"I can believe it."

"Believe what?" Marcus is back.

Fausta shakes her head, stands up. "Nothing," she says. "Now what?"

"Now we sail to Pompeii."

I gape at Marcus. "Sail to Pompeii? Who will take us?"

Marcus is already walking towards the chariot. The horses look downcast, the grass and leaves they might have nibbled on are layered over with ashes. "With enough money, anyone will take you anywhere, you must know that. Fausta, you stay here and watch over the camp in case Livia or any of our team arrive." He holds out a hand with a few coins. "Eat. Sleep. Rest. We will be back soon."

Fausta follows us to the chariot. "Surely by now all the survivors will have left?"

Marcus backs the horses round to rejoin the road, then gestures to me to climb into the chariot. "There may be many survivors. They may be searching for loved ones themselves and if so, they would not leave the area. And if the soldiers have seen the city only from the deck of a ship…" He steps into the chariot beside me, our bodies once again pressed together. I have stopped noticing it by now, there is no intimacy in it, only desperation.

Fausta steps away from the horses. "Neptune grant you safe passage," she says and then steps forward again, one hand on the closest horse's neck. "Come back safe, Marcus," she says, and her loud voice is very small.

Marcus doesn't reply, he only whips up the horses to the fast gallop that I am almost used to. "Where are we going?" I ask, gripping onto the front of the chariot, not daring to look back at Fausta for fear of growing dizzy.

"The docks of Puteoli," he says.

THE DOCKS OF PUTEOLI STINK. Not the normal stink of any docks, of fresh or frying fish and sweating men, smoking braziers for warming hands, garum sauce and whatever has spilled on the quayside that morning whilst being loaded and unloaded. This stink is everywhere and overwhelms everything. It is the stink of vast quantities of rotting dead fish.

"Never seen so many dead fish washed up on the shore," says a man when I ask. "We couldn't clear them away fast enough, they just kept coming. There's still loads of them floating on the sea. Most of the fishermen's boats have been wrecked and those that haven't won't go out again, they're too scared. They say Vulcan hasn't finished with us yet. They're afraid Neptune might have been angered too, there was a giant wave that came up. The men are saying sea monsters might rise from the deep at his command. They won't risk it."

I look at Marcus, but he doesn't seem bothered by this information, by the idea that there might be nobody to sail us to Pompeii. He settles himself down on the quayside, as though he has all the time in the world and looks up at the man. "Spread the word," he says. "My name is Marcus and I will pay a month's wages to whoever will sail me to Pompeii tonight."

"No one will sail to Pompeii tonight," says the man. "It's already growing dark. I doubt they'll even sail tomorrow."

"A month's wages," Marcus says again. "But I must be there before dawn."

"What's the rush? Want to feel the wrath of Vulcan for yourself?"

"I'm looking for my wife and son," says Marcus. "A month's wages," he repeats.

THE MAN WATCHES US FOR a while, but Marcus doesn't move and eventually I settle down beside him to wait. I cannot imagine that anybody will set sail tonight, in the dark, to a place that may or may not have been cursed by Vulcan, that may or may not still exist. I look up at the sky, which is still grey. A sailor would need the stars to help him navigate, surely, they would not risk going out without them at a time like this. The man wanders away.

"Are you hungry?" I ask Marcus but he shakes his head, as I expected. I ignore him and boldly hold out my hand. "Money," I say, as firmly as I dare.

He doesn't argue and hands me his purse. I take it, make my way along the quayside until I find a popina. It looks deeply disreputable, with lewd graffiti everywhere suggesting that the barmaid and several of her sisters are for hire, at cut rate prices. I pull my cloak around me and quickly place an order for bean soup and bread, along with two cups of wine. I take them back to Marcus and all but force him to eat, returning our cups, spoons and bowls to the popina when we are done.

"What if no one will take us, what will we do?" I ask.

"Someone will come," he says.

Hours pass, although it's hard to tell the time with no stars. It grows dark and the only light comes from two windows of a house nearby and from the popina, where I can hear raucous laughter and the gurgle of cups being refilled. Occasionally I take a deep breath to try and steady my constant nerves, and when I do, I retch at the smell of rotting fish, which I thought I'd got used to. Every so often, a man will wander out of the popina and stare down the quayside at us, our huddled shapes barely visible. Clearly the word is being spread, but there are no takers as yet.

I MUST HAVE FALLEN ASLEEP, though I don't know when. I wake when Marcus digs me in the side and I find that I have been sleeping slumped against him, my head on his shoulder, although he has not moved away from me. Standing over us is the shape of a man.

"A month's wages?"

"Yes." Marcus' voice is not eager, only flat. Perhaps it convinces the man he is telling the truth, that the offer is genuine.

"And it can't wait till tomorrow?"

"No."

"Why not?"

"I'm looking for my wife and child."

"You can't search for them in the dark."

"No, but I don't want to waste more time. You can get me there by dawn?"

There is a pause. "Have you heard what happened?"

"Yes."

"I've seen it," says the man. His voice changes, I can't see his face in the dark but he sounds as though he is about to cry. "It's like nothing you've ever seen before. It's like the opening to the underworld."

Marcus stands up and I follow, although one of my legs has gone completely numb so I almost fall over again. "Let's go."

THE BOAT IS SMALL. I stand on the quayside looking down into it, while the man holds a flaming torch up so we can see to get in. Marcus climbs in and then turns to me, holding up a hand.

I want to refuse.

I want to say I will wait here.

I am afraid we will never make it, that the fishermen are right and sea monsters will rise from the deep. I want to tell Marcus that the last time I was on a boat I saw my mother die and my father become a slave. Perhaps ordinarily I might tell him I am afraid, but I look at his face, white even in the flickering yellow light, and I cannot let him go alone to search for his wife and child. I take his hand, wondering if he can feel my fingers shaking and find myself aboard the boat, the rocking under my trembling legs bringing tears to my eyes. I lower my head and sit down as quickly as I can, huddle into my cloak and murmur a prayer to Libertas under my breath.

"Watch over me, Libertas, as I enter the realm of Neptune, intercede with him for me, for us. Beg him to let us pass, we need to know the truth of what we must grieve for."

HADES

I SLEEP, BUT ONLY BECAUSE MY eyes close against my will. I cough often and sometimes so hard that I wake myself up in a panic, clutching at the side of the boat, forgetting why I am rising and falling. When I remember I stare blearily about me and can vaguely make out the shapes of the fisherman and Marcus by the still-flickering torch, but I cannot see any details, and my eyes close again even as I search for a glimpse of light on the horizon.

A fit of coughing wakes me again, shaking me to life. A pale hint of light is growing in the sky, and when I turn to spit over the side of the boat, I see my spit is dark. Marcus is still in the same position. The fisherman has his back to me, standing in the prow of the boat. I try to make out something, anything, but I cannot, perhaps it is still too dark. The fisherman looks over his shoulder at me and when he sees me peering to the left, he shakes his head.

"There it is," he says and his voice cracks. He gestures ahead to the left as though we are unaware of where the shoreline is and indeed, he is right, for the water is grey and the land is grey, there is no difference. It is like seeing by night, when even a full moon cannot show the colours of the day, only a strange shadow copy of it.

He must have made a mistake. What is in front of me cannot be Pompeii. He has erred in his calculations; this is some other place. The shape of Vesuvius is wrong, the mountain is a third less tall, its outline different. Where its summit was once a tall cone, now it is a broken flattened ridge. The port is changed too, vast black rocks jut out of what used to be a clear stretch of blue water, an easy mooring for ships to come home to. And beyond the water there is nothing. No city walls, no houses. There is only a dense and endless grey. I look back at the man and shake my head.

"This is not Pompeii," I say with certainty. "It must be further down the coast."

"Pompeii is gone."

"The people…" I begin, but he shakes his head before I have finished.

"Gone," he repeats. "All gone."

"They didn't run?" I ask.

"Some ran," he says. "The heat reached out and touched them and they died there and then."

"From heat?" I say, uncomprehending.

"The anger of the gods is hotter than any fire you have ever known," he says. "Hotter than the white heat of a blacksmith's iron."

"No-one escaped?"

"Some," he says. He swallows and when he speaks again his voice is croaked. "A few," he manages. "There are refugee camps further down the coast."

I clutch at Marcus' arm. "They will have escaped," I say, my voice too high and too joyous. "For sure, they will have run and…" I trail away, unsure of what I am saying. I look again at the grey world spread out before me and shake my head. "A

125

fisherman," I start again, "Livia will have asked for help and one of the fishermen will have taken pity on her, since she had a child, he will have rowed with her and his own family to safety, to Stabiae, or…" I look to my right, down the coast as though I might spot fresh green trees and a sandy beach where all the inhabitants, save perhaps a very few unlucky ones, will be gathered. But there is nothing to see, only the smoking mountain to my left, the ashen nothingness before us and to my right, the sea leading onwards into still more devastation.

Marcus says nothing, does not move. Suddenly I am afraid to touch him again. I pull my hand back. He stays still and silent while the fisherman sails closer to the shore, using a pole to guide his way around the larger rocks.

"Can't get much closer," he says at last. "You'll have to wade."

Marcus stands, unsteady in the boat, then slips over the side. The water reaches his chest and I am afraid, for I stand shorter than him by at least a head's height and I cannot swim. Once in the water he holds out his arms to me and I dare not refuse. I clutch at my satchel, but Marcus shakes his head.

"You will wait for us," he tells the fisherman. I have not heard his voice for many hours, it comes out as a croak. The fisherman nods. Reluctantly, I leave my satchel in the boat and slip over the side into Marcus' arms. The water is cold and my feet scrabble to gain purchase, but he holds me until I have found my footing, his face blank. The water is up to my chin, but I can feel the bottom, and Marcus keeps one hand on me as we wade towards the shore. I go under once, tripping over a rock beneath the surface, but he yanks me upwards and I find my balance again. We have to crawl to get out of the water, for the shore is littered with rocks. I touch something soft and yelp, then see a dead sheep floating, its wool trailing in the water, eyes white and body bloated. I pull back in disgust, scramble more quickly, scraping my knee. I still don't really know where I am. The harbour was always a bustling place, there were jetties and walls with heavy iron rings where the boats were tied up. I cannot see the walls. There are no jetties, only the odd floating plank of wood, another dead sheep's body drifting past, rocks everywhere.

At last we are both standing on solid ground, if it can be called that. The ashes here are so thick they have mixed with the sea and formed an oozing mud. My feet sink in and soon my shoes have all but disappeared, the paste clinging to my calves. We trudge through it, heads down to take care over each step we take. When we are further from the water, the ashes become dry. They are too soft, though, each step we take sinks us down until a rock finds us. One patch comes up to my knees before I hit rock. I panic, thinking I will sink down into endless ashes and suffocate, try to take a deep breath to steady my thoughts and then realise that this is the fate that befell the people of Pompeii, the soft soft ashes filling their houses and mouths. I have to take a few more quick breaths, panic rising in me at the thought. I put my hand on a large rock, try to calm myself and look around me, the invisible sun behind the yellow-grey sky lending me some light with which to see.

This is Hades.

This is the land of the dead.

Everywhere is grey and black. There is no other colour. I shake my head, blink my eyes, for they seem to have lost the ability to see colour. But there is no colour. The sky is grey. The broken mountain is grey and black. The whole of the land beneath the sky, no matter where I turn, is grey, with black chunks of rock here and there. What used to be trees are now black charred arms stretching out of the devastation, reaching out to the gods to beg for their forgiveness, to placate their anger. Behind me is the sea and that, too, is grey, a silver-grey that shifts while before me is a soft grey that also shifts with the wind, clouds of it billowing. The air smells of rotting eggs and occasionally another smell drifts past, the harder sweeter stench of rotting flesh, from the fallen. I try to think only of the bloated sheep I saw bobbing in the bay and not of the people who stumbled while trying to escape, who ran but were felled by raging heat or trampling feet in the darkness that followed, who did not rise again. Now only the smell rises.

I should not have thought of it. My body is forced over as though by a blow to the back and bitter yellow bile spews from my mouth onto the ground, mixing with the soft grey. I straighten up, spitting the taste from my mouth, sweat trickling under my eyes. Ahead of me Marcus does not turn at the sound of me retching. Has he just walked over the top of the city walls? Is he walking up one of the main streets of the city? Or is he trampling over the rooftops as though he were a cat? I keep trying to find an anchor, an understanding of where I am, of where Pompeii is, but it has vanished so completely I am adrift. I stumble after him. If the mountain is there, if the sea is behind me, then is this the Marina Gate? If I walk after Marcus and we head that way, will we come to the gladiatorial barracks again, will we find his house nearby? And how will we judge how far we have walked when there are few landmarks and we stumble at every step, slowing us so that we lose track of how far we have come? If we used to say walk fifty paces, how many paces through the thick slow ash is that?

Marcus is still walking, now a long way off, stride by long stride, sometimes stumbling a little, once falling. He walks as though he is certain of a destination, as though he is in a hurry to reach it and all these ashes are merely in his way. Because I do not know what else to do, I follow him. I cannot hope to keep up with him, he has too great a head start and his legs are far longer than mine. I walk as fast as I can, falling often until I slow my gait. I cannot catch up with him, so I had better save myself from further scrapes and bruises.

"I AM SO SORRY," I keep saying, as though it were a chant, as though if I say it enough times there will be nothing to be sorry about; the ashes will rise back into the sky and uncover Pompeii just as it was before, its inhabitants crouched safely under its weight, scared of course, but relieved beyond measure to see us. Marcus will embrace his wife and child; he will smile and nod permission for me to run to Lucius' villa and find Myrtis and Felix, and all the others in the household. Myrtis will grumble about the state of the house, with all this damage and ashes everywhere, and want to know who is going to clean it all up, and Felix will hug me without words, glad I have been spared their experience. Marcus has finally stopped. I've only just caught up with him. He walks so much faster than I, even in this landscape.

"I am so sorry," I say again to his back.

He turns towards me, his face full of such rage that I step back, afraid that my words have offended him, that my helplessness is a burden to him. He reaches me in a few quick steps and for a moment I think he is going to beat me, or rape me, or something else terrible and I do not know why, nor how I can escape. I stumble, lose my footing, and fall into the ashes, their softness pulling at me. Marcus grasps my wrist, but he is not pulling me to my feet. Instead he jerks at my arm, impatient, while I struggle to stand but he pulls me off balance again. There's cold

129

air on my wrist and a soft thud and then he lets go of me and walks away again, each footstep sinking, a grey cloud following him. I look down at my arm. He has undone my gold cuff, which is now half-buried in the ashes, the tiny pin on a chain beside it. My arm feels cold and light without it. I claw the cuff back out of the ashes and rock from all fours onto my knees and then stand, precariously.

"What have you done?" I call out to him. "Why have you taken it off?" I don't understand what he means by it. I don't know what I am to do. Is he taking it away as a punishment? But he left it lying in the grey softness as though it were of no importance. Clasping the cuff in my left hand, my other arm outstretched for balance, I follow him to where he stands looking out over the endless grey. When I am only a few steps away I stop. "Why?" I ask.

He turns to me, stares at my puzzled face and then reaches out a hand. I hold out the cuff, but he shakes his head and gestures that I should give him my right hand. I hold it out. He takes it roughly, pulling me closer to him.

"I, Marcus Aquillius Scaurus, do give you, Althea, your freedom. This is your manumission. You are a freedwoman from this day forward. Now go." He drops my hand, strides away to the right, his head still turning this way and that, as though he will suddenly see something he recognises.

I drop the gold cuff and it lands in a soft puff of ashes. My hand is shaking so hard I can barely lift it. I stand in the hellscape, looking down at my wrist, the cuff now gone. I am free. I have been set free by my master. I am a freedwoman. *My father on his knees. I beg you, I beg you will buy my daughter also, I will serve you loyally if you will only buy her, if you will only take her as a slave. I beg you.* My tears fall into the ashes at my feet and stain them, tiny black blotches of happiness and wonder amidst the devastation. I scoop up the cuff. Its weight will assure me of money for a long time to come, I need only find a jeweller who will buy it from me for a fair price. After that… I am not sure what I will do. I can offer myself as a paid scribe to a rich household or live a simple life and write letters for those who cannot write for themselves. But I am free and nothing else matters.

Except those who have been lost.

The wild thrill dies as I look about me again. The landscape shocks me, over and over. I have seen some form of it for days now and the worst of it for many hours, and still it is so shocking, so horrible, that I cannot comprehend it. I think of the layers upon layers of stones and ashes beneath my feet and below them crushed invisible bodies. I step to one side as though to lift my weight away from them, yet for all I know I am now standing on another person, unknown to me or worse, known to me, their body crushed still further under my unknowing weight, their lungs unable to breathe because of my ignorance of their whereabouts. I begin to walk, unsure of where I am going, only that I cannot keep standing in one place in case I am causing further torment, even though I know that the suffering is gone now for the dead and is felt only by the living.

Marcus.

He has made his way to a place a little way off and is on his knees, scooping up ashes and throwing them to one side. I wade towards him, the soft ashes fooling me so that I step on hard rocks more than once, fall over twice.

"Marcus?"

"The apartments were here, I have worked it out." He coughs. The ashes he is scooping up are filling the air. I pull my head wrap across my mouth.

"How can you be sure?"

He sits back on his knees, suddenly eager to tell me, eager to be certain. "That must be the barracks because there is the very top of the roof of the theatre and I took fifty paces this way and then I would have turned left and entered the courtyard there, you see?" His arm flings out in a wide arc, points to the endless grey, to a place that in his mind is the entryway to his home. "And so, the roof must be below here, I think it must have fallen in, because it should be higher than the ashes, but perhaps the weight of the rocks and ashes caused it to give way. But we were only on the first floor, so it's possible that the second floor protected our apartment…"

I kneel next to him. My tears start to fall. The sight of this man, alone in this devastation, who has chosen a spot which might, or might not, be the right place, who has started digging without any possibility of finding his loved ones, is too much to bear. "Marcus," I say, as gently as I can, "Marcus, they are gone."

"No," he says and digs again, the air around us growing ever thicker with clouds of ash so that I cough and cough again.

"Yes," I say. "Marcus, please. They are gone." I touch his arm.

The shove he gives me is so hard I find myself rolling with the force of it. My mouth fills with ashes. I crawl onto my knees, spitting and coughing, desperate to get the ashes out of my mouth. When I have wiped down my face I see Marcus is still on his knees, trying to scoop away the ashes.

HE DIGS FOR HOURS. BUT the ashes shift with the slightest breeze and he makes slow progress. He finds what seems to be a rooftop, but it is broken and crushed and even though he lifts away tiles and beams, grunting and sweating with the work, it is only a tiny part of what would have to be excavated. He will not let me come near him. In the end I sit watching him, as though by witnessing his efforts I am somehow helping him.

I pray. At first, I am not sure to whom I should be praying, other than Vulcan, god of fire, who must have been angered. The sun moves across the sky and I have to sit and watch a man I barely know search for his wife and child, even though I am already certain they are dead, like all the rest of the people who used to live in this city that has disappeared, buried beneath the grey. Myrtis and Felix.

I start at the beginning. I pray to Jupiter to strengthen this man and to Juno to care for his dead wife. I pray to the Great Mother Cybele for the tiny child I only saw for a few hours. I pray to Vulcan, apologising for whatever has angered him. I pray to Mercury, messenger of the gods, to bring us mortals a message to tell us what to do, to take back to the gods a plea from us begging for forgiveness. I pray and pray, I think of every god I can, beg each for forgiveness, I beg for their influence in taking away some of this horror, in whatever realm of life they control. I pray to Mars, who watches over soldiers, for Marcus was once one of his men. I pray to Venus for the love this man has lost. I pray to Libertas, at first thanking her that she protected me, an insignificant slave, from certain death, but I also pray to her for Myrtis and Felix and other slaves I have known, now lost in the choking ashes and then it is hard not to berate Libertas, not to ask in anger why they had to die.

"We need to return."

The fisherman's voice startles me from my prayers. Marcus pays no attention; he is still digging. I twist round to look up at the fisherman, his arms and legs coated with ashes where he has stumbled and fallen on his way to find us.

133

"There is still digging to be done," says Marcus, without stopping.

"We need to return now, there is not long until twilight. I will not sail in the darkness again."

Marcus ignores him. The man looks at me and I stare back at him, as though what he is asking is impossible, though I know he is right. Livia and Amantius have not escaped. Now that I have seen the horror that was once Pompeii, I can no longer believe in happy endings. Myrtis and Felix are dead, Lucius, his wife and daughter also. This desolate landscape is why so few refugees have arrived. If everyone had escaped, there would have been fifteen thousand or more from Pompeii alone, and there have only been a few hundred, perhaps one or two thousand at best so far. The truth is that Marcus' wife and son are dead, buried far beneath the ashes that he is helplessly digging through. He will not reach their bodies alone, and, even if he were to, what joy would that give him? And yet his desperation is so strong that if he were to believe them dead, I fear he would take his own life here and now, with the fisherman and I as his only witnesses. My only choice, if I wish to keep him alive, if I wish to keep him safe as I promised his wife, is to lie. The promise I made her, so fleeting and casual, has in the past few hours taken on the strength of an oath in my mind, unbreakable. I swore to a woman who is now dead that I would look after her husband, 'keep him safe', and now I feel the burden of the promise I made so lightly.

"Marcus," I say.

He does not stop digging. Perhaps he knows what is coming, what I'm about to say.

"Marcus," I say again. "We need to sail back to Puteoli while we still can."

"No," he says.

I take a deep breath. I have to lie; I have no other choice. "They cannot possibly still be here," I say. "They must have fled at once; they will have seen what was happening and asked for help. Perhaps from your assistant, perhaps from someone at the amphitheatre. They would have thought to reach Fausta in Misenum. You said yourself she was your right-hand woman. Livia would have thought of her in your absence. She would have known Fausta would look after her until you sent word or came back. She must have found a boat to take her to Misenum or, even better, Puteoli. She knew that would be on your route back from Rome when you came to look for them. You need to be at one of the refugee camps, ready to receive them when they arrive from wherever they sought shelter. And besides," I add, "now that the soldiers have arrived, they will be registering more and more people, and crosschecking them. We need to be there. You need to be there."

Marcus sits back on his heels and turns to look at me. His face and arms are covered in ashes. He looks like something unearthly and I want to draw away from him. Instead I lean forward and touch his arm, as though to draw him back to the realm of the living from this dead place. "We have to go," I repeat. I lie again, more forcefully. "They will be in one of the refugee camps," I say. "You must go to them there."

I see my lie in his eyes. I see that he knows the truth already, that he has been digging for their bodies, not to save their lives. But I also see that he wants so desperately to believe me, to still cling to hope that they are alive, that he will do anything, go anywhere, if I might only be proven right.

I LOOK BACK, ONCE WE are in the boat. Twilight is beginning to fall, and this will be the last time I ever see Pompeii. I stare at the unending flat grey, trying to remember the city that lies beneath it, trying to lay that image over the grey, and failing.

Pompeii has gone.

IN THE BRIEF TIME WE have been away, the military camp has expanded. As Pompeii has disappeared, so a new city of tents has risen. The regimented rows and uniformity of the tents promises order, promises safety from the chaotic wrath that has gone before. The tiny mismatched shelters are beginning to disappear, as family after family are transferred into the military encampment. A cohort of Praetorians has arrived and is busy creating a second camp, to accommodate any leftover from the first and any further refugees who may arrive. Vast outdoor kitchens have been set up, with vats of savoury porridge, flatbreads, hot soups and bean stews. But back in the administrative tent first one scribe and then another shakes their head, checking their lists of names both here and at the other main refugee camp in Stabiae.

"We can't guarantee we have everyone," they admit. "But we've tried to consolidate all the refugees into these two camps, so that we can more easily look after them and help them find their missing families."

"But it might take a while for people to get here?" I ask.

There is a shrugged nod, but by now the explosion from Vesuvius was six days ago. Even on foot, most of the refugees should have reached one camp or the other, depending where they started from. Arrivals of new refugees have slowed to a trickle, many of them were staying with family or friends until they heard about the camps. The scribes do not say so, but there is little chance of many more survivors. There are messengers on the roads between here and Stabiae twice a day, every day, making their way through whichever routes are still passable, reports are returning the information that most survivors have now joined one or the other of the two camps. Even those with other places to go to have made themselves known, if they wish to trace relatives or friends. The scrolls at the scribes' feet are growing longer and more numerous, but Livia's name is not among them.

WE FIND FAUSTA.

"You're back." She embraces Marcus, who stares over her shoulder at the lines of tents, then embraces me. "Did you reach Pompeii?"

"Yes," I say, when it appears clear that Marcus will not reply.

"How was it?" she asks, her voice low.

"She can tell you," says Marcus. "I need to search the tents." And he is gone, striding towards the first tent in line, ready to check each one again in the hopes of finding what he is searching for.

Fausta turns to me. "Tell me about it," she says, pulling me by the hand to sit under a tree.

I sit and look into her expectant face. And my shoulders heave, the tears pour out of me that I held back for too many hours whilst Marcus dug. Fausta leans towards me and takes me in her arms. I bury my face in the folds of her toga and weep as I have not wept since my father died.

WHEN I HAVE TOLD HER everything, Fausta sits for a long time, staring out across the fields. "I didn't know such a thing could happen," she says at last. "I can't really imagine that I will never see Pompeii again." She takes a deep breath and exhales, her shoulders dropping. "And the people…"

"I lied to him," I confess. "I didn't know how else to make

137

him come back. But they can't have escaped. The only people who can have escaped were those who were out of the cities for some reason, like you and me and Marcus, or traders, fishermen who saw the danger and left quickly. All the others…"

"What else could you do?"

"I was afraid he would…"

Fausta turns her head towards the military encampment, watches as Marcus makes his way from one tent to another. "He would," she says. "What else is he to live for now? Better an honourable death than a miserable life when you've lost everything you hold dear."

"I promised his wife I'd keep him safe," I say. "I can't let him do that."

We sit in silence for a little while.

"Why aren't you wearing the gold cuff?" asks Fausta suddenly.

I search in my satchel and hold it out. "He – he set me free."

Fausta stares at me. "When?"

"In Pompeii, in the ashes."

"Why?"

"I don't know," I say. "He just took it off and said the words. I think he wanted me gone, he didn't want to have to look after me, he wanted to be alone to search."

"Was there a witness?"

My stomach dips. "No," I say reluctantly. "Does that mean it's not valid?" The thought of it, of having my freedom taken away from me just when I thought it had been granted, is almost too much to bear on top of everything else that has happened.

Fausta shakes her head. "No," she says firmly. "It doesn't matter, there doesn't have to be a witness. So long as he stands by his word, which Marcus would." She thinks for a moment. "But then why are you worrying about him? That bracelet would be enough to live on for a couple of years if you're careful, you can just travel back to Rome and become a scribe to some rich man, you'd be paid well."

"I can't do that," I say. "I watched him digging through the ashes to find his wife and child and I knew all the time they were dead. I can't leave him to discover that for himself, all alone."

"You've a good heart," she says. "There's plenty wouldn't stand by him."

I look down at the cuff, heavy in my hand, knowing what she says is true. There is no reason for me to be loyal to a man who's been my master barely a week. I am free now, I could do as I wish, I could simply leave, return to Rome, and take up life as a freedwoman. But I can't find it in myself to leave a man whose whole life has been shattered in one instant, and besides, the idea of being utterly alone, without friends or family, is frightening. A slave who has been set free is normally regarded as part of their past master's circle. At the very least, he would be their patron, they would take his name, and his family and friends would become part of their own extended social connections. If I left now, I would have nothing but a piece of gold and it does not seem enough, with all that has happened. I want to know that someone would search for me if I were lost among the ashes, that someone would mourn for me if I died. I shake my head, tucking the cuff back in my satchel. "I can't leave him," I repeat again. "I promised his wife I would keep him safe."

"That's going to be a hard promise to keep," says Fausta, not unkindly.

"I have to try," I say.

She nods.

"And the others?" I ask, not having dared to before now.

"What others?"

"The people you and Marcus used to work with," I manage. I don't know how else to describe them. Gladiators, whores, dancers, slaves.

Fausta shakes her head, her face set as though she has already accepted this new grief. "Gone," she says and even though her tone is harsh two tears fall from her eyes which she quickly dashes away, as though, if she starts to cry, she will not stop. She takes a deep breath. "This contract he signed to manage the amphitheatre," she says, "what happens if he breaks it?"

"He wasn't even allowed to leave Rome," I say, lowering my voice in case someone can hear us. "There will be punishments just for that if they find out. If he abandons the job, he'll be a wanted man."

Fausta watches as Marcus begins checking the last line of tents. "So," she says at last, "it comes down to this. You, Marcus and I have nothing and nobody left except that gold cuff and the management of the amphitheatre. If they think he's abandoned that job, he'll find himself in the arena and you and I will have no man to protect us. You may find a job as a scribe, but I'll be back in a brothel, on my knees to earn a living. We have to stop Marcus from taking his own life and we must get him back into the amphitheatre to continue his work. If we don't manage that, he will die, and you and I will struggle to live."

I know what she is saying is true, but I have not allowed myself to state it so baldly until now. I think over her words, trying to find another way, but there isn't one. Marcus has secured a job which carries with it both money and, if he succeeds, a certain level of respect, if not status, given the nature of the job and the people he will be associating with. Fausta and I will be a great deal safer if we have a man who will protect us. If he is working, Marcus can pay me to be his scribe, so I will have a job ready made for me.

"What do we do?" I ask.

"How much money does Marcus have left?"

"I'm not sure," I say. "He can't have very much left. We had to change horses all the way down here, he'd have to pay to get back the ones we left after the first change. And he paid a month's wages to the fishermen to take us to Pompeii."

Fausta grimaces. "Then we have no choice," she says. "Marcus must return to Rome and continue the job. We have to make that happen or all three of us will suffer for it."

"But he won't want to leave," I say. "He will want to stay here until he finds Livia."

Fausta nods. "I know. He won't leave until he believes he's done enough to find them, and if he believes they're dead…"

"So how – what do we do?" I repeat.

Fausta takes a deep breath. "You must return to Rome," she says. "When you get there, you stall them, make them believe Marcus is still in Rome and that he is still doing the job." She holds up a hand to stop my interruption. "I'll stay here with him until he has searched this camp and perhaps the one at Stabiae to his satisfaction. Then I'll suggest that there's still a slim chance Livia is alive and that if she were, she would head to Rome to find him, she knows where Julia's insula is, she would go there. I'll tell him we must return to Rome, continue the work and Livia will find us there."

"But she won't," I say and feel tears welling up again at the thought of it.

"No," says Fausta, and her firm tone wavers for a moment. "But if we can keep him alive long enough, he'll see that he must go on, for our sake as well as his. Marcus is loyal to those with whom he works," she adds. "He'll come to see that his death would only cause more misery. For you, for me, for other people who depend on him. But we must keep him alive until then. Even if it means lying."

I open my satchel and pull out the gold cuff again, pass it to Fausta. "Can you get money for this?" I ask.

"Yes," she says. "If you're sure?"

"I've got no one else," I say. "I'm too afraid to be alone."

Fausta lays her rough hand against my cheek for a moment. "I know," she says. "It's a hard choice, but it's the only one I can think of right now. Let's hope it's the right one." She stands as Marcus comes towards us, squaring her shoulders and lifting her chin, ready to do what must be done.

He tries to argue with us of course, he says he will not return to Rome, that he does not care about the job, that Livia is all that matters. But Fausta keeps calm and works on him. She reminds him of the binding terms of his contract, but only briefly, preferring to remind him that he must still provide for Livia and Amantius when he finds them, and how will he do that with no job, given that his savings are now lost beneath the ashes of Pompeii? In Rome at least he has a job and a place to live, Julia will welcome Livia with open arms when she arrives. He has a scribe in me and Fausta, as she was before, will be his right-hand woman to help run the amphitheatre, if she is needed. She appeals to his sense of loyalty, to his protection of us as two women who will otherwise be alone in the world. She emphasises the importance of keeping the job at the amphitheatre, before suggesting that I return to Rome and stall for time, freeing the two of them to search for Livia. She holds up the cuff and tells him that even though he has freed me I have proven loyal and thrown in my lot with them, that the money they get for it will allow them time to search, as well as feed us until he is next paid.

There's a moment where I think he will refuse, that he will tell her what we already know, that Livia and Amantius are dead and therefore there is nothing left for him to live for, that he will walk away from us and take his own life, somewhere out here in the field, an honourable death allowing him to follow his wife and child into the underworld. But somehow, I find Fausta pressing a few coins into my hand, enough to keep me in food for a couple of weeks. She finds a trader heading north back to Rome with a wagon of goods which he reluctantly agrees I may ride on. I don't like the way he looks at me, running his eyes up and down my body before agreeing to take me. I want to refuse, but Fausta leans close to him and whispers in his ear. I watch his face drain pale and he nods hurriedly, backing away from her, gesturing to me to take my place on the wagon without any more glances at my body.

"What did you say to him?" I ask Fausta.

"I said if he so much as laid one finger on you, I'd put a curse on his dick and it would fall off the next time he tried to use it. Sleep in the wagon when he stops at an inn, don't relieve yourself anywhere near him. When you get back to Rome, go straight to Julia and tell her what happened, she'll help you for Marcus' sake. I'll bring him back as soon as I can. Until then, hold your nerve and stall for time. I know you're scared, but you have to do this."

"What will I say to stall them?"

"You'll think of something. You've got four days of travel to come up with something clever. Work hard and think quickly."

Marcus' words, I think, he must have used them to her too. I clutch at her hands a little too tightly, afraid of letting go. "May

Feronia keep you safe until I see you again," she says and turns away.

I look at Marcus, somehow hoping that he will intervene, that he will decree that he will come back to Rome with us now, take charge so that I do not have to be sent on this mission alone, but he is standing looking over the hundreds of tents now being erected by the Praetorian cohort.

"Goodbye," I say. "I pray you find Livia quickly," I add and Fausta nods at me.

He tries to focus on me. "Stay safe," he says. "I will be back as soon as I have found them. Julia will care for you." He turns away again, lost in his own desperate need.

FREEDWOMAN

WARY OF FAUSTA'S ABILITIES TO curse his genitals, the trader keeps his hands to himself, but he also refuses to talk to me or be pleasant in any way. I spend four lonely days travelling back to Rome and, by the time I reach Julia's, my very bones feel cold as well as thoroughly shaken by the endless trundling of the cart. The courtyard feels like a homecoming.

"You're back. Where's Marcus?"

I look up at Maria. Sat in her usual place, she has spotted me at once. "He's still in Puteoli."

Julia appears in her doorway. She takes one look at me and waves me indoors without a word. I nod to Maria, then follow, grateful to be taken in.

"What happened?"

I CRY, TELLING HER. I try to describe Pompeii and fail; it cannot be described to someone who has not seen it. I can only tell her that it has gone, there is no hope of recovering it. I repeat Fausta's descriptions of the events from the viewpoint of Misenum and I falter when I have to describe Marcus searching through the ashes. I sob and Julia does not pat or hug me, she does not tell me not to cry. She sits apart, watching me solemnly; she knows that not to cry for such an unthinkable horror would be a horror in itself. She lets me cry as though it were my sacred duty to do so, like a ritual at a ceremony in a temple and, having held back as many tears as possible for Marcus' sake and then been all alone for the journey home, the relief in crying without restraint is comforting in itself. By the time I have finished, darkness has fallen, and I sit, exhausted, silent.

Julia stands and lights candles at her household shrine. She lifts her palms and prays silently for a while. Then she puts a thick vegetable porridge in front of me and I eat. The heat in my belly is soporific, I find myself almost falling asleep while I eat.

"I have to make them believe he is here in Rome," I say, and I almost sob again at the thought of it, it seems like such an impossible task. "I have to convince them he is working on the amphitheatre when I don't even know when he'll be back."

I want Julia to give me a ready-made plan, to tell me exactly what to do, but she only clears away my bowl and spoon. "You need to sleep," she says. "You cannot think when you are so tired."

"But how will I convince them?" I ask.

"Sleep," she says. "The roof hut is yours until Marcus returns and tells me what he wants to do. He would not have freed you if he did not believe in you, Fausta would not have sent you back here alone if she did not think you could do what must be done."

I stare at her, my eyes sore with crying and tiredness. "How do you know he freed me?"

She looks down at my wrist. "Your cuff has been taken off. You would not have removed it without permission. Now go and sleep."

THE SKY IS NOT EVEN light when I fetch cold water and,

shivering, wash myself. I put on a clean tunic and wrap up my hair, pull my cloak around me before packing my satchel with my tablet and stylus. I walk down the rickety stairway shivering more with nerves than the cold.

"You look like a slave girl," comes Maria's voice.

I startle, having not seen her, already at her place on the balcony despite the early morning hour. She is munching on a hot fruit roll and looking me over, none too satisfied.

"I'm clean and neat," I say, slightly offended.

"That's all that a mistress expects from a slave girl," agrees Maria. "It's not what a freedwoman aspires to."

I hesitate. "What would you change?" I ask in the end.

Maria puts her head on one side. "Brighter colours," she starts. "You need different clothes; those look like the slave livery of a well-to-do household."

"They are," I say. "And they're all I have."

She tuts and then lifts herself heavily from her seat and disappears into her apartment. I stand waiting, unsure of whether she is about to return or not but, after a brief pause, she reappears holding something in her hand. "Wear these."

I approach her and look at what she is offering. A delicate pink tunic, a head wrap in dark blue, with tiny shells attached to the edge. "I can't take those."

"Consider them a loan," she says, pushing them into my hands. "You'll never fool them if you look like a slave girl. You need to look like you have some authority."

"Thank you," I say and hurry back upstairs, where I change as quickly as possible and then come back downstairs feeling absurdly overdressed.

But Maria is still displeased. "You *move* like a slave girl," she says, frowning. She crosses her arms under her ample bosom and stands her ground, blocking my way.

"What do you mean?"

"Head down, shoulders hunched, quick little steps like you're worried you're going to bother someone," she says brutally. "Get your head up, shoulders back, *stride*."

"I'm not a man," I object.

"Oh, you don't think the great ladies of Rome stride? Think about how Julia moves."

"She's – was a Vestal Virgin," I say.

"And nobody messes with her," says Maria triumphantly. "Try to walk like her."

I think about Julia, how she moves. I lift my head so that my neck feels like it has doubled in length, stick my breasts out so my shoulders go back and then walk down the stairs as if I'm approaching a temple altar, slow and solemn, my very person sacred. I can hear Maria laughing from above me.

"That's more like it, my girl. Bona Dea watch over you and Minerva give you quick thinking."

"Thank you," I call. I look up, but her features are hidden in the morning gloom. I can only see the solid comforting bulk of her, seated at her favourite spot, waiting for her watchdog duties of the day to begin.

IT TAKES ME OVER AN hour to walk into the amphitheatre. It is just too big, I think helplessly, pacing back and forth along the Forum, trying to summon up my courage while the sun rises ever higher. How can I hope to hold my own against the architect, the various heads of the guilds, even the Aedile, should he take it upon himself to conduct an inspection? How will I convince them Marcus is still in Rome and working on the project? They will know I am lying for sure. And if I fail, then Marcus will be a wanted man, Fausta will be forced to work in a brothel, and me? I will be some rich man's scribe, and I can't guarantee I'll be lucky a third time. I'll find myself a plaything against my will, possibly even enslaved again, for I have no paperwork to prove I am not a slave. And a rich man does not much care for a freedwoman's protests, if she has no man to protect her. I have no family, no friends, no-one to protect my honour except myself.

I try to think how it would be if Marcus were here. He would be asking one awkward question after another; I think to myself. He would be enraging the architect, who doesn't get a moment to think when Marcus is here. At last I stand outside the shadowy arches of the imperial entrance and take a deep breath. One day at a time. I need only fool them for one day at a time. Work hard and think fast.

"Ah, the scribe girl."

The architect is standing behind me, scowling. His scribes stare at me with undisguised dislike.

"Good morning," I say with a bright smile. "I am delighted to see you. Marcus has given me a list of items I should check with you."

"A list? Is he not here himself? Where is he?"

"Did you not receive our message? I sent a messenger boy. Marcus has been ill for over a week," I say. I lean a little closer. "A bad oyster at a dinner party."

The architect isn't quite sure how to respond. Oysters suggests Marcus has been dining with a well-off patron. He hesitates.

"So, my list for today," I say, forcing my smile a bit wider. "Shall we go through it now?"

"When will he be back at work?"

"Oh, he is back already," I say. "Didn't you see him? He

walked the whole amphitheatre at dawn this morning, gave me the list and went off to Ostia to see some contact. A beast-hunter, I believe. It'll probably take a few days, what with setting up exactly what will be needed, as well as the journey."

The architect looks disgruntled. The port of Ostia is most of a day's journey from Rome and all the best beast-hunters operate out of there, so that they can coordinate shipping of animals from Africa. He can't really argue with my story and I have just bought myself three or four days. My smile becomes brighter all by itself.

I ASK ENOUGH QUESTIONS AND make myself irritating enough to the architect over the next three days that he starts actively avoiding me, arriving very late on the fourth day and leaving for the baths extremely early.

"I assume I can at least expect to see Marcus tomorrow?" he asks before he departs.

"Of course," I say. "He may wish to try out the flooding soon," I add cheerfully, knowing this is one of his pet horrors, and watch him blench at the very idea.

ON THE FIFTH DAY I arrive at first light and hurry up to the architect as soon as he arrives. I can see his eyes roll at the sight of me as I approach.

"Marcus has gone to seek housing for his family today," I say. "He may be a little late. Meanwhile, he says that the pens under the arena are not suited to purpose."

"In what way?"

"Not strong enough," I say. "He says they must be remade entirely. Also, he thinks they should be spaced out better or the animals will fight, even through the bars."

The architect splutters with rage. "Those pens are the finest – strongest – he cannot –"

I shrug, looking down at my tablet, which is full of meaningless scribbles. "I don't know what to tell you. That's what he asked me to raise with you. He said it was very concerning. He can't have expensive wild animals getting damaged before a show, especially if the Emperor will be in attendance, which of course for the inaugural Games he will be most days, I should imagine. I mean, it would look bad, wouldn't it? And they'll want to know who built them, won't they? Which won't be Marcus, will it? I'll leave it with you, shall I?"

FOR ALL MY SMILING BLUSTER at the amphitheatre, when I return to the rooftop hut each day I sit and cry. I am so afraid that Marcus will not come back at all. I am afraid that at any moment the Aedile might visit, or the architect will absolutely demand to see Marcus and I will be unable to produce him. I try to keep myself busy at the end of each working day, washing myself and my clothes, buying stuffed bread and olives or nuts, eating, sitting on the rooftop to catch the last light and writing notes to myself of other awkward requests I can make at the amphitheatre. I'm not sure how long my money will last, either, I have enough for perhaps a week more of food. If Marcus and Fausta do not arrive by then I will have to ask Julia for money, and she is already housing me without asking for rent. How long should I stick with this plan before I have to give up and go and seek work elsewhere, revealing the fraud I have helped to perpetrate? And can I manage to pass as a freedwoman with no paperwork proclaiming me so? I wonder whether I can fake some paperwork, falsify Marcus' signature. The thought of becoming a slave again makes my stomach turn over.

"Not back yet?"

I look up to see the old Jewess, Adah, standing over me. I've not seen her since my return. "No," I say. "I don't know when he will be back," I confess.

"Is it like they say? The mountain of fire?"

I nod.

"The cities gone?"

I nod.

She lowers herself to sit next to me, her knees making a loud clicking noise as she does so. "Did you lose people?"

Myrtis, Felix. I nod. I can't say their names. I'll cry, and I am afraid to cry, I have to stay strong.

She pats my arm, her hand a mass of wrinkles. "I'm sorry, child," she says. "It's a hard thing to lose those we care for."

I swallow. The tears are already welling up in my eyes.

"No shame in crying."

A sob escapes me and now it is too late, the tears are falling.

Adah does not keep her distance as Julia did, she puts her bony arms round me. I put my face into the cloth of her dress and cry. It is a different kind of crying, it is not a sacred grief for Pompeii or any of the other cities, not for Marcus and the frightened refugees. Instead I cry for Myrtis and Felix, for my own terror and loss over the past days, for my constant fear that I will not be able to do what is asked of me and will end up enslaved again, just when freedom was so close.

Adah rocks me and murmurs something in a language I do not understand, but I recognise the words a mother murmurs to a child who is hurt, the same sounds in all tongues. When I end up hiccupping and pull away, sniffing, she uses the edge of her shawl to wipe my face.

"He'll be back. How many days have you kept them at bay?"

"Five."

She chuckles. "Cunning girl."

"I can't think of anything else," I say, hiccupping again. "I worry they'll find me out."

"Make them worry," says Adah. "Then they won't have time to think about you." She gets up, using my shoulder as a support, letting out a little groan as she straightens up. "Goodnight, child."

"Goodnight, Adah," I say. "Thank you," I add, though I am not sure she heard me, already halfway across the rooftop and back to her own little hut.

"You want to do *what*?"

"Test the toilets," I say, as though this is obvious.

"They've *been* tested. They work perfectly. The plumbing of this amphitheatre is second to none. It's better than some of the finest villas in Rome."

"Not with a high volume of people."

"What?"

"They've not been tested with lots of people," I say, peering into one of the toilets in the third tier. "Sponges for wiping," I add out loud, making a note on my tablet.

"How many people would you like to test them with?" he asks.

"Three hundred?"

"*What?*"

I spread my hands, stating the obvious. "We can seat fifty thousand people. There's what, fifty toilets on each tier. The full day goes on for several hours. How many people do you think will be using them at any one time? Especially during the breaks, or the less popular parts of the show?"

"And just how are you going to test them?"

"Gather up three hundred people and get them all to use one of the toilet rooms as quickly as possible. We can see how long the queues are. Whether we get any blockages. How quickly an attendant can clean the room again with people coming and going. How fast we run out of sponges if they fall off the sticks and go down the drains."

He stares at me in horror.

"Tomorrow, then?" I ask. "The foremen can get all the men to use the third-floor toilets tomorrow morning, as a test. We must have more than three hundred men on site at the moment?"

He wants to refuse; I can see it. "Where is Marcus? I want a word with him."

"Racing stables," I say.

"What's he doing there?"

"We need chariots and some racing teams for the opening Games," I say, making it up as I go along. "Re-enacting a battle."

"Is he going to oversee this ridiculous test tomorrow?"

I make an appalled face. "I shouldn't think so," I say. "Why would the manager oversee a toilets test? He has much more important things to organise. By the way, the imperial box looks awfully plain. Is it going to be decorated at all?"

The architect looks harassed. "The mosaic-makers are late delivering," he says. "I've commissioned a magnificent floor for the imperial box but most of the best makers are working on the imperial palace at the moment, Titus is having works done."

I raise my eyebrows. "Well, as long as it gets done in time…" I say doubtfully. "It would be awkward if the Emperor came to see the works and thought his own box wasn't being included in the decorations. I mean, you're already decorating the arena wall,

154

which is hardly the main priority, and his box isn't even carved or painted yet?"

The architect swallows and I depart, head held high.

The toilet test buys me a full two days, as the first round is a disaster, queues blocking the corridors, the attendant barely able to keep up, so that we now know we will need two slaves per toilet room. I insist on a second day of tests which fortunately go better, although the architect doesn't even turn up on the second day, having developed a severe headache after watching the first day's shambles. Eight days. I have managed eight days. I feel oddly proud at the antics I have managed to force on the poor man, although I still worry about how much longer I can keep going.

On the ninth day I ask rather pointedly how the statues to decorate the outer arches are coming along, given that there are over one hundred and fifty to be made and painted, featuring various past emperors, august personages and divinities. The architect launches into a spirited defence of the time they are taking, to which I respond by grimacing and taking notes on my tablet in my most unreadable shorthand, before shaking my head and saying that surely we are due an inspection very soon by, at the very least, the Aedile and quite possibly the Emperor himself. After all, he can see the building from his palace windows, he must be curious about our progress? The architect looks as if he's going to be sick.

"ALTHEA! ALTHEA!"

I'm washing, the cold water nothing like the warm baths I'd like to be in, but I can hear Maria's bellow even from inside my little hut. Opening the door, I peer over the edge.

"He's back!"

I stare down. In the courtyard below me are two figures, recognisable even in the evening gloom. Marcus and Fausta. I run down the stairs and nearly hug Marcus, then settle for embracing Fausta instead.

"You're back! The gods be praised!"

Fausta smiles broadly. "The gods be praised indeed. The horses are almost dead, but we made it back."

"I'll take care of them." Celer has appeared on the walkway above and now he makes his way down the stairs and out of the courtyard gate, with a quick pat on the shoulder for Marcus.

"Come inside." Julia is beckoning.

"I'll be with you in a moment," says Marcus. His voice is quiet and so hoarse I barely recognise it. He walks to the toilets and I turn to Fausta, lowering my voice as Julia joins us.

"Livia?"

Fausta shakes her head. "We searched everywhere, even went to the family farm in case she'd hidden herself there." She shakes her head again. "They're dead, they can't have survived what happened. You can tell just by looking at the refugee camps. If a lot of people had escaped there should have been many thousands. There weren't many more when we left than when you did," she says to me.

Julia keeps her voice low too. "How is he?"

Fausta sighs. "He still maintains she's alive. He won't accept the truth. In the end the only way I could get him back here was to agree with him and say that he'd better come back here and hold down the only means he has for making money at the moment. That she would know where to find him. I thought I wouldn't be able to convince him but, in the end, he gave in. Maybe he was just too tired to fight me anymore. Neither of us has slept properly since it happened."

I FETCH WATER FROM THE public fountain so they can both wash, offer Fausta my spare tunic so she has something clean to wear. Julia gives Marcus a faded green tunic that used to belong to her husband. While they wash and dress, I run to the bakery for bread, then sit in Julia's kitchen chopping up cabbage, carrots, garlic and onions to add to soaked beans and sprouted barley. By the time they join us the stew is bubbling fiercely. Without her toga Fausta looks smaller somehow; the usual bulk of cloth stripped from her frame makes her appear more delicate.

"Smells good," says Fausta. "I haven't had a hot meal since – in weeks. It's been snatched mouthfuls of bread and a bite of cheese, if we were lucky."

They sit and I serve everyone. Marcus stays silent, but he eats as if he's eaten nothing since I saw him. The food is good, the hot stew filling and heating us all at once. When we've eaten our fill, Julia sets a bowl of nuts on the table and some sweet wine cakes.

"Here," I say, passing Marcus a scroll of papyrus.

"What's this?"

"A list of lies I've told as well as questions and issues you've raised in your absence," I say.

He looks down the list and a small smile reaches his lips, the first time I've seen him smile since we saw the ashes begin to fall in Rome. "You're very inventive," he comments. "I'm dissatisfied with the hinges on the Gate of Triumph?"

"And the Gate of Death," I confirm. "Both of them are prone to squeaking despite being re-oiled three times. The squeaking noise will detract from the sense of occasion."

He shakes his head, still smiling. "I don't like the green arena sand sent in for my approval?"

"It was the wrong shade of green," I say firmly. "So was the blue. They're sending new samples tomorrow."

"And I've requested two women go onto the payroll as my assistants? Is that you and Fausta?"

"Yes," I say.

Fausta laughs out loud. "She's a better negotiator than you," she says. "I think from now on she should be the one to talk money when there's money to be talked. You better learn that list off by heart."

"Agreed," says Marcus. His smile fades, he looks as though maintaining a conversation is about to finish him off.

"You should sleep," I say hurriedly.

He stands, nods to the three of us and then leaves. I can hear the rickety stairs creaking as he walks up them.

"I should get some sleep too," I say.

Julia and Fausta nod.

"Is he all right?" I ask Fausta, pausing in the doorway to look back at her.

She looks away, then shrugs and meets my gaze. "No," she says bluntly. "He must know they're dead, but he won't admit it and I didn't dare say it out loud in case he took his own life. So I kept my mouth shut and he keeps talking about her possibly still being alive. Maybe he has to do it to survive each day, but I'm still afraid for him. I'd feel better if I knew he'd accepted the truth."

"The truth can take a long time to accept," says Julia.

Fausta nods.

I stand in silence for a few moments. "Goodnight," I say at last.

"Goodnight," they chorus.

WHEN I REACH THE ROOFTOP hut, Marcus is already lying down. I blow out the lamp I've carried up, casting the room into instant blackness, lie down and pull the blanket over myself. I try to stay very quiet, thinking him already asleep, but he speaks.

"I'm sorry," he says in the darkness.

"For what?"

"Setting you free."

I lie still, hardly breathing at what I am hearing, my heart thudding. There was no witness to my manumission, just the two of us in the landscape of horror that used to be Pompeii. If Marcus wishes, he could claim he never set me free and it would be the word of a woman against her master, a slave against a citizen of Rome. I would stand no chance. I think of the gold cuff closing around my wrist, of a life ahead of me bound back to slavery after a confused taste of freedom.

"I do not mean to enslave you again," he says, when I don't speak. "I did not mean that."

I take a deep breath, feel my muscles relax.

"I meant to free you with honour," he says. "It should have been done before a lawyer, with witnesses, you would have been given a scroll with the details. I would have given you my name and a freedwoman's cap, a purse of money. I thought it would happen some years from now and that Livia…" He stops. There is silence for a few moments before he starts again. "Livia would have held a feast and given you new clothes."

"I don't need –" I begin but he cuts me off.

"I wanted to do it with honour, not in anger and despair. But when I did it, I just wanted to get rid of you, to have no burdens, no responsibilities, so that I could hunt for Livia without any hindrance. It was not right, nor auspicious for your new life as a freedwoman. And I am sorry for it, especially as you have shown me such loyalty."

"I have only done what anyone would do," I say.

"No," he says. "You could have fled, you could have gone anywhere and done anything with that gold cuff."

I stay silent.

"I will do right by you," he says at last. "If you will stay by my side as we planned, I will do right by you. I do not have much for now, but I made you a promise. And…" He pauses again. "I told Livia I would look after you." Another silence. "I did not mean it as an oath," he says at last. "I meant it only as a reassurance to her. But I said the words to her, I promised to look after you until she should arrive." He takes a deep breath. "Perhaps she is still alive," he says, and tears fall down my cheek at the hope in his voice. "And if she is, I must stand by my promises to her."

"I promised too," I say.

"What?"

"You left the house so quickly and I was running after you, but she took my hand and said I should look after you. And I promised I would." I swallow. "I did it as you did, I said it quickly, I said it without thinking, only out of politeness to my new mistress. But they were my last words to her. I will not break my word to her, wherever she is."

The dark is very dark. I turn my head and can barely see any shape at all, even though I can hear Marcus' ragged breathing and I know tears are falling. He takes a deep breath. "We are sworn to each other then, is that it?"

I do not know if he is making fun of me, but his tears tell me otherwise. "Yes," I say.

In the dark I feel his hand seeking me out and I tense, unsure of what he is doing. He finds my arm and follows it to my hand, then takes it in his. "I swear to care for you, Althea, and do right by you, by Libertas who cared for you as a slave and Feronia to whom you passed as a freedwoman. I do it in the name of my wife Livia, who asked it of me and to whom I made my promise. When I see her again, I will be able to tell her I did as she asked."

He makes to pull away, but I hold onto his hand and speak into the night. "I swear to stand by your side, Marcus, and keep you safe as I promised your wife Livia, my last mistress before I became a freedwoman. May Feronia help me in this, my new life and undertaking."

Our hands unclasp and we lie in silence. When I sleep, it is the first deep sleep I have had in weeks.

KARBO

L ATE NOVEMBER DAWNS ARE BLEAK things, cold and misty. But they begin to take on a shape, a regularity, which, after all that has happened, I find comforting.

I rise first and fetch water, carrying the heavy amphorae back up the rickety wooden staircase. By the time I reach the rooftop Marcus has awoken. He washes and dresses quickly, then heads to the popina, while I do the same. By the time I reach him, my still-damp skin shivering from the early morning cold, there will be a hot pancake waiting for me, or sometimes a fruit-stuffed bun, a speciality of the bakery. Fausta prefers the bread and cheese that Marcus favours and she makes short work of it, knocking back a glass of wine and then striding along with us as we make our way to the amphitheatre. She has gone back to wearing her toga, though she could have disguised her origins on moving here, to a new city. I suppose by now it is part of how she thinks of herself, a she-wolf through and through. She has taken a tiny room on the top floor of the insula, just below the rooftop. I wonder what Adah would make of her if she knew she was indeed now sharing a dwelling with a prostitute, but perhaps she hasn't found out yet, I don't see her often. Maria, meanwhile, seems to treat Fausta with a kind of formal respect, not warm enough to be friendly, not cold enough to be disparaging. Maybe she can tell she is not a person to argue with.

Every day that passes is a day taking us closer to the by now almost-legendary hundred days of Games that we must deliver. The inauguration will be on the sixth of July. Every year between the sixth and thirteenth of July it is customary to hold the Games of Apollo, an annual week of theatrical shows, feasting, races and gladiatorial combats, so it makes sense for the inauguration to tie into these festivities. If we begin the hundred days of consecutive Games then, it will take us through the two weeks of Roman Games honouring Jupiter in September and we will finish by mid October. After that the weather will not be on our side anyway.

"THINGS HAVE TO BE DONE right," says Fausta.

She has Marcus and me leave work early one day and, instead of heading to the baths, she takes us to the Forum, to the colonnade where the lawyers wait for clients. There she has Marcus repeat his manumission of me and, in just a few moments, I hold in my hand a witnessed scroll proclaiming me a free woman. I look down at the papyrus, see my name Althea, now accompanied for the first time by Aquillius. It is customary for a slave to take her master's name when she is freed and, although Marcus shrugs and says I may choose whatever name I wish, he looks a little pleased when I choose his.

"Well, give her the gift," prompts Fausta.

Marcus hands me a small parcel. "It's nothing," he grunts.

"It is everything," retorts Fausta. "Open it," she adds to me.

Inside a small piece of linen is a pretty woollen cap in a fresh green. I run my hand over it, unsure of whether I should wear it at once. "Thank you," I say to Marcus, though my eyes take in Fausta as well, for organising it.

"You're a freedwoman, you should have a freedwoman's cap," says Fausta. "The colour suits you. Pop it on."

I pull it shyly over my head.

"There you are," says Fausta with satisfaction. "Don't you look grand?"

"Thanks be to Feronia," I say.

"Thanks be," Fausta echoes and Marcus nods.

MARCUS WANTS OUR OWN IN-HOUSE group of musicians. He picks them from here and there to form a group that suits his purposes, then has them rehearse, endlessly, for all kinds of different situations, from the Emperor arriving in the imperial box to beast hunts, gladiatorial bouts, dancing girls and even the execution of criminals.

"Creates atmosphere," he says.

"I can't make myself heard," I complain. "How are you supposed to hear me, or I you, when you're under the arena and I'm up here in the seating? They never stop playing."

"She needs a whistle," says Fausta from several seats above me.

I twist in my seat to look up at her and she pulls a leather thong out from under her tunic, to which is attached a bronze whistle like the ones centurions use in battle to signal different formations. I look back at Marcus, thinking he'll laugh, but he pulls out a matching one from around his own neck and nods.

"I'll get you one," he says. "Useful things. You can hear them even above the roar of the crowd when they get overexcited."

"Yes, but can you hear them over the sound of your musicians?" I retort.

A few days later he presents me with my own whistle. At first, I'm hesitant to use it. It seems very loud, even compared with the musicians, and I feel silly blowing it but, after a few times when I've tried and failed to catch Marcus' attention by any other means, I get used to it. One long blast to call for him, two short puffs to tell everyone else to shut up. I'm tempted to use the two short puffs regularly with the musicians as well as the carpenters who are constantly hammering. But the work must go on, our ears sacrificed on the altar of this amphitheatre's future success.

WINTER EVENINGS COME ON EARLY. We stop work soon after lunch, then go to the baths to warm our bodies in the hot water. After that, Fausta and I head back to Julia's, the courtyard a safe haven on the early dark nights when no-one respectable likes to roam Rome's pitch-black streets. In the courtyard at least we all know each other, a stranger would be spotted at once. Flickering lamps and torches keep daylight lingering longer than the sun and often we share meals together, with Julia or Maria. Sometimes we eat at Cassia's popina, elbows on the counter, chatting to each other, and Cassia when she's not too busy. Sometimes we discuss work, other times just gossip about the locals.

But Marcus does not return to the courtyard in the evenings. Each night full darkness falls and still there is no sign of him. When I have yawned once too often, I take up a lamp and make my way up to the rooftop. Every evening I look over the edge, down into the narrow street below, hoping to catch a shadow that moves like him, but I never do. I lie on my mat, huddled under our rough blankets, my cloak added for extra warmth, and I wait. Sometimes I fall asleep waiting and only wake again when Marcus trips over me, cursing under his breath. He snores when he sleeps and sometimes lets out a cry. He works without stopping every day, even smiles and jests, but his pale face and the dark rings under his eyes in the mornings, as well as his wine-soaked breath, tell Fausta and me all we need to know about his nights. I want to stop his night-time wanderings and drinking, but I don't know how. The streets of Rome at night are a dangerous place to be, dark and full of people one would rather not meet, even by daylight.

WE SEEM TO SPEND OUR days collecting waifs and strays. Then there are those craftsmen who realise that an amphitheatre of this size, holding regular Games on this scale, will bring in a good income, and that they should therefore not turn their noses up at the kind of people they would normally avoid associating with. There are a few sly looks and comments at Fausta's presence but, after a carpenter gets his nose punched for putting his hands on her without her permission, they stop abruptly. After that, for the most part they seem to treat her as a man, exchanging bawdy banter and heavy-handed slaps on the shoulder as greetings or farewells. This suits Fausta. She relishes the wider opportunities of this role, using it here and there to help her own kind.

It takes her only a few weeks to seek out and identify the most suitable women to join our team. We need a group of dancing girls who will provide entertainment between the main Games. The girls must be pretty, good movers and not easily offended by lewd comments from the crowd. Those best suited are prostitutes and Fausta makes it her mission to find those who fit the bill. We will pay for their costumes, prostitution licence fees, and a small stipend. In return they will learn the steps, perform as and when required and enjoy the added bonus of being called up into the stands after the shows if a spectator happens to take a fancy to them. It suits them, for their days are mostly quieter than their nights and they view it as easy work. Fausta commissions the costumes in bold bright linen with decorated ribbons, leaving precious little to the imagination. They use the arena to practise, occasionally moving to one side when the carpenters come too close with their scenery or scaffolding, exchanging banter and rude gestures, laughing boisterously.

"Fausta here?"

"Who's asking?" I ask, looking up from my tablet and abacus, where I am currently calculating the wages of the scenery painters.

The woman standing in front of me is a prostitute without any doubt. There is something of Fausta about her, a fierce stance that speaks of a woman who has had to stand her ground more than once and won more often than not. "They call me Acca," she says.

The name of the she-wolf or prostitute who suckled Romulus and Remus. A professional name. "What do you need?"

"Want to know if I can have my girls outside after shows without any trouble from the management."

"You need to speak to Marcus, not Fausta."

She gives me a look that tells me Fausta is already known to the she-wolves of Rome, that she is seen as the right person to talk to, if it concerns prostitutes.

"Over there," I say, giving up and waving a hand towards Fausta, who is sitting on the topmost tier, wrapped in her toga, surveying the arena floor. She says you have to sit where the plebs sit to truly see the arena. Acca lifts her chin to me and strides up the steps, swiftly reaching Fausta and sitting beside her

"What did Acca want?" I ask Fausta later.

"Wants us to know her girls will hang around dressed as

gladiatrix when the Games are over, waiting on customers coming out. Doesn't want any trouble about it."

"Dressed as gladiatrix? Why?"

Fausta shrugs. "Says the men like it after they've seen armed combat, think it's sexy."

I shake my head.

"Oh, it goes on all the time," says Fausta. "Men and women. Plenty of pretty boys dressed as gladiators get called into carrying litters by the rich women of Rome, and the men, come to that. They know they're not the real thing, haven't got the scars, but it's wonderful what a bit of shiny armour does for a man's looks."

She looks thoughtfully out over the arena and then changes the subject. "Where was Marcus last night?"

"I don't know."

"Not with you?"

"It's not like that between us," I say, blushing slightly.

"Not ever?"

I shake my head.

"Where was he, then?" she asks. "I didn't see him come home, after the baths, did you?"

"He didn't come home until very late," I say reluctantly.

Fausta's eyes narrow. "Is he coming home late every night?"

I nod.

"Cack," says Fausta.

"Do you think he's gambling?"

She snorts. "Not with their family history. His father took him out and flogged him once for gambling. He barely tolerates it in the amphitheatre. He wouldn't get caught up in it after what happened to their farm."

"Women?" I ask awkwardly.

She thinks. "I'd have said he'd come to you for that, the way he looks after you. But maybe I'm wrong." She considers. "He knows he's always welcome at my door, I'd not turn him down after what he's been through, but I'm not sure he thinks of me in that way."

It's the first time I've heard Fausta speak of sleeping with men for money, and I feel awkward, but she speaks of it as if it were nothing, a simple fact of life, which it is, I suppose.

Fausta sighs. "Well let's keep an eye on it," she ends. "He can do what he likes, I just don't want him getting into trouble, that's all."

MARCUS GETS PAID AND THIS, at least, removes some money worries from all of us for the time being, since Fausta and I, as his assistants, also get paid. I take a coin to Feronia's shrine, in gratitude for my first payment as a freedwoman. Then, mindful of Maria's kindness to me, I buy bright woollen cloth and make myself new clothes, so that I can return those she lent me, along with some honeyed walnuts as a thank you.

"Keep them," she says, when I try to return the clothes, washed and neatly folded. "They don't fit me anymore, haven't worn them since I was a girl and had a waist like yours. Get off," she adds as I hug her, but she looks pleased. Sometimes I sit with her on her balcony in the evening and we watch the comings and goings of the courtyard, so that she can impart the latest gossip to a fresh ear. There is nothing she does not observe, nothing she does not know about everyone who lives here.

"There's a street brat I keep seeing," she says one day. "Fast as a rat he is, scampering in and out of here, trying to steal things."

"What does he look like?" I ask. There are plenty of children who come in and out of our courtyard, some who belong here and others who are their playmates and treat the place like their own home.

"Black as soot," says Maria. "Brought over from Africa, I should think."

"Does he have a family?"

"Doubt it. Probably a runaway slave."

"I'll look out for him," I say.

"You'll never catch him, much too fast," she says.

I think for a minute. "If you can catch him, I might have a job for him," I say.

SATURNALIA IS BEING CELEBRATED ACROSS Rome but none of us much feel like celebrating. Fausta and I give each other little cakes and the amphitheatre is quiet for a few days while the workmen have time off. But Marcus does not speak of the festivities, nor show any sign of wanting to take part in them.

I wait up for Marcus one night, hoping to find out where he's been. The moon is halfway across the sky by the time he returns, I can hear the wooden stairway creaking as he makes his way up it. The door opens and he stands in the doorway, blinking at the light of the lamp.

"What are you doing up?"

"Where have you been?"

"Out," he says.

"Have you been gambling?" I ask.

He snorts as though I've said something funny. "My father took me out and flogged me when he found me gambling once."

"I know," I say, pulling at his arm. "Then come home earlier."

"Home?" he asks. He's swaying on his feet. "Pompeii?" he adds.

I stare at him. There are tears trickling down his face. "No," I say more gently. "Just back here."

"I can't go home," he says. "It disappeared. Livia disappeared. Amantius…"

I know," I say softly. "I know. But you need to rest. We have so much work to do, you can't do it if you're drunk every night and don't get enough sleep. Please come home earlier."

"Home," he says. "Home."

"Yes," I say. "Please. If street robbers see you like that, you'll have a knife at your throat for sure."

He shrugs as though this doesn't worry him, then kneels and looks about the room. "Lararium," he says.

"What?"

"Household shrine."

"I know what a Lararium is."

"We don't have one."

I nod. "I know."

"Why not?"

I want to say we are not a household, but then I suppose we are. Fausta installed a shrine in her room as soon as she arrived here. "Do you want me to set one up?" I ask.

"No, don't worry," he says. "I have one in Pompeii. We can use that, Livia will have found it, I suppose."

I sigh. "You need to sleep," I say again. "Lie down."

He doesn't even bother to remove his shoes, just slumps down on the bed and closes his eyes. I unfasten his shoes and place them to one side, then cover him with a blanket.

"Livia," he says, eyes still closed.

"Goodnight, Marcus," I say.

For a couple of nights, he comes home earlier, one night he eats with us, even talks a little and I think perhaps he has heeded my words, but the following night he does not come home until almost dawn, sleeping an hour or two at most, then rising again. I do not know how long he can keep it up before he makes himself ill with exhaustion.

"BEEN WAITING FOR YOU. GOT him!"

I've only just walked back into the courtyard after the day's work. I look up at Maria, who is holding a struggling boy by the earlobe. "Is that the child?"

"It is," she says with smug satisfaction.

"You must be faster on your toes than I realised," I say, laughing.

"Don't you be cheeky to me. I caught him by my wits, not by running around like a dithering hen."

I make my way up the stairs to her. The child looks to be less than ten years old, scrawny. His skin is truly almost black, as she said, though dull with lack of care and right now he looks furious.

"What's your name?" I ask.

He shakes his head.

"I'll shake your ears off if you don't tell her," threatens Maria.

"Karbo," mutters the child.

"Karbo?" I check.

I get a sullen nod in response.

"Maria said you're fast. Just how fast are you?"

"Let me go and I'll show you."

"He thinks I'm an idiot," Maria says.

I squat down, so that I can look the boy in the eye. "Have you seen the Flavian Amphitheatre?"

"Everyone's seen it, stupid," he says.

172

"Less of your cheek, you street rat," says Maria, shaking him by the ear again.

"I work there," I say. "And I need a messenger. There is work going on all the time, and once we get spectators, we won't be able to call to one another. We will need a quick boy who can run and find people in our team and pass on messages, or tell us if we are wanted for something. But the boy I choose must be fast. The amphitheatre is huge, it takes a long time just to walk from one end to the other. So how fast are you?"

"What makes you think I want a job?" he asks.

"I think you're a runaway slave," I say and his eyes widen in fear. "I don't think you have a family of your own, or a job in any household, or you wouldn't be running in and out of our courtyard all the time, trying to steal food. If you can show me how fast you are, I would pay you board and lodging to be our messenger boy."

"For how long?" he asks.

"At least a year, maybe two," I say. "Perhaps longer than that, if you're good at your job. You can live here with us. Fausta has space in her room. You can sleep there, and we will feed you."

He stares at me and I wait for an answer. Maria doesn't loosen her hold on his ear.

"Fine," he says at last. "Now let me go."

The minute her fingers leave his ear he streaks past me and down the stairs, bolting for our courtyard gate exit.

"I thought he'd stay," I say, disappointed.

"He'll be back," says Maria, settling back into her usual position, vast bosom leaning on her crossed arms.

"Will he?"

"You offered him food," she says simply.

THE NEXT MORNING I'M BLEARILY tucking into my pancake at Cassia's when I feel a tug on my arm and turn to see Karbo standing beside me.

"You promised me board and lodging," he says.

"You ran off."

"I'm here now," he objects.

"Bread and cheese for this boy, Cassia," I say.

"I'd rather have a pancake."

"Pancake it is."

"Two pancakes."

"What he said."

Cassia lifts her eyebrows, but swiftly cooks two pancakes, douses them in date syrup and hands them to Karbo. He demolishes them both before I've even finished my single one.

"Now you owe me a day's work," I say.

He trails behind me all the way to the amphitheatre.

"Huge, isn't it," I say to him, expecting him to be overawed by the size of it inside.

"It's a cold place to sleep," he says. "Nothing soft, just stone."

"Sleep?"

"Lots of people sleep here at night," he says as though this were obvious.

"Why?"

He shrugs. "Easy to get in. Lots of room in the corridors, can't rain on you. Some people sleep under the arena floor, say it's warmer there, but you get all sorts down there at night, can't trust them."

Marcus has been watching us, head on one side. "Right, boy, let's see what you're made of. Show me how fast you can run around the amphitheatre through the corridors. Quick as you can."

He manages it in an impressively short space of time.

"You might have hit on something," says Marcus to me. "That is, if he doesn't eat his weight in pancakes every morning."

Karbo turns out to be what we were looking for. He carries messages from one end of the amphitheatre to the other, with no need for whistles or yelling. He keeps an eye on strangers entering the building and finds out what they want and who they wish to speak to. At first, he is jumpy, not letting any of us touch him for any reason, but as the weeks go by and he is fed a hearty breakfast and dinner every day, as well as a good portion of bread and cheese for lunch, he seems to relax in our presence. He does not sleep in Fausta's room at first, only taking up a spot under the wooden stairs in the courtyard and accepting a sleeping mat, but one night it rains heavily and Fausta simply picks him up under one arm and dumps him in her room despite his protests. After that he seems to find her presence acceptable, curling up in a corner of the room. I can't persuade him to join us at the baths each day after work. He seems to find washing himself in the public fountains more acceptable, occasionally returning dripping wet but approximately clean. I think his skin could do with oiling but since he won't allow that I make him a new tunic, since his is both falling apart and woefully short. Maria watches over him, combining an odd mix of feeding him honeyed walnuts and boxing his ears, according to what she thinks he most needs.

"So, the basic structure of each day is the same. Beast hunts in the morning, gladiatorial procession before or after, depending. Then a bit of light stuff, dancing girls, actors, that sort of thing. Then the execution of criminals. Some of the audience will leave during that part. Haven't the stomach for it.

Gladiator bouts in the afternoon. All of the audience will come back for that. In fact some people only attend the combats, not so interested in the animals. So the audience changes a bit over the course of a full day. Now the mornings, that's for showing off some of the rarer animals and hunting them, so we have beast-fighters in the morning and sometimes add them to the gladiator sessions in the afternoon if we want something different. Most of the gladiatorial bouts, we don't want anyone dying. Blood, yes, death, not so much. If we do a fight to the death, the trainers would rather we put up criminals against the real gladiators, or occasionally they've got gladiators who are troublemakers or on their way out, whatever. Point is, you don't want to lose your best fighters. But the audience gets bored if it's the same people all the time, so you need to spice it up. We use the speciality acts for that, also the re-enactments of past battles, myths and legends, that sort of thing, makes it more interesting, allows us to get away with fewer actual deaths, because you can pop some criminals in there to be killed off and, also, you can have a bit of fakery, acting dead rather than being dead. So we'll visit the two gladiator trainers we'll be using the most. No doubt there'll be others, but these two will be important for us." He thinks for a minute. "We'll get regular deliveries of criminals, but it would help if we knew how many we have before they arrive, it allows us to plan. We could ask them to save up a larger group for the first day, I suppose. Titus will want a good show, we can't just have a handful, which is all you get some days."

I'm supposed to be making notes, but I'm distracted. Marcus has come into work with a black eye, which he refuses to answer any questions about. His night-time excursions, whatever they are, have to stop or he'll end up with worse than a few bruises. I consider asking one more time, but I know he won't answer.

THE FIRST GLADIATOR TRAINER WE meet is a grizzly older man, standing in his training ground, much like the barracks of Pompeii. "Well, if it isn't Scaurus!"

"Paternus."

The two men embrace.

"This is my assistant and scribe, Althea," says Marcus.

The man gives me a look from under bushy eyebrows. "Always a female assistant, eh? What happened to the other?"

"Fausta is still with me. The Flavian Amphitheatre needs all hands on deck."

"Always liked the look of her," muses Paternus. "May have to pay you a visit one day and renew our acquaintance. Anyway, you're here for my men, is that right?"

"Can't run the greatest amphitheatre in the Empire without you," says Marcus.

"Flatterer."

Marcus shrugs. "Truth," he says. "I'm going to be your best client."

"Glad to hear it," says Paternus. "Hundred days of consecutive Games, that's what I'm hearing. Is that right?"

"Yes."

"That'll keep us all busy. I might have to get some new talent in."

"You do that. I'll take everyone you've got. And I want to discuss the first day's Games with you. I need something no-one's ever seen before."

"I don't do speciality."

"I know," agrees Marcus. I'll go to Labeo for that."

Paternus shakes his head. "Labeo would wet himself if he met a real gladiator."

177

Marcus shrugs. "He knows his side of the business, just like you know yours. There's room for everyone. But I don't want speciality on day one. I want legends. Can you get me Verus and Priscus?"

"Both of them?"

"Yes."

"Who do you want them to fight?"

"Each other."

Paternus stares, as do I. Verus and Priscus are legendary gladiators, undefeated, now close to retirement. They've never fought one another. Seeing them fight together would be a spectacle the whole of Rome would want to see. Paternus shakes his head. "And what kind of money's available for that? For one of them to lose their undefeated status, you're talking serious gold."

"Plenty of money in the purse if you can get them. And their freedom."

"For which one?"

"Both."

"That's unheard of."

Marcus grins. "I know."

A MAN NAMED STRABO JOINS us. He will be in charge of the dark under-arena area, supervising deliveries of animals and criminals, as well as keeping the space tidy and ready to receive the performers. He is cross-eyed, a large man with a deep voice, taller even than Marcus, pale-skinned with thick black curls.

"He used to manage the slaughter of livestock," says Marcus. "He can kill a bull with one blow of a hammer. We can probably use him for Charon, he's got the height for it."

I shudder. The role of the hooded Charon is to finish off any gladiator who is not fully dead, by a hammer blow that will see him to Hades in an instant. Strabo, a kindly enough man, seems ill-fitted for the role, but someone has to do it.

"Time to meet the other trainer," says Marcus.

"You don't sound keen," I say.

"A different sort entirely," says Marcus. "You'll see."

Labeo is a young man, his hair excessively curled and primped, even his eyebrows plucked, wearing a tunic in a bold blue and red stripe. He's wearing more jewellery than most women. We visit his training ground and are shown into a large room with doors at each end. The walls are painted with scenes of gladiator fights.

"I have heard so much about you," he says to Marcus. "A great appointment. I hope we can work closely together. My gladiators are guaranteed to create a real spectacle in any arena. In yours... it will be unforgettable. His eyes flicker over me, there's a hesitation before he flashes a dazzling smile. "And this is your... assistant," he says. "Delighted."

"Althea Aquillius," says Marcus, giving my full name so that Labeo is aware I am not a slave, although he will work out that I must have once been Marcus' slave, given that our names match.

"Delighted," repeats Labeo, waving us to a seating area. "Let me offer you some refreshment. Some hot wine on this cold day."

Marcus accepts wine for both of us and I take a small sip. It's not very good, a cheap wine overly sweetened and spiced.

"Now then," says Labeo enthusiastically. "Can I show you some of my fighters?"

"If you wish," says Marcus.

"I have *everything*," says Labeo. "And anything I don't have, you need only say the word and I will have it sourced for you specially, within a week at the very most."

"Glad to hear it," says Marcus. He looks tired.

Labeo gives a quick gesture and the room before us begins to fill up while he provides a running commentary. The men and women are wearing processional armour, highly elaborate and polished, not the battered items real gladiators wear during bouts. It almost looks like a play.

"So, first of all, my women. I have the greatest selection of female fighters in Rome. Fierce, they are, you wouldn't credit it from women, but they really can fight! I have some excellent trainers who work for me."

"They look like they've come from a brothel," mutters Marcus to me. He has a point. Their armour is deliberately skimpy in parts, showing off their bodies in a way that would make them extremely vulnerable to an opponent, their long hair left to hang down loose rather than tied up in what would surely be a more practical hairstyle for fighting.

"I also have dwarfs, always popular as you know," says Labeo, when over fifty women have paraded past. More than a dozen dwarfs make an appearance. "I swear there isn't a dwarf in Rome who can handle a sword I haven't managed to recruit. Then I have those of the opposite persuasion, shall we say?"

Four men shamble into the courtyard. They're tall, taller than any man I've ever laid eyes on, they make Marcus, who is tall, look like a dwarf himself. Their armour is designed to emphasise their size, with vast padded shoulders in leather broadening their already considerable chests.

"Impressive, aren't they?" smiles Labeo. "Crowds *love* them. We did an Odyssey re-enactment with one of them playing Polyphemus. Made a fantastic giant, well, I mean, he *is* one, isn't he?"

Marcus nods. "I can see you have what we need," he says.

180

"I'll send a list of requirements, day by day as we draw up the schedule. You'll have plenty of advance warning, a couple of weeks at a time." He seems keen to leave, as though he finds the parade wearying.

"Oh goodness, you've hardly seen anything!" cries Labeo. "They're just the regular specials. I've got some really *particular* items to show you." He gestures and two men enter the courtyard.

I have to narrow my eyes to be sure of what I am seeing. They seem to be joined together, where each man's chest should end, it is instead joined to the other. They have four legs between them, but only two arms, one on each man, as well as a strange protuberance, like a hand without an arm, which pokes out from the shoulder of the man on the left. The fingers move. I lean back, making a gesture against evil spirits.

Marcus grimaces. "So I gather," he says. "I think we have seen all we need to."

"When they fight, they look extraordinary, but *imagine* when you slice the two of them apart! No one will ever have seen anything like it. It would be expensive, of course, because I'm not going to find another one like that in a hurry, am I?"

"We'll send you the list of what we need," says Marcus.

There is still a good part of the day left, but Marcus points me back towards the amphitheatre as we leave. "Make my excuses," he says. "I'm going to the baths."

I want to ask him to come back to the insula, to eat with us tonight, but I know he won't listen to me. I make my way back to the site, my stomach turned by Labeo's enthusiastic demonstration of his wares.

THE BEAST-HUNTER WE ENGAGE TO keep us supplied with animals is less well presented. Bestia is a hunched, lumbering hulk of a man with little interest in the welfare of the animals he sources.

"Shitting giraffes? Really? What in Hades do you want them for?"

"Giraffes are impressive, hardly anyone's seen them," says Marcus calmly.

"Bollocks are they impressive. They die if you look at them. Sodding scared of ships, if you ask me. How about rhinos instead? Solid buggers, reliable."

"As well as," says Marcus.

"You bastard."

"You want the job or not?"

"Got enough shitting work on."

"Fine," says Marcus. "I'll find someone who can get me what I need."

"Jupiter's dick. I'm the best and you know it."

Marcus shrugs. "I wouldn't call you that. I'd call you adequate. I'm going to need over three thousand animals a month. You show me the amphitheatre that's using that many animals and I'll show you a liar."

"You going to use Carpophorus in the beast hunts?"

Marcus nods. "Not on the first day, I've got something else planned. But yes, of course. He's the best beast-fighter there is."

Bestia sighs. "He'll be the ruin of me. That cackhead has no consideration for how difficult some of those animals are to get over here. Just kills them like they're no trouble at all."

"The crowds love him."

Bestia rolls his eyes. "Cackhead."

JULIA TAKES ME ASIDE. "MARCUS is not paying the rent he owes," she says. "It's not like him. Why doesn't he have any money?"

I stare at her. "He gets paid a good wage," I say. "He hasn't paid the rent?"

She shakes her head.

"Leave it with me," I say. "How many days is he behind?"

"Almost thirty," she says.

I tell Fausta and she looks troubled. Between us, we put together enough money to pay Julia what she is owed, but it leaves us with very little.

"But what's he doing with his money?" I ask her. "He can't spend that much on wine. And women…"

Fausta shakes her head. "Don't think it's women," she says. "But it's a lot. He's doing something with it."

It's February and the days of the dead are being celebrated. Tonight my cloak isn't thick enough for the protection I want it to give me. I hesitate before leaving the safety of our courtyard and the flickering torches that light it in the evenings. The street outside looks very dark. There is no lighting, only the odd small gleam coming from household windows, not enough to give me any sense of safety. The streets of Rome at night are known for being dangerous, people make truthful jokes about going for a stroll at night if you wish to end your life.

But I have to move quickly, or Marcus will disappear. Already I can only just make him out, striding northwards up Virgin's Street, about to disappear into a network of small streets where I will lose him for sure. I feel cold, colder than the night air warrants. I have to keep up with him or I'll be lost and if I get lost out in the night-time on my own, I'm in a lot of trouble. But I need to know what's going on.

The street is horribly empty. The bakery is shut up for the day, its wooden shutters pulled to. Cassia's popina, further behind me, is open, but the light from it quickly fades as I make my way to the end of the street and see Marcus turn left.

I keep my footsteps quiet, afraid he will notice me following him, but I needn't worry, he never looks behind him.

Three streets in, he turns into what looks like a popina, lewd graffiti all over its frontage. Clearly there is no father here to threaten customers with a stick for touching the barmaids. I hold back, then edge forward, closer to the street counter when I see that he has gone all the way inside. There's a largish drinking room in the back, from which I can hear the rattling of dice. Perhaps Marcus is gambling after all, I think. Perhaps there is something in his blood that draws him to the betting tables, something dark left over from his grandfather's disastrous loss of the family farm.

"Help you?" The barmaid, wearing a tunic that has slipped down over one shoulder to give a, perhaps deliberate, better view of her cleavage, is staring at me.

I hold out a coin. "Cup of wine."

She obliges but can tell I don't belong here. "You looking for someone?"

I point discreetly to Marcus. He's sitting at a table with two men. I can't see any dice but perhaps it's only a matter of time.

"Oh, the Pompeiian man."

I frown.

"Isn't he from Pompeii?"

"Yes," I say. "How do you know that?"

"Half of Rome knows him, love."

"Why?"

"If you go around paying good money for nothing, people get to know you pretty quick."

"What's he paying for?"

The girl tips her head to one side. "Do you actually know him?" she asks. "Or has someone sent you looking for him? Though you're a funny person to send," she adds. "Is he in trouble with someone I should know about? The authorities? I don't need trouble in here, not with, you know," she winks, "my customers liking the sound of rolling dice."

"He's gambling?"

Again, the girl looks at me as though she finds my questions odd.

"Look," I say, desperately, afraid Marcus will spot me. "Just tell me what he does here, will you?"

"He pays for information," she says.

"What sort of information?"

"Anything related to Pompeii," she says.

"Like what?"

"Names of any new refugees from the area who've recently arrived in Rome. He'll meet anyone claiming to be from there, pays them money to sit with him and tell him exactly where they've been, who they've seen. Looking for a woman and a child, that's what I hear."

I drop my head onto my hands. I'm relieved but also saddened that Marcus is engaged in this endless, fruitless search, that all his money is being used up on useless information.

"You alright?"

I lift my head and sigh. "Yes."

"You know him, do you?"

"I work for him."

She pauses in wiping down the counter. "Seems like a decent man. Doesn't gamble though he gets plenty of offers. Never seen him with any of the women that hang around here."

"He is. But…"

185

"But?"

"He's searching for his wife and child," I say. "And…"

The girl grimaces. "No chance?"

I shake my head.

"Sounded like a bad business."

"It was."

"He put the word out he'll pay for information. And there's a few who might be able to really help, but…" She leans forward. "There's a lot of others who are just fooling him. They put on the Pompeiian accent, they say oh, they knew so-and-so, some common name that could be anyone. They say my brother's cousin's sister-in-law knew someone who said something… and he pays for their nonsense. Can't you stop him coming?"

I shake my head. "I've tried. He won't listen. Does he know they're fooling him?"

She shrugs. "Maybe. Maybe not. He's pretty drunk when he leaves here each night. Probably believes all sorts."

"He had a black eye the other day."

"Someone said Pompeiian women were all whores, didn't know he was here. He went for them, but he was too drunk to handle himself properly, got a wallop."

I sigh. "Can I try and take him home?"

"Be my guest."

I make my way into the back room, aware that the prostitutes are sizing me up, a possible competitor intruding on their turf. The men, fortunately, are mostly focused on their gambling. I reach Marcus and touch him on the shoulder.

He looks up and frowns. "What are you doing here?"

"I could ask the same question."

"Not your business."

186

"You can't go around giving your money to liars who claim to know anything about Pompeii."

"Who says they're liars?"

"I do. Come home."

One of the men at the table raises his eyebrows. "Oh, a woman come to take you home, is it? Worried about walking through the streets by yourself, Scaurus?"

Marcus ignores the taunt, keeps his eyes on me. "I don't have a home. It's buried under ashes and rocks, remember? You were there."

"Julia's is our home now."

He shakes his head and knocks back his cup of wine. "It won't be a home until Livia is with me again."

My eyes fill with tears and I blink them away. "Let's leave this place."

"There was a man who said he knew something, he left a message for me, said he'd be in tonight."

"But he's not here now, is he? Let's go."

He shakes his head, stubborn. "I need to hear from him."

I squat down by his bench, look up at him. "Please, Marcus," I say. "This is a bad idea. People will take advantage of a man who will give out good money for rumours, for half-lies and hearsay. Fausta and I had to pay your rent and we'll run out of money if we have to do it again. We can't go hungry or end up on the street because you're giving away your wages to every hustler in Rome."

He looks away from me.

"Oh, tell her to get lost," says another man at the table. "Why do women always have to ruin a good game with their whining?"

"Please," I repeat, touching Marcus again, this time on his hand.

He stands. "Fine. If you'll stop nagging me."

I stand up and walk swiftly out of the popina, looking back once to make sure he's following me.

"Thank you," I say in a low voice to the girl at the counter as I pass, and she gives me a quick nod.

OUT IN THE STREET MARCUS overtakes me and walks ahead, his strides fast and angry, shoulders hunched. I follow, grateful he has made so little fuss, and also glad to know what has been going on all this time. Perhaps, now I know what he has been doing, I stand some hope of stopping him in the future.

"You the Pompeiian?" A dark figure steps out in front of Marcus.

"I am."

"Heard you might be interested in what we do."

"And what is that?"

"Business in Pompeii."

"Business?"

"That's right."

I stand still in the shadows, heart beating fast, listening. I don't know if the man realises I'm here, it's very dark, I can barely make him out.

"Tell me about it."

"I heard you pay for information."

"I haven't heard any yet."

"I don't share without seeing what's on the table."

Leave, I think. Don't pull your purse out, this is the kind of man who will slit your throat and take everything you have.

But Marcus is pulling out his purse, I hear the coins clink together. "I want information on anything that's happening in Pompeii," he says and my hands ball into fists with fear of what is about to happen. "If you can tell me something that will help me find what I'm looking for, you'll find me more than generous."

I'm waiting for the man to attack, but he stays still.

"There's some interesting activity in Pompeii right now," he says. "Worth anyone's money to know about."

"Which is?"

"There are... goods available."

I frown. What's he talking about?

Marcus sounds confused too. "Goods? Speak more clearly. We're alone here."

The man lowers his voice a little, I struggle to hear him clearly. "There are tunnels."

"Tunnels?"

"That's right. Got a good crew. Discreet, quick, hardworking. You wouldn't believe the stuff coming out of there."

"Such as?"

"Jewellery, gold, money. Art. We tunnel into the big villas mostly, easier pickings. But we've found valuables in all sorts of places. People must have collected everything they had when they were thinking of escaping. There's good money to be made, if you want in on it. I could put a lot of work your way, easing the goods out, you know."

There's silence in the dark street. The man must gather something is wrong from Marcus' silence, because his tone changes. "So? Are you the man I took you for? Or am I talking to the wrong person?"

It's so fast I scream. Marcus shoves the man up against a wall, a blade to his throat. He's trying to struggle free, but Marcus has him in too tight a hold.

"You are tunnelling into the houses of the dead, stealing

their goods?" he says, and I cringe, I've never heard his voice so full of rage.

The man tries to reply but Marcus must have his throat so tightly pressed against the knife it comes out as a guttural sound rather than real words.

"Marcus," I say, my voice shaking. "Let him go, Marcus." I'm afraid he is going to kill the man. I don't doubt he's capable of it, the rage I heard was that of a man on the edge of sanity and he's no doubt killed men while in the army, but right now, if he kills a man in peacetime, he'll be a murderer and end up in the very arena we're building.

"He's scum," Marcus says. "He deserves to die."

"Yes," I say, because I agree with him. "But you don't deserve to face the punishment for murder. Please. Please."

He hesitates, still holding the man against the wall. I wait for a cry, for the man to slump to the ground lifeless, but Marcus suddenly lets go of him. "If I ever see your face again, I will kill you," he says. "And no woman will stop me."

The man is already running, away down the street from us, his footsteps fading into the distance.

"Thank you," I say. My teeth are chattering against each other, I have to grit them together to make them stop.

"Don't follow me again," he says and walks away.

I trail him in the darkness until we reach Virgin's Street and Julia's insula. In the darkness, we enter the rooftop hut and lie down to sleep, though I stay awake long into the night, even after he is asleep.

A Visit from Titus

I F I THOUGHT MARCUS WOULD stop his night-time wanderings after the encounter with the grave robber of Pompeii, I was mistaken. I tell Fausta what he is doing, and she nods, grim-faced.

"I don't know how to stop him," I say. "He's so desperate to find Livia, but she can't still be alive, she would have come here by now for sure."

Fausta shakes her head. "He can't admit she's dead because then he'd have to grieve properly. And he can't do that because he has all of this," she sweeps her arm across the site, "to make happen. So it's easier to keep doing what he's doing."

"For him, perhaps," I say. "But not for us when he's arriving at work hungover and half asleep and sometimes not at all. And what if he gets his throat cut in a dark street one night? We won't even know about it; they'll throw his body in the Tiber and that will be the end of him. And of us."

"The Aedile is coming to inspect progress next week," says Fausta. "Let's just keep him going till then, shall we? After that we can think about what to do next."

THE AEDILE'S VISIT IS A tense one for all of us. Marcus is on time to work but his breath smells of wine and he looks white-faced.

"Jupiter strike you for the idiot you are," mutters Fausta when she sees him. "Chew on this." She stuffs mint in his mouth. He turns away and spits it out, but at least he's eaten some of it. "Now get your head up and be polite to the Aedile," she adds, as the senator and his entourage come into view, stomping through the Gate of Triumph as though they think they're part of a procession.

We huddle together, watching as Marcus greets the Aedile, manages to turn on something approaching charm, walks around the arena with him, answering questions and pointing to various items: the lifts under the trapdoors, the pens below, the names being carved into the seating, and so on.

"It looks like it's going well," I say to Fausta.

"Perhaps," she says, still frowning from her exchange with Marcus. "He better not bugger this up."

The Aedile departs, apparently satisfied and for that brief morning I think that perhaps this signals a change in Marcus, that he has turned a corner. But I'm wrong. After the visit, he barely comes to the site at all. I wake in the mornings to find him asleep and snoring. He will not rouse even if I shake him and he does not appear at the amphitheatre most mornings. The work of the manager falls more and more to Fausta and me.

"THERE'S A MAN WANTING TO see you," says Karbo.

I look up. Fausta and I are checking over the merchandise that twelve different stallholders have brought in for us to approve. These will be the official stalls, I've no doubt there will be many dozens of unofficial sellers of every possible kind of product, but these at least need to be good quality. We have examined a range of pottery items, including tableware and lamps, all featuring gladiatorial scenes and animal hunts, followed by painters who specialise in fast portraits of gladiatorial heroes and their fans.

"So we have a pre-prepared portrait of the gladiator Verus, for example," says the painter, explaining how they do their work. "And then if you want, we can do your portrait, right alongside him, see, we leave an empty space there."

I think of the speed at which Lucius' triclinium was painted and then repainted, at Marcus' instruction. "Very nice," I say. "Do people buy a lot of these?"

"Oh yes, very popular. People like having pictures of their favourite gladiators."

"There's a man wanting to see you," repeats Karbo.

"I'll leave you to it," I say to Fausta. "There's still the leatherworkers and then we have to approve the food and drink providers, who will be allowed to roam between the seats. I'll try and get back to you soon."

The man Karbo leads me to is tall and wiry, with light-coloured hair. At his side stands a tiny woman, who barely reaches his waist, but who looks just like him, the same light floppy hair and long nose, same light brown eyes and skin that only turns pale gold in the sun.

"Fabius," the man introduces himself, "and my daughter, Fabia."

I nod, waiting for an explanation.

"Marcus sent for me."

I tilt my head. "Did he?"

The man frowns. "I'm to be the physician for the amphitheatre. My daughter will be my assistant."

"Oh," I say, "I'm sorry, I didn't know to expect you."

"Marcus didn't tell you?"

"No," I say. "I'm sorry, he's not here today."

The man looks disappointed. "Ah, well never mind, never mind, we will find lodging somewhere nearby and return tomorrow. We served together; I was an army physician. I retired from the army when I married but my wife is no longer with us and so, when Marcus sent word, well, it was too good an opportunity to miss."

"My father finds ordinary ailments boring," says Fabia. "He misses sword wounds."

"I apologise for Marcus not being here to greet you himself since he sent for you," I say. "He is... not quite himself these days."

"We heard, of course,' says Fabius. "Terrible thing. It must have left a mark on him."

"Yes," I say. "But perhaps seeing an old friend will help. Will you come for dinner?"

I send Karbo to find Marcus and tell him he must stay at the insula tonight, that we will eat with Fabius and Fabia, but when we return from work, he has already gone out and he does not arrive. Fabius arrives with gifts of delicious food: a large platter of freshly cut fruits as well as pickles and sliced hogshead. Julia steps in as hostess and looks after us well, but the meal feels awkward. Fabius and his daughter seem kind and make pleasant dinner companions, but Marcus, who should be here, is nowhere to be seen.

"So do you work at the amphitheatre too?" Fabia asks Karbo.

"Yes," he says proudly. "I'm the fastest boy in Rome."

I hide a smile.

"I'm sure you are," says Fabia. "Perhaps you will show me round the amphitheatre one day? You must know it better than anyone and if my father and are to work there, I will need a good guide."

Karbo's chest inflates. "I'll look after you, show you what's what," he assures her.

"If you need an apartment, let me know. If one comes free, I can keep it for you," says Julia at the end of the evening.

"I would be most grateful," says Fabius. "Perhaps I can keep Marcus company, bring him out of himself a little by talking of the old days in the army?"

I nod, grateful for his understanding.

The next morning, I take Fabius on a tour of the under-arena space.

"I will need an area to lay out my tools," he says. "Stitching and amputations must be done as quickly as possible."

We identify a suitable space for him, far enough away from most of the cages for safety.

"Althea!" Fausta is kneeling on the arena floor above us, her head poking down through one of the trapdoors.

"What?"

"The Emperor is here."

"Now's not the time for pranks," I say, rolling my eyes.

"Not joking," she says, her face serious, voice flat. "Get up here, quick."

I climb up a ladder set into one of the trapdoors. The bright morning sunlight hurts my eyes after the gloomy space below but there's no mistaking a crowd of Praetorian Guards and lictors, deferentially surrounding a man in a toga trimmed in purple. "What do we do?" I ask Fausta.

"Go and talk to him, of course," she says. "Show him around. Reassure him that everything is going very, *very* well."

"With Marcus not even here?"

"Say he's beast collecting."

"Why can't you go and talk to him?" I ask.

She raises her eyebrows. As usual, she is wearing her toga. "The Emperor will not be impressed at being shown round the site by a prostitute," she says. "Go!"

TITUS IS A PLUMP MAN, his toga adding to his bulk, two chins wobbling when he laughs, which he does often.

"I hope the acoustics are good in here," he begins, as soon as introductions have been made. "Can't bear it when you can't hear properly at the theatre. You want to tell them to SPEAK LOUDER!" he adds, finishing on a bellow. "There, see, perfect sound," he says, pleased with his test.

I try to keep my eyes on him, but find myself flickering a quick look towards Fausta, sheltered in the centre of the huddled team, everyone watching us. She nods and smiles encouragingly.

"And where is this manager I've heard so much about? Scaurus something?"

"He will be devastated to have missed your visit," I say. "He is at – in – Ostia, there is a new animal they have found that may be suitable for a beast hunt. Some sort of water-creature," I finish weakly.

"Can you flood the arena?" he asks over his shoulder, turning on the spot to look around the whole space.

"Of course," I say, thanking the gods for all the conversations I have overheard between Marcus and the architect. "We can have a naval battle whenever you command it."

"Marvellous," says Titus. "I shall think when would be best."

"Of course," I say brightly, making a note. Marcus will curse me for agreeing to such a thing when we've not yet tested the plumbing to see if it could cope.

"Ah, shorthand, very good," says Titus, coming close and peering over my shoulder. "Pass me a tablet and let's have a race. I'm told my shorthand is as good as any scribe's."

I stare at him, but an aide, evidently used to this sort of thing, has already passed Titus a fresh wax tablet and a stylus while another has pulled out a choice of scrolls, which Titus inspects, then selects one.

"Good choice," he says. "The Iliad. Ready, Althea?"

The aide begins to read out a battle scene from the Iliad and I try not to think what an absurd situation I find myself in, focusing on the words and getting them down as fast as possible. When the man stops reading Titus holds out his hand and I put my tablet into it. He compares the two, then holds them up so the gathering can see them. "Well, well, Althea has beaten me!" he declares. "Why, I shall have to hire you for imperial service!"

My stomach rolls over. What if Titus decides to take me as a scribe and removes me from Marcus and my work here? I can hardly refuse the Emperor, even if I am a freedwoman. "I am already in imperial service," I say, trying to put a smile on my face and opening my arms to indicate the amphitheatre all around us.

"Quite right, quite right!" bellows Titus. "You are indeed. And I am glad to see it looking so well advanced. Although I shall expect more decoration, eh? Looking a little plain at the moment."

"It will be magnificent," I say. "There are hunting scenes planned in all the corridors, I can show you the designs –"

"I really think I should take you as my own scribe," he interrupts, beaming. "So efficient, not to mention very pretty."

I keep my smile fixed on my face. "Perhaps you should see the first day's Games before you make that decision," I say.

He laughs. "I am sure everything will be wonderful. Oh yes, before I forget, I saw two excellent executions of criminals, years ago, now. One was a criminal playing the part of Icarus, they made these extraordinary wings from real feathers and had him dropped from a great height, with scenery above him showing the sun. The other one was based on the legend of Prometheus stealing fire from the gods and being punished for it, they actually trained an eagle to eat his entrails until he died. It was very clever. Perhaps they could be incorporated into one of the days."

"I will see to it myself," I say, slightly appalled that he would want such grim spectacles repeated.

"I'm going to inspect the baths today as well," says Titus. "Building a whole new complex, just over the road from here, you must have seen it."

"It looks magnificent," I say, although the baths site looks like it is running behind to me. It has been built using some of the plumbing and heating systems left over from Nero's palace, the Golden House. Apparently, it was supposed to coincide with our inauguration, but I don't see that happening. They're still building the main pool, none of the mosaics have been put in yet and the gardens surrounding it are just bare earth. They'll have to do some serious transplanting of ready-grown trees and bushes if it's to look at all impressive. Still, if they're behind schedule they'll make us look better.

"I hope you will enjoy using the facilities when it opens," says Titus, allowing his gaze to travel over me.

"I'm sure our whole team will be very grateful for it every day after work," I say.

Titus finally departs, happy and with many promises to visit regularly, which I try to look enthusiastic about. When the last marching feet of the Praetorian Guard fade into the distance, I sit down on the steps, my legs weak.

"Good job," says Strabo, his large hand on my shoulder.

"Thank you," I mutter.

A few more people touch my shoulder and there are murmurs of congratulation as the team disperse, moving back to their jobs, chattering about the visit.

Fausta sits down next to me. "Bastard."

"Titus?"

"Marcus."

I want to disagree but she's right. My shaking turns into anger, my fright turning to rage at being put into a situation so fraught with danger with no warning, no support from the man who should have been in my place.

"Althea."

"What is it, Karbo?" I ask wearily.

"I found Marcus and brought him here."

I look to where he's pointing. Marcus is standing in one of the arches, looking over at me. I'm on my feet and striding towards him before I realise it.

"Where were you?" I ask, and my voice comes out low, shaking with anger.

He looks away. "Asleep."

"I know that!" I say. "You are out every night, chasing shadows, and then leaving me in the shit the next day. I have had enough!"

"I have to find Livia…" he begins and something in me snaps.

199

"Livia is dead!" I say too loudly, and the site falls silent around me.

The team forms into little huddles, pretending not to be there, but listening to every word. I want to stop but I have to say what must be said or Marcus will sink ever deeper into his hunt through the halls of Hades.

"She is dead, Marcus, and so is your son. And I am sorry for it, truly I am. If I could bring them back I would do so, no matter what it took. But I cannot, no one can. And you will get yourself killed wandering the backstreets of Rome at night, drunk and with a purse of money on you for some cutthroat to lay hands on. And then all of us will be screwed, because a man with less heart than you will be appointed, and we will be nothing to him. He will not care what becomes of us. Not that you seem to!" I'm almost running out of breath.

"I –" he begins but I cut him off.

"You put me in danger! You put this whole project in danger! If Titus had been displeased, it would be all of us in the arena, being mauled to death!" My voice has risen to a shout, echoing around the amphitheatre.

"Althea –"

"No! You can't fob me off with half-baked promises. You owe all of us an apology, you owe all of us your time and your presence here, doing the job you were hired for. Your wife and son are gone, there is nothing you can do for them. But we need you, Marcus. *We* need you." I let my tablet, full of the absurd shorthand rendition of the Iliad, fall to the ground. The wood splits in two, held together only by the wax inside it. I open my mouth, then control myself. What I am saying is true, but it is also cruel, and I am exhausted. I walk past Marcus and out of the amphitheatre, through the Forum, heading back to Virgin's Street.

I arrive in our courtyard with tears rolling down my face.

Maria peers down at me. "Back already?"

"Don't ask," I say.

"Did someone hurt you?"

I shake my head. "The Emperor visited the site."

She nods, serious. "And Marcus didn't make it in time? Karbo was trying to get him washed and over to you."

I shake my head. "Shame on him for making a child come and fetch him to his own workplace."

On the rooftop I find a half-full amphora of water and wash my face. I feel too hot, as though the sun has burnt me, although I know the heat is from the rage and fear of the past hour, as well as the fast walk home.

"Althea."

"Oh, leave me be!" I cry out. "Can you not stay on the site, where you're supposed to be, for once? Just once?"

Marcus shakes his head. "You're more important. What you said was more important."

"He could have had us thrown to the lions," I spit.

"He loved you," says Marcus with a grimace. "Fausta said you charmed him; he was delighted with the visit. You rose to the occasion better than anyone else could have done."

"Except you."

He nods. "It should have been me. And I am sorry, Althea. I have mistreated you, have poorly repaid your loyalty."

I look down. "I'm sorry for what I said," I say. "About Livia –"

"But you were right," he cuts me off.

I raise my eyes. His are swimming with unshed tears.

"She is dead," he says. "And my boy. They are both gone. I know it."

"Marcus," I start, moving towards him, but he holds up a hand to stop me.

"I will stop searching," he says. "I am done with that now."

"I am so sorry," I say, and the relief of finally being able to offer him sympathy for his loss, so long denied, makes my own tears fall. "She was a kind woman, Anna said so, she said Livia was the best mistress, she was glad to serve her. I am sorry I never knew her better. And Amantius was so much like you, he was a little copy. I know it must be unbearable. I do not know how to make it bearable for you." I'm talking too quickly, trying to say everything all at once.

He walks to the side of the rooftop and for a moment I feel a sudden lurch of terror that he will jump, that now that he has acknowledged his loss, he will want to end his misery. But he places his hands on the wall and looks down, then across the rooftops. "I have you and Fausta and Julia," he says. "I could not ask for better women to surround me."

I move to his side, rest my own hands on the wall. "I will do anything to help you," I say. "And Fabius is here now, he said he would spend time with you."

He nods. "He's a good man. We're lucky to have him."

We stand in silence for a while, side by side. "Will you eat something?" I ask at last.

He nods, a weary movement. "I am so tired," he says, his voice low.

"Food and sleep," I say.

"And work," he says.

"And work," I agree. "But better those three and nothing else than wandering Rome at night."

He nods again. "I am done with that," he repeats. "I swear it."

FEVER

THE FIRST WARM MONTHS COME, bringing longer days but also interrupted nights.

"Explain to me why I am covered in bites and you haven't even one?" says Marcus, irritably scratching at his leg.

"I don't know," I say, a little smugly. "They don't bite Julia, either."

"Oh, so they only bite men, is that it?"

"They bite *me*," says Fausta. "I just don't moan about it."

"I haven't been bitten," I say, "but the whining noise they make keeps you up all night. You keep waiting for it to stop, waiting for a bite so you know where they are and can slap them."

"When the noise stops, you can take comfort in the fact that they've landed on me," says Marcus.

Fausta shakes her head, exaggerating the gesture so that the man standing on the other side of the arena can see her. "Can't see anything written on that board," she complains. "The writing needs to be a lot bigger, else you can't see the gladiator scores from this distance."

"They looked fine to me this morning," says Marcus.

"Yes, that's because you're always in the Emperor's box. I've told you before, you have to sit where the plebs sit. They need to see those scores clearly if they're going to place bets."

"I thought there were more than three scene painters due in today," I say, looking down at my list and frowning. "We've got over two hundred pieces of scenery to get ready, and only two months left. Someone explain to me how that's going to get done?"

Marcus grins at Fausta. "Getting good at this, isn't she? Hardly needs us at all. Got it all in hand."

Fausta nods encouragingly at me. "Once you've told the boss off in public it gives you a bit of confidence, doesn't it?"

I frown at her. I still worry that Marcus may do something stupid, should a black mood descend on him.

But Marcus takes it well enough, he shrugs and smiles, then walks away to find out why we only have three scene painters today. We watch him speaking to the foreman for a while.

"At least he's not drinking any more, nor seeking out trouble. He comes home at a reasonable time now, doesn't he?" asks Fausta, her eyes on Marcus' distant figure.

"Yes," I say. "He comes home and eats, but then he just sits on the rooftop, all alone. He doesn't want to talk. Sometimes I'm afraid I'll come up to the roof and find…"

"I don't think he'd jump," says Fausta in her usual blunt way. "More likely do it with a sword, soldier-like."

"Let's not talk about it," I say, keeping my voice low.

"He's just sad," says Fausta. "I think he's got past the stage of taking his own life. But he's grieving. He puts on too much of a front at work, it has to come out sometime. Better alone on the rooftop than the back room of a dirty popina on a dark street."

Marcus is climbing back up the steps towards us. "Five men off sick," he says, frowning. "Three scene painters and two more from the decoration team in the corridors. Some sort of fever. Have to hope it's not catching."

We all make a gesture to ward off bad luck, Fausta muttering under her breath to whatever god she feels is most likely to protect her.

"Are we supposed to wait for them to get better?" I ask. "Or do I need to find new painters?"

"They'll get better," says Marcus. "Don't worry about it."

BUT THE NEXT DAY THERE are ten men missing from the site, and the day after that thirty. Meanwhile, in Julia's insula, five of her tenants on the top floor, in the smallest rooms, go down with a fever, as does the elderly mother of the baker.

"She burns up and then she has shaking chills," says the baker's wife, her face worried as she returns early from work to spend time with her mother-in-law.

"Some sort of pestilence," says Julia and disappears for most of the day, praying at Vesta's Temple, perhaps speaking with her old colleagues.

The architect is beginning to look stressed again, just when he thought he had everything in hand. The stonemason sends word that over thirty of the statues destined for the arches around the amphitheatre will be delayed thanks to the pestilence.

"Put them at the back," says Marcus, unruffled, when he hears about it.

"The back's already full!"

"That is unfortunate," Marcus agrees. "Can't you shift them round?"

"That will take even longer!"

"You'll just have to wait then," says Marcus. "Presumably the men will be better soon."

"You don't seem very worried," spits the architect.

"Not my building," says Marcus with a smile.

"It is!"

"No, it's *your* building, they're *my* Games. Your statues are none of my business, they don't affect the spectacle."

"You are so mean to him," I say, as the architect stalks away. "Don't you feel sorry for him?"

"He has the easy job," says Marcus. "The building is mostly finished. It's our lives in the arena if the Games aren't up to scratch."

"I doubt they'll finish the decorations in time," I say, looking around me.

"They'll be decorating this place for years to come. They haven't even done the velarium, and that's not decoration, it's essential in the summers. Not to mention the under-arena space, which has just been thrown together, no proper building there at all, just a basic floor with some scaffolding over the top, lifts and pens around the edge. He hasn't even finished the waterproofing layer, tested the plumbing for flooding the space or ordered waterproof doors to seal off the entrances. Much he cares about us and our promise to deliver a naumachia."

"He might care more if you didn't antagonise him."

Marcus only laughs.

But none of us laughs over the next few days as the amphitheatre falls quiet and even the streets of Rome, so noisy, begin to empty. The pestilence spreads rapidly, and it does not respect anything, nor anyone. Senators and bricklayers, whores and priestesses, all of them fall ill. The patrician families hurry away to their countryside villas, certain that it is Rome's dirty air and streets that are the problem. Traders and farmers from the surrounding countryside, usually so keen to supply Rome and its hungry citizens, stay away and the market stalls grow empty.

Fabia and her father have begun their work earlier than expected, seeing to the many gladiators who have fallen ill.

"It starts with a fever, then the chills and shaking take over. But there are so many symptoms. Coughing, headaches, vomiting, diarrhoea, pain in the chest and limbs. I've seen all of them," Fabia reports to us.

"But most people are getting better, aren't they? Especially the gladiators? They must be stronger than most people."

"Doesn't matter how strong you are," says Fabia. "It comes in cycles. Fever, then chills, then sweats. Some people get better after the sweats, some die during the fever. Children and old people get it worst, but that doesn't stop strong men getting it. And pregnant women. I've seen eight die in two days now, couldn't save the child except in one case and that was touch and go." She sighs, rubbing her hands together against the morning chill. "And now I'm starting to see people who get through the sweats, they seem cured and then, the cycle starts again. Worst one I've seen had three attacks and then he died."

"Where is it coming from?" I ask.

She shakes her head. "I don't know. I can't tell. Sometimes it seems like it must spread in households, one person to the next, because a whole family goes down with it. But then you'll get a family and only one person falls ill, the rest go untouched. Some say it's the water in the public fountains, the old people say it comes from the marshlands outside of Rome, but they can't explain how it gets here. The air? The water? People who are already carrying the illness without knowing it? I just don't know. I've been working day and night, trying to help, but there isn't much we can do."

She rubs her hands over face. "I better go," she says. "Too much to do." She makes her way down the steps, which are too steep for someone of her size; she has to keep one hand on the wall to steady herself.

A FEW DAYS LATER THE architect goes missing and word comes that he, too, has fallen ill. Work on the amphitheatre has slowed to a trickle. No more statues are arriving from the stonemason's, the mosaic makers have left half of the imperial box unfinished. In the architect's absence, Marcus takes over, directing the few remaining craftsmen to to those parts of the arena most visible to those who matter most. The upper tiers, at this rate, will get no decorative flourishes whatsoever before the opening; all such works will be concentrated where the Emperor and the richest families of Rome can see them.

"So, we're carving family names into the marble seating, but the upper corridors won't even be painted? It's the plebs who take the Games seriously, attending day after day," Fausta points out.

"The Emperor is paying, and he wants his cronies impressed," says Marcus. "Stop whining and find out who the second-best mosaic makers in Rome are, because right now, they're the people I need. If nothing else gets done, the imperial box has to look magnificent."

Fausta grumbles, but she knows he's right and within two days a new team of mosaic makers are working on the floor. "It's the section behind his throne, so he won't be looking at it much," she comforts Marcus, who is still fretting.

"Fabius says more than a third of the gladiators might not be fit to fight during the inaugural Games," he says, appalled at a note he has just received. "I've been trying to get more gladiators from the south, promising them it's a big chance for their careers, but most of them are refusing. They're too scared of getting the pestilence themselves." He snorts. "So much for bravery. Bunch of cowards, under all those muscles."

"No Fausta this morning?" Cassia asks, expertly flipping pancakes to feed Karbo and me.

"Lazy lie-abed," I say. "When you see her, tell her to come straight to work. We don't have time to wait for her, there's hardly anyone on site as it is. At this rate it'll be Karbo and me doing the painting and carving. We should have made and stored most of the scenery by now, we're falling behind. So much for telling Titus everything was going well, the gods must've heard us and decided we were too full of ourselves."

Much to my surprise, the architect has returned, although he looks as pale as his toga.

"I'm not sure you should be here yet," I say, keeping my distance in case he is contagious. "Are you sure you're better? You don't look it. Marcus can look after everything, you know."

"That's what I'm afraid of," he says sourly. "Jupiter be praised, I am well. I recovered quickly."

"As you wish," I say. "I'll leave you to it."

"Please do," he says.

But by early afternoon the architect is staggering and has to return home. Karbo comes to tell me in the nearby warehouse, where I'm making an inventory of the scenery that is complete and what still needs to be done, a depressing task given how much is missing and how fast time is running out.

"He shouldn't have come back to work so soon," I say. "He clearly wasn't well enough."

"And Fausta?" asks Karbo.

"What about her?" I snap, trying to hold two scrolls under my arm while making notes on a third.

"She never arrived," says Karbo.

I drop everything I am holding, leave scrolls and tablets fallen on the floor and run through the streets back to the insula, Karbo at my side. When I reach the courtyard, Maria is not in her usual place, instead she has moved up two floors and is keeping watch outside Fausta's door. I run up the wooden stairs, clutching at the bannister.

"It's the pestilence," says Maria. "I've left water for her just inside the door, but I won't go in."

"Thank you," I gasp. "Karbo, you stay outside."

"He sleeps by her bed every night," points out Maria.

Inside, the room is dark. I open the tiny window trying to get fresh air in. Fausta is lying on her bed, blanket crumpled at her side, naked. I touch her skin.

"She's burning up," I say to Karbo, who is hovering in the doorway.

I SPEND ALL OF THAT afternoon attending to her by the flickering light of a lamp. Karbo brings cold water more than once from the public fountains, I dip rags in it and lay them over her forehead, her breasts, her belly, her feet. I wipe her hands over and over again. Maria moves back to her normal spot and warns the others to stay away when they come home. Julia ignores her and comes to stand in the doorway.

"There are more than twenty people ill now, just in our insula," she sighs. "I'm doing what I can."

"Take Karbo to help you," I offer.

Fausta alternates between burning up and then shaking with cold, her hands like claws reaching out for the blanket and clutching it to her desperately. I add my cloak and tell Karbo

211

that he must sleep, he has been helping Julia for hours. I send him to sleep in the rooftop hut with Marcus.

"Let me help," says Marcus.

"Someone has to go to work tomorrow," I say. "Go and get some sleep."

"Hot," croaks Fausta, and she throws my cloak and the blanket aside again.

THE NIGHT IS ENDLESS. SOMETIMES I sleep, but I am woken by Fausta's moans when she is too hot and by her teeth chattering when she is too cold, her whole jaw shaking so hard that I am afraid she will bite her tongue. Julia brings me slices of early cucumbers, still tiny, but I cannot make her eat. Instead I put the slices in her water cup and make her drink. Julia brings a tea made of marigolds and fennel, Fabia sends one of honeysuckle. They should reduce fever, but nothing makes any difference. By the morning I am exhausted and Karbo tells me that Marcus told him to stay with us while he goes to work.

"He said you are not to come," he says solemnly. "You must sleep. Cassia has sent you food."

I sip some water, try to eat a fruit roll and only get halfway through before I feel my eyelids droop. "Watch over her," I tell him. "Any change, wake me."

HE SHAKES ME AWAKE AND I blink at the sunlight streaming in through the window. Sweat is pouring off Fausta, as though a river were washing over her. I pull away the blanket and mop her with my rag, washing away the sweat as it seeps out of her. I trickle water into her mouth again and she opens her eyes, focuses on me, then Karbo.

"Bona Dea," she mutters, "Get the boy out of here."

212

I gesture to Karbo to leave us, though I think Maria is right, surely he would be ill by now if it were contagious. "Drink," I urge her.

She swallows more vigorously, and I get more than three cups of water down her, though she will not eat. When she falls asleep again, the sweating having eased, I pray to Juno to look down on her and bring her back to health, promising to sacrifice at her altar if she will do so.

My prayers are not so easily granted. Fausta becomes feverish again, then cold, the chills shaking her whole body.

"He found me," she mutters, her face turning from one side to the other, seeking a cool side of the pillow to rest her cheek on.

"What?" I say, unsure if I have heard her correctly.

"Vulcan," she mutters.

I make a sign against evil spirits. "What about Vulcan?"

"He found me in the end," she says. "I escaped his wrath, but he found me, even in Rome he found me."

A chill runs through me. "It is a fever," I say. "The pestilence is not from Vulcan." I say it more firmly than I believe. I have heard the same from others, that Vulcan is still displeased, that not content with obliterating city after city, he has come here to Rome to exact a greater punishment.

"Where is it from then?" she asks, her breath too fast.

"The bad air," I try. "The marshlands have bad air and everyone knows they sit too close to Rome, the air drifts here and…"

But her eyes have closed, she turns her face away and I do not think she is listening to me anymore.

By the morning of the third day I begin to have some hope. Once again, sweat has streamed from her body, but after a few hours it stops, and she gulps water as though her life depended on it. She sleeps, and when she wakes, she manages to eat a little soup made of spring greens, which I spoon into her, mouthful by mouthful. She gives a small smile at the sight of Karbo and when Marcus visits in the afternoon, she even props herself up on one elbow to talk to him.

"Amphitheatre falling apart yet without me?" she croaks.

"Getting on better than ever," he says promptly. "Should have got rid of you years ago. You've been holding me back."

She manages a small laugh and then sinks back onto the bed. I am cheered by the exchange, but Marcus appears at nightfall on the same day, and gestures to me to come outside.

"The architect died last night."

I stare at him. "But he came to work. I know he came back too early but…"

"The fever came back and he couldn't breathe."

I can't think what to say. "What will we do?"

Marcus shakes his head. "We can manage. So long as one of us instructs the craftsmen, it can be done."

"In the time we have left?"

"The parts that matter."

WE ATTEND THE ARCHITECT'S FUNERAL, ashes from the pyre fluttering through the hot air. Marcus looks grim and I wonder whether the ashes remind him of Livia, of the day when the sky turned ashen above the amphitheatre, when the architect's immaculate white toga grew speckled all over. Outside the city, where the burials take place, I look around in horror at the number of burials under way, not just dozens but hundreds. The road we are on is as busy as one of Rome's main streets.

"How many people have died?" I ask.

Marcus shakes his head. "They say almost a thousand just yesterday and more every day," he says. "Let's go. This is no place to linger."

To my vast relief, Fausta seems to be recovering. I insist she should have sunlight and fresh air, so I wrap her up in my cloak and seat her on the balcony, two floors up from Maria. They don't talk to each other but there is some sort of companionship as the two of them watch the comings and goings of the courtyard. The baker's family get well again, but five families within our insula lose one or more family members.

The city feels strangely quiet, people keep to their homes if they can and everywhere there is the smell of burning incense, many people believing that the perfume may drive away the unseen pestilence. We must all get water from the public fountains but there is fear of coming too close to others, as well as the worry that perhaps the water itself is tainted. Candles burn constantly at all the street corner shrines, lit hurriedly in thanks for recovery or as desperate requests to avoid the illness.

Rumours are everywhere. Besides the water and the air, the older people blame the marshlands for carrying illness into the city, but they are waved off by other more frightening rumours.

"It's the ashes from Vesuvius, they are cursed with the spirits of those who died and now they have created a pestilence." Those who believe it wrap cloth round their faces, only their fearful eyes showing, hoping not to breathe in the spirits of the dead. They make sacrifices and offerings to Hades, asking that he collect up those who belong to him, asking that he prevent them from wandering the streets of Rome. "They were never properly buried or cremated," they say, and some even ask the priests to hold empty funerals for the dead of Pompeii, of Herculaneum, of Oplontis, and all the other towns and villages smothered under the unending grey ashes. They say that if there were funerals to guide the spirits of the dead they would not reside in the poisoned ashes; they would not seek out bodies and set them to burning them internally.

"It is Vulcan, trying to reach those who escaped his wrath and fled here." And those who believe it shun the refugees who escaped, will not speak with them or serve them and make gestures behind their backs and even to their faces to ward off evil spirits and curses.

Some say the refugees had a pestilence in their own region and now they have brought it here, that is why the pestilence descended not long after they came to Rome. And those who say it go one step further than shunning the refugees, they seek them out and let out their fear through anger, meting out violence, from spitting to beatings and worse.

The Jews whisper amongst themselves that this is their Almighty's revenge on Emperor Titus. He burnt their Holy Temple. Now he is being punished through the fire spewing from Vesuvius and the fever in his subjects who are burning up. When the whispers are heard by others their retribution is swift. "The Jews are to blame. They prayed for retribution on us for burning their holy places and now their vengeance has brought down a pestilence on us." And Jews are sought out and beaten or killed, in the dark nights when more and more bodies have been taken to the outskirts of the city and burned or buried, sometimes so many there is not even time to carve their names, and so they will be forgotten.

Some believe those who died deserved it. They say the fearful and the ill have brought it upon themselves, that they are being punished for something they have done. They claim that good people have nothing to fear, that the illness is a sign of impurity, or impiety, or improper respect for the gods. They make a show of their lack of fear, laughing at those who cover their faces and seeking out the refugees or the Jews to drink with, boasting of their own fearlessness, their certainty that they will not be touched. They celebrate the warmer days with picnics and sailing along the Tiber in barges with much wine-drinking and defiant merriment, while the more careful tut and suggest that meeting in large groups can only aid in spreading the pestilence.

And it does not matter that the fearless and the refugees sicken, and the Jews also sicken, nor that the ashes of Vesuvius have not been seen for many months now. It does not matter because everyone in the city has lost someone and everyone who is not ill is grieving and angry. When those who were already grieving and angry fall ill they cannot even summon the strength to fight the illness and so die even quicker.

I WAKE IN THE NIGHT, too hot. Summer is bringing warm nights. I shrug off the blanket that covers Marcus and me, leaving my half of it between us. But now I feel too cold. I pull the blanket back towards me and as I do so, a wave of heat comes towards me from Marcus' side. Despite sleeping side-by-side for all these months, we never touch while we sleep. Now, tentatively, I reach out a hand and touch his shoulder where it emerges from the blanket.

He is hot. So hot.

I get onto my knees, feel around me in the dark until I find the lamp, then strike the fire steel against the flint, the sparks falling to the floor more than once, my hands trembling. At last, the kindling catches fire and I use a taper to light the oil-soaked wick, which eventually flickers into life. Jupiter make me wrong, I pray. Let it be nothing, just the blanket too heavy for June. I pull away the blanket. Marcus mutters. I touch him again and there is no doubt. Fever. He has the fever.

Outside the hut is a full amphora of water, cooled by the night. I hurry outside, stub my toe against it, the pain shooting up my leg. I bite my lip to keep from crying out. I drag the amphora inside and look for something to use as a rag. There is nothing, I have left them in Fausta's room. I reach for my spare head wrap, dip it into the cold water and begin to wipe him with it. He lifts a hand to push me away.

"You're burning up," I say to him. "You have to let me cool you."

"Burning," he murmurs.

For the next few hours, until the dawn comes, I talk to him and continue to use the damp head wrap to cool him. He does not speak again. Sometimes he moans, turning from side to side, sometimes towards the coolness, sometimes seeking to escape it. The lamp flickers and goes out, but I do not refill it, only continue wiping him. When the first light comes through the window, I take a deep breath, the sunlight rescuing me from the lonely darkness. Now I can see Marcus better. His skin is flushed, his breathing shallow.

The door swings open and Julia stands in the doorway. Her eyes flicker across the pair of us, her face serious. "How long has he been like this?"

I shake my head. "Several hours."

"The chills?"

"Not yet."

"What can I bring you?"

I try to think. "More water, more rags. The teas. They didn't work for Fausta but they might help him. Send Karbo for Fabia."

Julia comes and goes all morning, bringing everything I ask for. When Fabia arrives, she shakes her head and prescribes everything we have already tried. I follow her outside the hut as she leaves.

"What else can I do?"

"Nothing," she says. "Keep him cool when he is hot, keep him warm when he is cold. Pray for the sweats, they may herald the end of this."

I want to ask her to stay with me, I am afraid of her leaving, but I know that she must see many others and that there is nothing that will magically cure this illness.

I make my way down the stairs to Fausta. She is pale, but has managed to get up by herself and take up a position on the balcony. Karbo has brought her food and water.

"You look better," I say.

"I feel dreadful."

"At least you are up. I promised a sacrifice to Juno for you if you recovered, I will do it as soon as Marcus can be left alone."

She gives a snorting laugh. "You asked Juno to heal a prostitute? Isn't her job to look after respectable Roman matrons and their households?"

"She can watch over anyone she cares to," I say. "I need to get back to Marcus. Will you be all right?"

"You can't kill a she-wolf that easily," she says.

I smile at her fierceness and turn away.

"Althea."

I look back at her.

"Take good care of him. You know what men are like, all

219

bravado, then when they get sick, they turn into babies who need a nursemaid."

"I'll tell him you said so," I say.

"You do that. Tell him he's a lazy bastard that needs to get out of bed and do some work or find himself face-to-face with a lion in the arena. One month left, tell him, pestilence or no pestilence."

I'M RELIEVED AT FAUSTA'S CONTINUING recovery. If she can recover, so can Marcus. I make my way back to the hut and find him shaking with the chills. I cover him in blankets, in both our cloaks and still he shakes. There's nothing else to cover him with, so I lie next to him, pressing my body against his to give him my own heat. Eventually, I fall asleep, exhausted from a night spent awake. I wake up when he pushes me away. The fever is back.

"Livia," he mutters.

I pull away the blanket, our cloaks, reach for the water and the rags. "Drink," I say, filling up a cup and holding it to his lips.

His eyes suddenly open. "I'm burning up," he says.

"I know," I say. "Drink the water, it will make you feel better."

"Was it like this?" he says.

"What?"

"Was it like this?" he asks again.

I don't know what he's talking about. Perhaps he is delirious. "I don't understand," I say, wiping the damp rag across his face, dipping it in the cold water again and wringing it out. "Was what like this?"

His eyes are open but he's not looking at me, he is looking at something else, something not in the room. "Vesuvius," he says, and a chill runs through me. "Was it like this, Livia? Did you burn up inside? Did you die like this, is this how it felt before you died, before they all died?"

I fumble, wiping the rag across his dry lips as though to stop the words coming out.

"My boy," he says.

"Don't talk." I wipe his lips again. He's frightening me, he is making me think of everybody who died in Pompeii and all around, it is like hearing a spirit speak. "Don't talk," I say again. "Try to rest," I add, hopelessly.

"They burned up," he says. "All of them. Livia, my boy, my baby boy Amantius. This is what it felt like for them, isn't it? A heat ripping through them that got hotter and hotter – until they died."

"I don't know," I say, my voice cracking. I take a deep breath, trying to stay calm. He is delirious, only delirious. He doesn't know what he's saying. But he does, of course, I know he does. This burning fever is exactly what it must have been like, but worse. I think again of the woman who described it, even from a distance, as opening an oven, the heat rushing across your skin and nowhere to jump back to, no way to escape it.

"It would be the right way to die," he murmurs.

"What?" I ask.

"I could join them," he says. His eyes close. "I would know how they died, I could join them."

I shake him, my hands reaching out and grabbing him by the shoulders before I can think what I am doing. "You're not to join them!" I say, my voice too loud for the tiny room. "Stay here! You have to stay here!"

"How is he doing?"

It's Julia. I snatch my hands away from him, my breathing too fast. Marcus has kept his eyes shut, giving no response to either my words or actions. I stand up, make my way outside, closing the door behind me. I'm glad to leave him, his words are frightening me. I tell Julia what he said.

Her usually serene countenance creases in a grimace. "He needs to fight," she says. "To be ill when you are grieving for your wife and child..." She pauses. "He must not long to join them, or the fever will take him for sure."

"What am I supposed to do? How can I keep him here?"

"Give him something to live for," she says.

"He has nothing to live for!" Tears start falling and I wipe them away too hard. "Everyone he loves has died and he is doing a job he hates."

"He may hate his job, but he is good at it. And there is still the farm."

"The farm he can't afford to buy, now he's lost all his savings?" I say. "The farm he was supposed to make a home of with his wife and child?" I shake my head. "I have nothing I can say to him. Nothing!"

Julia takes me by the shoulders, looks into my face. "If there's one thing Marcus is," she says, her voice certain and calm, "it's loyal to those to whom he has made a commitment. You have to remind him of those people. Fausta, you, Karbo."

"What if we are not enough?"

"You have to make it be enough," she says.

"They say two thousand have died in one day. How is that possible?" I think of the amphitheatre, slowly filling with the bodies of the dead.

Julia shakes her head. She spends her days going from room to room, offering cold water and cold wet cloths on the faces and bodies of those who are ill, offering her coolness and calmness to those who are afraid. "It must abate soon," she says. She looks out over the city, hands on the wall, face turned towards the south east and the temple where she once served, though she cannot see it from here.

"Have you ever seen a time like this?"

"No," she says.

"What if everyone dies?"

"They won't."

"How do you know?" I ask, begging her, as though she were a speaker of oracles, a seer, as though she might look into the future and see Rome and her citizens healthy and well again.

She turns back to me. "We should visit the island."

I follow her along Sand Street and down to the river, over the bridge that takes us to the boat-shaped island in the middle of the Tiber river, home to the temple of Aesculapius. I've never had to pray at his shrine before, but now it is swarming with people come to ask the god of healing and medicine to help their loved ones. The snakes that usually live here, symbols of his powers, have slithered away to quieter parts of the site. We catch sight of one in the grasses near the entrance and another hiding beneath an altar. People are queuing to fill cups with the healing waters of the temple and some carry children in their arms so that they can be licked by the dogs of the temple.

Julia and I carry back two small pots of sacred water, giving the sick inhabitants of our insula a few drops each, in the hopes that it will help them.

"How is Marcus?" Maria asks as I pass.

I shrug. "He sleeps and I think he might wake up better but then he talks and sweats and he is back in the fever."

"What does he say?"

I don't answer.

"Livia?"

I nod. "I think he actually wants to feel the fever," I say miserably. "I think he feels closer to her and Amantius. He believes he knows what they suffered, he wants to feel it too."

"None of us know what they suffered," says Maria. "None of us can even imagine such a death."

I have made a mistake. For a moment when Maria spoke, I allowed myself to imagine Myrtis, the heat and the ashes choking her. Tears roll down my face. I try not to think of her, only of the moments when she scolded me or fed me, teasing me by calling me by the dog's name, saying neither of us knew the meaning of hard work. I think only of things she did that made me laugh. Nothing more. I wipe my face with a corner of my tunic and Maria catches my movement.

"You can only do what you can," she says. "Take the water to him, it will help."

THE DAY WINDS WEARILY ON. Marcus does not speak again, but I do. I talk about Fausta, passing on her insulting comments and inventing more, trying to recreate their ribald banter. I talk about Karbo, how well he has come on, how his face has filled out from one too many pancakes, how eager he is to learn from all of us, how he follows Marcus around like a lost puppy.

"If you die," I say, "I'll have to work for some dreadful rich man, who will forever be pinching my bum and worse. I'll have to live in some fancy villa and I certainly won't see any of the team again, a scribe working for a patrician family can't be hanging out with the likes of whores and gladiators, nor street waifs and strays. Think how lonely I will be." I say all of it only to provoke him, but there is a truth in what I'm saying. I have to pause to wipe away tears and collect myself. "See what you're doing to me?" I add. "You should be ashamed of yourself, making a woman cry over you. How am I supposed to work hard and think quickly with you lying around in bed like some softie? I thought army men were tougher than that."

He doesn't answer. I leave the room only briefly, to fetch more water and accept some soup from Julia. While I'm out, I look in on Fausta but she's already asleep, which is good, she needs the rest. I tell Karbo to stay with Maria tonight. I do not want Fausta disturbed.

I WAKE EARLY. THE SUN has already risen, for the mornings are at their lightest now that we are in June. Twice I sit up, then lie back down, uncertain. The third time I look down at Marcus, his breathing is still laboured. I reach out, touch his forehead, the skin still hot to the touch. I stand up, leave my shoes where they are, my headwrap on the bed mat, my hair uncombed. I feel inside my satchel, pull out a couple of coins, then run down the wooden stairs.

Vesta's Temple is already surrounded by women, all of them barefoot with dishevelled hair. Some hold fruit or cloth, bread or cakes. A few richer women hold jewellery in their hands. Their elaborate hairstyles abandoned, they can only be identified by the quality of their dresses, though it looks as though most have dressed in their simpler clothes, linen and wool rather than their accustomed silks and gauzes.

I hang back in the crowd, heart beating too fast. I am not sure if what I am doing is wrong. Vestalia is the one day when the shrine is opened to view and mothers may approach to beg favours of Vesta. I am not a mother. I hope no-one will ask any questions. In my hands I hold flowers, bought in the market as I made my way here, my feet tender on the dirty streets. But the crowd begins to move forward and I am in the queue now, there is no going back.

The six Vestal Virgins stand before Vesta's own fire, each one upright in her bearing, even their youngest recruit, a little girl barely eight years old, only two years served out of her thirty years of duty. The women in the crowd bow their heads, lay down their little offerings, whisper something, then move away, their faces lightened by the chance to beg the goddess herself for help.

Only five women in front of me, then three, then one, and suddenly the flowers have left my hands as I whisper the words I have prepared.

"Goddess Vesta, I come here not as myself but as a woman now gone from us, her name was Livia, mother to Amantius, wife to Marcus Aquillius Scaurus. He lies sick, Lady Vesta, he burns with fever and he will not fight it because he wishes only to join his wife and son. But I made a promise to Livia, Lady Vesta. I said I would look after her husband and now I ask for your help in doing so, for I can no longer do it alone. I bring you flowers, for Livia wore flowers in her hair. I beg for your help, Lady Vesta. Bring Marcus out of the darkness that surrounds him."

Behind me another woman is waiting, my time is over. I stumble away from the temple, narrowly avoiding stepping in mule droppings and almost end up being trampled by a donkey cart. I stop to gather myself, still uncertain whether I have done the right thing. Lady Vesta knows all, will she be angry that I came to her when I am not a mother? Is it wrong to come on behalf of another woman? Is it bad luck to come in the guise of a dead woman? I am not sure. I look down the Forum, seeing the amphitheatre standing at the end of it, vast and gleaming in the early light. I made a promise, I think, and I am not sure whether I mean the promise to Livia to protect her husband or to Marcus to help him see through the inauguration of this vast building, this all-consuming monument. Either way, I have work to do. On the way back I collect breakfast rolls and wine, as well as a treat of fresh plums from one of the only market stalls that still has fresh fruit from the countryside. The owner stands well back from me, keeping a cloth wrapped around his face.

"Can't be too careful," he says apologetically, gesturing to the covering, but I smile, grateful for the promise of fresh fruit. It will cheer Fausta and Karbo. And perhaps I can persuade Marcus to drink more water if I lace it with wine, or I could boil some of the plums to make him a juice. Perhaps Adah will even accept some. She has barricaded herself away during the pestilence, continually burning incense. Once or twice, I've worried, thinking her hut is on fire because there's so much smoke coming out of the window, but she seems well enough when I see her although she won't have anyone come near her. She allows the bakery to bring her loaves and she must collect water before dawn when there's no-one about, for I never catch her at it. I will lay some plums by her doorway; perhaps she will eat them when they have been smoked for long enough in her clouds of perfumed incense. The fresh air and sunshine, the short walk and the plums, all make me smile. There is hope yet. Perhaps Lady Vesta will intercede for Marcus and all will be well.

I HEAR KARBO WAILING BEFORE I even enter the courtyard and I run, scattering plums from my basket. Karbo. Karbo, standing on the balcony, tears pouring down his face, a wordless wail coming from his open mouth. One door after another opens, there are heads, shouts, half-dressed men and women asking questions and I see only one thing behind Karbo. Fausta's open door, darkness within.

Julia takes over, caring for Marcus while I wash Fausta's body, still warm, one hand lifted up over her face in the convulsions that must have come in the night, the fever returning when she was all alone. I strip away her clothes, soaked in sweat, not even telling Karbo to stay away. He crouches in a corner, clutching her toga to him, his face pressed into it, the white cloth collecting his tears. Occasionally I hear him sob and I turn to touch him, to stroke his head and murmur words, but most of my actions are done in a daze.

Maria sends for an undertaker and, when they arrive, I let them carry Fausta away, one last glimpse of her black curls before she will be burnt up, before Vulcan claims her for his own. When they are gone, I want to run after them, to tell them to bring her back. I did not kiss her. I forgot to say anything to her. I was so tired and confused and shocked that I only washed her and dressed her in my own clothes and let Karbo touch her face.

He is asleep now, exhausted in his grief. I sit on her bed and take up a little corner of her toga, which he has wrapped himself in. I put it to my face as he did and smell the smell of her, a warm earthy aroma of sweat and herbs from where she used to trail her hands down over the leaves of Julia's many pots of herbs every morning, holding her fingers to her face to inhale their scents, before brushing her hands over her toga. I think of her raucous laugh and her coarse banter with Marcus, her confidence each morning, striding out in the toga that marked her out as a prostitute, her refusal to hide what she was. I think that I saw her cry only once, when everyone she knew and loved in the world except Marcus had died. She rose from the ashes to protect not just herself but Marcus and me. Still racked with fever, he does not even know that his best friend has died.

I hold her toga to my face and weep.

THE MINT

I T'S BEEN TWO WEEKS SINCE Fausta died. A lifetime ago and yesterday.

"Take your place."

I hover, one hand on the balustrade. "Shouldn't one of us be below the arena?"

"Jupiter and Juno! Sit *down*. The whole point is to see if it can run smoothly without us interfering all the time. It has to run on minimal signals. Sit."

I sit in the exquisitely carved chair next to Marcus, who is currently lounging on Emperor Titus' throne. The imperial box is otherwise empty. The arena below is also empty. Only Marcus and I know that eyes are watching our every moment from the metal grilles set into the walls surrounding the arena floor.

Marcus raises a hand and the vast Gate of Triumph slowly opens. A single woman walks solemnly across the arena, coming to a halt at its centre. She stands still for a moment, then turns her head up to us.

"Like that?" she calls up.

Marcus stands and leans over the side of the box. "Perfect, Julia, thank you."

"Again?"

"No, it was fine."

She nods and walks away. A hidden door in the arena wall opens and she disappears into the darkness.

"You're sure it won't seem too empty? Shouldn't there be a big procession or something?"

"There will be," says Marcus. "But first there must be a sacred moment."

"And they'll agree to it?"

"Why wouldn't they? The Vestal Virgins, at the very centre of the inauguration? It's perfect."

WE LEAVE THE IMPERIAL BOX and make our way through the corridors. By the closest exit a sullen looking man is standing waiting to speak to Marcus.

"These five hundred doves you want dyed?"

"What about them?"

"What colours do you want?"

"As many colours as you can manage. Not blue though."

"We've already done a few blue ones as a test."

"Well, don't do any more."

"What's wrong with blue?"

Marcus sighs and points out of an arch at the sky. "You won't see them if they're blue, will you?"

"You could just keep them white."

Marcus shakes his head.

"Why?"

"Boring. Everyone's seen white doves."

The man walks off, shaking his head.

"Lazy," comments Marcus. "Right. So that's the birds taken care of. These giraffes, how tame are they? Can someone walk them to the Gate of Triumph on a leash? Because the height they are, I can't keep them under the arena. Also, I want them to stay down the far end of the arena. I'd rather they didn't die in the beast hunting scene, they're ridiculously expensive and they're always dying on sea voyages. So let's try and use them several times, make the most of them, shall we, now we've got three all the way here and they're still standing."

I nod, make a note, then slump back in the chair.

"Tired?"

I nod.

"Go home and sleep," says Marcus. "I can manage."

"You're as white as a freshly-washed toga," I tell him. "It's you that needs to rest longer, you shouldn't be back at work yet."

"With the days running out? I had to come back."

I nod. None of us had a choice, all of us have come back to work too soon, pale and quiet, counting the hours each day till we can stop work, lying in the baths like stranded seals, before shuffling home and barely managing to eat before we fall asleep. Karbo's skin looks grey, he crouches in the shadows where he used to play in the sun and says nothing unless he's asked a question. Mostly he follows Marcus or me about and does what he's told. My heart hurts for him, but I'm so tired I can barely get through the days as it is, I cannot care for him properly. I make sure he's fed, and I have him sleep in the rooftop hut with Marcus and me, leaving Fausta's room empty. Julia could rent it out, of course, but there's a lot of empty rooms in Rome just now. The pestilence has faded away leaving ten thousand dead, with no need for rooms. Sometimes Marcus wakes late, or I see sweat on his brow and I panic, thinking the fever has come back, that it has not released him from its grip after all, but he remains well, only weakened by the illness and saddened by another loss. We waited until he was definitely on the mend before telling him and his grief for Fausta was so raw I feared a relapse. He still does not mention her name much. I see him trip over it several times a day when we are at work, see him about to turn to her and crack some joke that will make her laugh. And then there's the pain when he remembers she is not sitting above us where the plebs will sit, watching over everything. She is gone.

THE TRUMPETS HAVE BEEN PRACTISING for more than an hour by now, the same fanfare over and over again, to herald the arrival of the Emperor. I'm beginning to get a headache.

"Can they not practise something else?" I snap at Marcus after I've written the same word three times. The list of things that must be done is unending and we have only a week left until the inauguration. I'm beginning to panic that it will not all get done in time. Even Marcus, usually so unflappable at work, is snapping at people and has developed a deep worry line between his eyebrows.

He shrugs. "If you like." He leans over the balustrade, twisting so he is looking up at the musicians, who are sitting nearby. "Hey! HEY! Switch to the hunting scene. Practise that for a bit."

I deeply regret my request after it turns out that this involves contrasting drumming with flutes pitched incredibly high, almost a screaming wail. It's a sound designed to instil a mixture of suspense and fear and it is doing nothing for my head, which is pounding. As the date of the inauguration creeps closer, more and more people want something from either Marcus or me. Stallholders of food, wine, merchandise and toys want to know exactly where they can pitch their stands and then argue about the spots we give them. The bookies are always slipping in to ask Marcus 'just a few questions' hoping to find out what animals will be used on the first day, the first week, the first month, which gladiators will be showing so they can check up on their track records. Marcus tends to give them short thrift. We have recruited cleaners, ushers, toilet attendants, armoured guards who will surround the arena when we use wild beasts, ready to catch, incapacitate or kill any animal that presents a danger to the spectators. We've made arrangements with undertakers who will attend all the Games, ready to remove bodies at speed. The dead gladiators will be taken back to their barracks, for some have families, criminals will be dumped in the Tiber. We will have the carcasses of animals to dispose of too, some of which may be sold for meat, some we may use ourselves to feed the meat-eaters in their pens, although they can't be overfed, or they won't fight or kill on demand. My days seem full of death and my spirit feels so heavy, it's hard to think straight.

KARBO APPEARS AT MY SIDE. "There's a Praetorian Guard wanting to speak with you."

"Me?"

"He wants you and Marcus to go with him somewhere."

I feel a flutter of panic. Have we done something wrong? Perhaps they have found out Marcus left Rome against the strict conditions of his contract, though surely, we would be able to argue he did so for his wife and child, so they might show mercy? Or perhaps they found out about Marcus' night-time drunken brawling and have decided he should be sacked? I make my way out to one of the corridors and see a man waiting for me, standing at attention.

He towers over me. "Althea Aquillius?"

"Can I help you?" I ask, trying to keep my voice light.

"Emperor Titus wishes you and Marcus Aquillius Scaurus to attend him at the mint."

"Mint?" In my confusion I think of the pots of mint in Julia's courtyard, the herb's bright strong smell in the perfumed waters of private baths.

"He's having a new coin struck. He wants you there to see it. It's to be thrown into the crowd on the inauguration day."

I gather my thoughts. "Of course, at once, a moment while I find Marcus." I pull out my centurion's whistle, dart back through the arch into the arena and blow it as hard as I can. There's a pause and then one of the trapdoors is thrown open and Marcus emerges.

"What is it?" he calls up.

"We're wanted by the Emperor," I call back. I walk down a few tiers so I can speak to him without the guard hearing me. "Titus wants us to attend the production of a coin showing the amphitheatre."

Marcus rolls his eyes. "We don't have time for cack like that, we're up to our eyes in this."

"We don't have a choice," I point out.

Marcus utters some choice words under his breath, mostly referring to the various genitalia of the gods and where Titus can go about putting them. Fausta would have sworn so the whole amphitheatre could hear. Tears spring instantly to my eyes. Every time she comes into my mind, I cry, and it upsets Marcus and Karbo, so I try not to think about her. Sometimes at night I dream of her and wake weeping, hold a blanket to my face and try to sob quietly before I fall back asleep and wake in the morning with aching eyes and swollen eyelids.

"So we cut small pieces of the bars of metal and then each is hammered into shape, creating 'flans', blank coins. They're placed into the oven to soften them up, then put into two-sided dies. When the men use a hammer on the dies, they imprint onto the coins, you see?"

Marcus is looking bored. I try to make a show of being interested. "How many do you produce a day?"

"A good team can produce twenty thousand strikes a day."

"Strikes?"

"Coins."

"All of them are made like that?"

"Yes, we make all the denominations."

Marcus looks around at the large numbers of people working. "No stealing?"

The man laughs. "Not a chance. There's a supervisor on every team watching the men work and all the men are strip-searched when they go home. If you're found hiding coins… let's just say you'll be finding yourself *in* the arena, not just making pretty pictures of it."

One of the men hands over a denarius to Marcus, who looks it over and then passes it to me. On one side, Titus' head, on the other a Jewish captive kneels below a trophy of arms. I think of Adah, what she would do were such a coin to come into her hands. Marcus passes me another coin, this time a sestertius. A seated Titus on one side, on the other, the Flavian Amphitheatre, each tiny arch perfectly portrayed. Inside, it clearly shows the steps between tiers of seating and includes tiny raised dots for the spectators. It is a work of art, but the endless metallic hammering is making me tired and fearful. These hundreds of coins being created show the amphitheatre in all its glory, they promise something that has not yet happened. It is not the building that will be glorified, it is what goes on inside it and that is down to Marcus and me. The pressure on us mounts through the constant blows ringing in my ears, the endless shining depictions being created. I hold one of the coins, trying to steady my breathing. I think of Pompeii and all its inhabitants, of the fever that took not just Fausta but thousands of lives, so much death and destruction in just one year and yet we are creating a place that glorifies and amplifies death and destruction.

I stagger. Marcus grabs my elbow. "What is wrong?"

"I feel sick," I whisper.

He looks appalled. "The fever?" He touches my forehead, then shakes his head, I am not hot. "Shall I take you home?"

"No," I say. "He will notice your absence. He won't notice me leaving."

He hesitates, glances towards where Titus is still beaming at the hammering men, turning one of the coins over in his hands, then nods.

The noise follows me almost to the gates, where it finally dims. I vomit in a nearby bush, the hot bile in my mouth choking my nose and throat, coughing and spitting to rid myself of the taste. When it is done, I squat down for a few moments, feeling weak. I touch my forehead again, but it feels cool. After a while I get to my feet and begin the walk home, slow and occasionally wavering.

When I reach our insula my head still aches, but I feel the urge to stop by Balbus' toy workshop on the ground floor before I climb the stairs to sleep. He is still there, although the shutters are half-closed. His wife Floriana is sweeping the floor and re-winding scraps of yarn while Balbus is sharpening some of his whittling knives, ready for the next day's work. I tell them what I want and they both nod solemnly.

"I know it is not your usual line of work," I say, "but I would like it done by someone who knows Marcus. The little figures…"

236

I swallow. "He was not yet able to run," I say at last. "And her hair was very light, like the shells of hazelnuts."

They nod, silent in the face of the tears that have filled up my eyes. I am too tired to be making this commission, I should be sleeping. "I will leave it with you," I say.

It takes me a long time to make my way up all the stairs to the rooftop, each step slow and tentative. When I reach the hut, I lie down on the sleeping mat and fall asleep almost at once. There is a moment when I think I hear Adah muttering, "Good child," and feel the blanket being tucked around me, but perhaps I am only dreaming.

FIRE

THE AREA BELOW THE ARENA is as dark as ever, the flaming torches along the outer walls only making it seem gloomier. The animals have been arriving all day yesterday and this morning, the pens are full to bursting. Some animals can be kept together for they find comfort in one another's company, but many must be kept apart in case they fight. Six lions, we have been assured, are all from one pride, five females and one male, but they've been kept near-starving. They could well turn on one another, so each must be kept in a different pen and none of them can be next to another animal, there must be spaces between each cage.

I fumble through the leather scroll holder at my feet, trying to find the right one to consult. "I have to personally check on over one thousand animals today. Karbo, you can accompany me. I'm going to have to teach you to read and write so you can take on this sort of task."

"I can read the date. The inauguration is in only two days after today."

"Don't remind me," I beg. "How can it be July already?"

"Is that all of the animals?"

I shake my head, find the right scroll. "Nothing like it, but we can't even hold all of them. We've just got most of the ones for the inauguration."

"But we've got lots of pens down here."

"For ordinary days, yes, especially in a regular schedule, perhaps one or even two hundred Games a year. Not for one hundred consecutive days. Nothing like enough. They're being stored down at the docks in a warehouse we've borrowed."

"Althea! Will you check the scenery?"

"Yes!" I call back to Marcus. "Last rehearsals tomorrow."

He lifts a hand in acknowledgment and disappears through one of the trapdoors.

"Come on, let's get this over with," I say. We make our way over to the towering man currently engaged in directing criminals into cages of their own.

"Strabo," I greet him.

"Althea."

"Have all the criminals arrived?"

"Most of them. There's a few women in this batch. They promised us one more woman and ten more men tomorrow, that'll take us up to the right number."

I swallow. There's a scroll detailing everything that will happen during the inauguration and I've had to make several copies so that different people can refer to it. The fate reserved for the female criminals is stomach churning. "Feed them properly, will you? They're in here for three days, don't starve them as well."

"Just as you say."

I pull out the scroll listing the animals and begin walking past each pen, counting and then annotating the list. "Antelope, seventy-five. Zebras, sixteen. Deer, fifty-nine."

I'M ABOUT TO FINISH FOR the day, the site is almost empty. I'm sitting in the stands where the senators will sit, sorting through a bundle of scrolls, trying to ensure everything has been correctly labelled and sorted into the right leather cases so that we know where to find everything. I unfurl one scroll, read off the details of which items of scenery need to be brought out of storage and into the under-arena tomorrow. They'll take up a lot of space, but we need to test that they all work smoothly, so we'll just have to put up with the inconvenience.

But the scroll is speckled with something, some sort of dust or… I brush it away, then stop.

Ash.

There is ash, floating through the air.

I look up but I cannot see the thick black clouds that came rolling in from the south when Vesuvius erupted. But there are still floating bits of ash, not as heavy as that cursed day but still…

I pack away the scrolls, dropping more than one, hands grown suddenly clumsy. Then I start climbing the steps between tiers of seats, legs aching, panting. Higher and higher till I reach the topmost corridor and outer arches, peer out of them. I think I see a faint grey cloud to the north west, but I'm not sure.

My legs ache as I clamber down the steep steps to the ground floor. But as soon as I get out of the building, I can see something is wrong. The Forum is not full of the usual crowds strolling about. Instead it is half empty and the remaining people are hurrying. I grab a passer-by.

"What's happening?"

"Fire in the Ninth," says the man, hurrying away.

I run.

The courtyard is full. Julia is standing on the steps, her hands raised for quiet.

"The fire has spread rapidly since it started last night," she says, "It's all around the Pantheon and the Baths of Agrippa and it's spreading both south and west. The Vigiles from our own region have been there since the early hours, others have been coming from every region all morning."

"At least our Vigiles were close at hand," Maria says. The Vigiles' station house in our region is just opposite the Julia Saepta.

"Yes, and there's a pool of water right near the Baths of Agrippa, they're trying to keep filling that so that the siphon pumps on the fire wagons can keep going and supply the main hoses. But they need a lot more people. Men should go and help, there is already a double chain from the river with buckets, but they need more. Take buckets and any other receptacle from each household. We need to contain the fire as soon as possible, or we will be in danger of a Great Fire happening again. Women, gather your children and valuables in case we need to vacate the building, but meanwhile we are all safest staying out of the way unless we can help."

The crowd quickly disperses, men rushing out of our gate carrying buckets and amphorae, whatever they can find. The women bustle about the balconies, in and out of doors.

"I brought your belongings down to my rooms," says Julia.

"Thank you," I say. "Where's Marcus?"

"Already gone to help," she says. "He led the first group of men."

"How bad is it?" I ask.

"Bad," she says, her voice low. "It's gone beyond some of the usual ways of fighting it, the soaked quilts and vinegar are already useless. They're pulling down buildings, trying to form a firebreak. They've been calling for cushions and mattresses to break the fall of anyone trapped in upper stories of the buildings that are ablaze. The streets are so narrow…"

I nod. The Ninth was spared the worst of the Great Fire sixteen years ago, which was to its benefit then, but after the fire was over, two-thirds of Rome had to be rebuilt, and that meant wider streets, stronger buildings and less wood. The Ninth is still a jumble of narrow streets and old buildings, many made of wood rather than brick and so more vulnerable to fire. Every building contains many lamps filled with oil, so any building that catches fire will find multiple sources of vicious fuel waiting to contribute to the blaze. The top tiers of most buildings are wooden, as is almost all the interior furniture. Many buildings already have a fire burning inside: popinas, temples, glassblowers, private homes, baths, bakeries, all of them with ample stores of dry wood, perfect for burning.

"Will this insula be safe?" I ask.

Julia grimaces. "If the fire is put out soon, yes. If not, we lie directly in its path to the south."

I hear shouts outside and run to the courtyard gate, just in time to see two fire wagons rush past, the horses whipped to a fast gallop. Behind it run a group of Vigiles, two of whom stop to commandeer a cart from a trader who happens to be passing; they ignore his refusal and turn the mules' heads down Virgin's Street and onwards.

"I can go and join the men," I say. "I can pass buckets."

She nods. "Be careful. Vulcan protect you."

I don't say that I don't much trust Vulcan after all that happened in Pompeii. I hurry out, only stopping to fully tie up my hair and cover it with a wrap, afraid that loose hair might be too tempting for stray sparks.

I RUN DOWN TOWARDS THE river and join the human chain, passing rope-and-pitch buckets hand to hand. The daylight hours pass in a haze of smoke and water. We can smell smoke and slowly the cloud of it begins to drift our way, a demoralising sight, telling us the fire is still raging. As we pass the full buckets, they slop water onto us, so that we soon have wet legs and feet which is almost welcome, given the heat of the day. The first days of July are not a time to be standing in the direct sun. With the return of the empty buckets comes news back down the line, passed mouth to mouth, some good news, mostly bad.

"Nero's Baths are saved, they used the aqueduct to protect it."

"They've used ballista to knock down twelve insulae and a bakery."

"The Horologium is saved."

But the news becomes more grim, even as water from the Tiber continues to head north, bucket by bucket and now the sun is sinking, making the Vigiles' work harder as they struggle to see what they are doing, blinded by the raging flames in one direction, by darkness in any other. We keep sending the buckets, arms aching, drained more by the news coming back than the physical effort.

"The Julia Saepta is on fire."

"The Diribitorium too."

"The Baths of Agrippa are burning."

And on and on through the night, the clouds of smoke only growing stronger, so that we cough and choke even as we pass buckets to unseen hands. People change places, new hands take the place of old. As dawn breaks I stagger back to Virgin's Street, unable to keep going without sleep. The courtyard is full of people sleeping on the ground, curled into corners. The bakery and all the shops are closed for the first time I can remember. Only Cassia is still cooking, feeding anyone who needs it, passing out bowl after bowl of greens and barley. I take a bowl, squat down to eat, then drag myself up the stairs. Looking out to the north makes me afraid, I can smell the smoke ever more strongly, the ashes continue to blow through the air. I can hear the distant crackling of the fire even from here. I want to help more, but I can barely stand. I stagger into the rooftop hut and lie down without taking off my wet shoes.

WHEN I WAKE THE SMOKE is stronger, I am already coughing.

I head back to the buckets again, not knowing how else to help. Past the courtyard of huddled women and children, the women trying to feed soot-faced men and find them a place to sleep. Maria has taken over the popina, Cassia presumably needed to sleep. She passes me a flatbread and a cup of wine and I try to speak through a mouthful.

"Have you seen Marcus? Is Karbo safe?"

"Karbo is asleep. I gave him strict orders not to leave the courtyard when he wakes, he's to help us feed people, not go running off to be a hero. He brought a message from Strabo last night, all is well at the amphitheatre, he will take care of the animals and the criminals."

"The rehearsals," I gasp. "We were supposed to hold the final rehearsals... what day is it?"

"The inauguration is tomorrow. If it happens."

"If? We've spent months..."

"If the fire comes further south it could reach the top of the Forum," says Maria. "And the amphitheatre's at the other end of it."

I shake my head. "The gods preserve us. And Marcus?"

"Marcus was at the Pantheon last I heard, but it wasn't looking good, the buildings are all too close together round there, all the craftsmen and traders have tiny little shops made of this and that, they're going up like tinder."

"I don't know what to do," I say miserably.

"Get back in the chain. It may not feel like it's helping, but it has to be. They need constant water."

I go back to the chain and the handles of the buckets rub against my already sore hands. My damp shoes grow wet as the sun's rays beat down on us. A couple of people in the line faint by mid-afternoon and a third and then fourth chain develop, although the receptacles grow less and less suitable, people using anything they have, even absurd things like water bottles. As twilight falls the news begins to frighten all of us.

"The racing stables are being evacuated, the horses are going wild, trying to stampede."

"The Theatre of Pompey's stage is burnt out."

"The fire's spreading east, towards the Auguraculum."

Nobody says anything, but if it passes that point, it will not be far from the Forum itself.

And then the news I've been dreading. "It's headed south, towards the Circus Flaminius."

Virgin's Street sits on the edge of the Circus. I run.

"Where is Marcus? Where is he?"

"I don't know. Celer went to the stables. He said the horses were all panicking, and they needed every man they could lay their hands on to lead the horses away one by one or they would have fled. I saw him just now with one of the horses. Maybe Marcus was helping him?"

I run outside the courtyard but there is no sign of Marcus in the crowd. I can see six different racing horses, all of them nervous, one rearing up which prompts screams from the women and children. The men holding the horses are struggling to calm them. I make sure to keep my distance and head through the streets to the main area of the fire. It feels like running towards Vesuvius, the streets getting progressively more blackened and ruined. Families wander the streets, confused and frightened, clutching their valuables.

THE PANTHEON IS A BLACKENED hulk. My hand shapes into the gesture against evil spirts almost without my knowing. To see a temple of the gods reduced to a smoking black heap is frightening. Who knows whether their wrath at being thus disgraced might fall on onlookers? I lower my eyes just in case. I think of Adah, her rage and bitterness at the Temple of her people in Jerusalem being burnt. Perhaps she is right. Perhaps her god has decided to punish Titus, and in so doing, punish Rome. I try and shake off the shiver that runs through me at the thought. Marcus. I must find Marcus.

In the half-light the ruins of the Baths of Agrippa look as though they are still smoking. I look around me, uncertain of whether I should call for help, for more water.

"Steam," says Marcus. He's sitting on the side of the road, face smeared in soot, tunic ripped at one corner and filthy. His hands are shaking and I wonder whether this blackened landscape reminds him of our hours in Pompeii, of the fruitless lonely search for his dead family.

"You're alive," I say.

"Barely," he says. "I think if I try to walk, I will fall asleep on my feet."

"We need you back at Julia's," I say. "The fire's spreading that way."

He's on his feet at once, though he staggers. We hurry back through the streets together and now I can feel heat coming through the alleyways, somewhere to the left of us, but coming closer, the shouts growing louder.

"Run," says Marcus and we run, reaching Virgin's Street just as the screams begin, the courtyard gate impassable as people run out, pushing into us as we try to force our way in. Finally, we enter, and Marcus pushes me aside. "Watch out!"

A burning section of the wooden rooftop railing crashes at my feet and I step back, clasping my tunic in case of sparks. Looking up, I see to my horror that our rooftop hut is already aflame, as is the topmost balcony, just below the roof.

"The building next door went up like a torch, it's all wood," says Julia, appearing at my side. "The fire leapt the street and the whole of the upper storey of this insula is wood. Get out Althea, now!"

I turn to follow her and then realise Marcus is not next to me. "Where is Marcus?"

"Outside?"

"He was here a moment ago!"

Julia's face is very pale. "There."

Marcus has reached the rooftop through the interior stairs and is pushing at the rooftop hut with all his strength. "What is he doing?"

"Trying to flatten it so the fire won't spread as fast."

I start running up the wooden stairs, every step shaking, unable to see above me because of the walkways.

"Althea! Don't! It's not safe!"

I hear crunching above me and come up the last few stairs to see the rooftop hut collapsing under Marcus' efforts. It's burning, but now that it's collapsed, the flames slow and a cloud of smoke emerges.

"And the other one!" he shouts, seeing me.

I turn and see Adah's hut, a flickering already beginning in one corner as more chunks of the burning wooden railing give way around the edge of the rooftop nearest to it. I run and open the door, to see Adah huddled in a corner.

"What are you doing here?" I cry, entering and grabbing at her arm. "We have to get downstairs right now!"

"This is the only home I've got, I won't leave it," she screeches, fighting me off, her hands clawed, her nails scratching my skin. "I won't!"

I grab again and this time I don't let go. She may be old and hunched over, but she's stronger than I expect. But I'm frightened and desperate and I force her out, just as Marcus starts shoving at the little hut, its wooden structure already rocking before we've made our way to the stairs.

"Not the inside stairs," calls Marcus, coughing as he rocks the little hut, the wood creaking. "Too much smoke!"

I turn to the wooden stairway and push Adah onto it. "Go down!" I shout into her face and she cowers from me and makes her shuffling way down the first set of stairs. I turn back to Marcus and hurry to his side, pushing against the hut with him. It gives way suddenly, so that both of us fall onto it and I feel a scorching pain in my calf. I yelp and then am yanked so abruptly to my feet by Marcus that I slam into him.

"They have hoses next door," he says and already I can hear the hiss from somewhere nearby and clouds of steam rise above us. "We have to break the stairway," he adds.

I gape at him. "What?" He points and I step back, horrified. The wooden staircase is on fire. "How will we get down? If the other stairs are full of smoke?"

"We'll think about that later. If we don't take down the staircase the whole building will burn. If we can get the stairway off, there's a chance of saving the rest." He moves cautiously to the edge and peers down into the courtyard. "Julia! Get the men to pull down the staircase!"

There's a pause and then I hear crunching noises from below, hammering and see the top of the staircase, now in flames, beginning to sway precariously.

"Help me," says Marcus and the two of us kick at the base of the staircase where it is joined to the roof. At first it seems as though the rickety wooden structure, that has always felt as though it was about to collapse at any moment, is actually going to resist our best attempts, but then it gives way, so suddenly that I almost fall with it but Marcus pulls me back. We hear it crash into the courtyard below and then shouts and the gurgling of water as people put out the burning parts.

"Now the other side," says Marcus. "Quick."

He has spotted what I missed, that there are Vigiles with ladders trying to climb up onto our roof from the outer walls. We help them steady two ladders, then a fast-moving chain of buckets of water pours out across the rooftop, the two huts hissing. One part of the roof has collapsed into the floor below, having burnt through the wooden ceiling, but the brick floors are intact. The fire has passed us, we are alive, most of the insula is still standing.

WHEN IT'S ALL OVER AND almost dawn, an odd quiet descends. The smoking wreck of the staircase fills the centre of the courtyard, and a chain forms without speaking to take it all outside the main gate. The inhabitants of the building cluster round the edges of the courtyard and talk to one another. Some sleep, too tired to care about where, or in what position, they find themselves. Julia, Cassia and Maria are trying to feed those who need it. I find Maria, who as usual already knows everything there is to know and follow her lead, pouring water and wine into cups, offering them to everyone.

"The fire's under control at last. It got as far as the Temple of Jupiter Optimus Maximus on the Capitol. The Circus and all the houses around it are a mess, but most people are safe, praise the gods. Praise Vesta for sparing her handmaiden."

"It'll take years to put right."

"Titus has already made a statement. He says he'll put his own funds towards rebuilding, that it will be done as quickly as possible."

"Our insula too?"

Maria shakes her head. "Julia didn't have insurance. Looks like we'll have to find new homes. She doesn't have the money to rebuild it and most of it's not fit for living in now. There'll be public money for public buildings, but not for private insulae. Still, you and Marcus saved it from being burnt to the ground, it would have done for sure if you hadn't cut off the wooden parts."

"Have you seen Karbo?"

"He was here a moment ago. He's safe. So is Adah."

I wander away from her, dazed with the news and exhaustion. There's nowhere I can go to sleep. The ground floor and first floor rooms are already packed with the insula's families and local neighbours, the second and third floors are soot-thick and uninhabitable. I look about me and spot a man sitting in one of the corners of the courtyard, knees bent, arms resting on them, shoulders slumped.

Marcus.

I lower myself to sit next to him. We stare at each other, our faces soot-stained, hair dishevelled, eyes rimmed red. I let my breath out in a rush. "Is that what you had in mind when you said we would have to think quickly and work hard? It's not quite what I imagined."

He shakes his head. "I don't know who could have imagined this past year."

"Well, I'm grateful to you. The whole insula is. And now you need to sleep."

"You're welcome. And no, we can't sleep. We have the small matter of an inauguration to take care of," he says, resting his head on his folded arms, voice muffled.

"How can we? We never even finished rehearsals!"

He lifts his head up. "Because no matter what else happens in Rome today, the amphitheatre will be inaugurated. And if it's not done to the satisfaction of the Aedile and the Emperor, you and I will not just be sleepy, we will be dead."

I gesture at him. "We're covered in ashes, our clothes are half-burnt, we have no possessions. We're going to inaugurate the greatest amphitheatre in the Empire? Stand in the imperial box when Titus sends for us, looking like this?"

Marcus stands up shakily. I put out a hand to help him, but he shakes his head and steadies himself. "May the gods watch over us today, Althea, we're going to need them. Come on."

"But –"

"We will manage somehow," he says. "Come on."

THE AMPHITHEATRE LOOMS OVER US, vast, shining white stone climbing into a bright blue sky, as though nothing happened, as though there had not been a fire for these past three days. Already in the colonnades nearby the ticket touts, prostitutes and bookies are gathering, ready to ply their wares. Closer to the building, more certain of their respectability, are the stallholders we approved, setting out their goods. I see the lamps and cups decorated with gladiators, the painters setting out their paints and brushes, boards on display already painted with local favourites from the past as well as current heroes.

Each entrance, as previously arranged, is guarded by a man under strict instructions to let no-one in unless they work here, no exceptions. Those who do have to show a special clay token painted red. Marcus handed them out as though they were gold coins.

"I don't have mine!" I suddenly panic. "It's back at Julia's."

Marcus shakes his head. "I'll have to leave you outside, then, won't I?" he says and pulls out two tokens he had tucked in his belt. The man nods and we enter.

The corridors are silent. I look through to the arena and am struck by the silence and calm. No-one would know today was the inaugural Games.

"Althea."

It's Karbo. He's standing holding a pile of cloth, with two buckets of water and a covered basket by his side.

"Karbo?"

"You need to be clean. Here."

The pile of cloth turns out to be a clean white tunic and a toga for Marcus. Under that is a woman's tunic in yellow and orange, a headwrap in red with tiny yellow flowers embroidered all over it, which I recognise as one of Cassia's very best outfits. "Where did you get a toga at such short notice?"

"It's Fausta's," he says, his voice small.

"Bona Dea bless you," says Marcus, giving the boy a swift embrace. He grabs one of the buckets and the bulky toga cloth and disappears around a corner.

"Thank you," I say gently.

I take the bucket and clothes and find a quiet archway. When

I'm sure no-one can see me, I wash myself and then dress in the fresh clothes. I carry the bucket and my smoked clothes back to where Karbo is helping Marcus adjust Fausta's toga correctly over his shoulder.

"Maybe I should just wear the tunic," he says doubtfully. "There's a lot to do."

"The Emperor is likely to call you to his box," I remind him.

"Just before he throws me into the arena?"

I start to laugh, then find it hard to stop and soon Marcus and I are doubled over laughing. Karbo watches us uncertainly.

Marcus straightens up, still laughing. "Ah, Karbo. You've saved us. Thank you."

"Breakfast," says Karbo. He uncovers the basket which is filled with still-warm bread from a bakery and a double handful of dates. Marcus and I grab them gratefully and chew as quickly as we can. Karbo eats too, then hurries away with the buckets. "I'll be back before the crowds arrive," he says.

I look at Marcus. His face is pale with lack of sleep but at least he's now dressed respectably, indeed far more smartly than he usually is. "How did he manage it all?" I ask.

He grins, shaking his head. "Thank the gods for good neighbours."

I nod.

Marcus takes a deep breath. "You ready?"

I nod.

"Let me hear you say it," he says, smiling.

"Ready," I say.

THE SACRED FLAME

THE CROWDS HAVE ALREADY BEGUN to gather even though the Games will not begin for almost two hours. Excited to be attending the inauguration, the plebians take their seats quickly enough, unencumbered by attendants.

The women on show today, however, are the very greatest of Rome, and each is accompanied by her personal body slave and one or two extra, carrying parasols, perfumes, cushions and goodness knows what else to ensure their mistress' comfort. They are appalled at how far they will have to climb to reach their seats at the top of the steep stairs. The richest insist on their manslaves carrying them all the way up, then send them back downstairs to wait till the show is over. It makes for mayhem as people flow in both directions rather than just one, as planned. Outside, the litters take up even more room as they deposit their mistresses before waiting nearby to be summoned at any time. Marcus has to send out three men just to manage the litter bearers and show them an area where they can dawdle.

We have been summoned by a disturbance in the top tier, which we had hoped to seat quickly and without incident before more senior attendees make an appearance.

Marcus is being berated by a woman who is insistent that she should be able to have more than four slaves with her, despite her ticket showing she can only have three. "He can crouch at my feet," she points out, indicating the smallest man in her retinue.

"I'm sorry, he cannot."

"Do you know who I am?" she asks, drawing herself up.

"No," says Marcus pleasantly. "But I am due to attend the Emperor's arrival. Would you give me your name so that I may explain to him why I am late?"

The woman looks this way and that, but gathers no support from all of whom are pleased her over-large entourage is being limited. "Very well, you may go," she says, shoving the unfortunate slave in the back and making him trip over. "But I won't forget your insufferable rudeness," she adds to Marcus.

Marcus bows. "Nor will I," he promises, smiling as though offering a compliment.

"Is this going to happen every time?" I ask.

"Hopefully not every time." He sighs as we make our way back down to the next tier, where the plebian men are taking their places. "They are our real customers," he says, indicating them. "They follow all the gladiators; they know their stuff and they come every chance they get. They won't make trouble for now, they're just happy to be here today, especially with all that's gone on."

The next tier is beginning to arrive, the equestrians, proud of their status, dressed in their finest. They beckon the refreshment sellers, settle down with snacks and drinks, talk business with one another.

We reach the ground floor and I peer out. The crowd-control ropes are in place, the queues seem mostly orderly. "It's working," I say.

Marcus nods, but he's looking out the other way, into the empty arena. "Let's get the senators and patricians seated, then we'll know we've got it under control," he says. "Once they're all in place there's only the ceremonial entrances and they're much easier. Fewer numbers."

WE SOMEHOW MANAGE THE ARRIVALS of the equestrians, the senators, even the Vestal Virgins, five of them accompanied to their seats with much bowing and scraping on everyone's part. I wonder how they picked lots to be here, since one has been left behind in the Temple of Vesta, so that the sacred fire does not go out. Is the sixth Virgin cursing under her breath at being left out, or does she consider it a lucky escape?

Finally, the stands are full. Marcus disappears, gone to give a signal to the Emperor's entourage that they may now enter. It would hardly do to keep the Emperor waiting in public; once he takes his place in the imperial box the show must commence.

TITUS IS A SHOWMAN, HE knows how to make an entrance. The trumpets ring out as he enters the imperial box alone to a standing ovation, waving and smiling to all sides, bowing his head to the Vestal Virgins. He takes his seat and only once the crowd has settled down does the rest of his entourage also arrive in the box, his younger brother Domitian with his wife, a few other people, the guards. They are not to take away from the attention on him, they must wait their turn to be seated.

I look down at my tablet, noticing that my hands are shaking. We have spent the best part of a year planning for this day through one disaster after another, we have persevered. Planning, preparation, rehearsals. But it all comes down to now, to these next few hours. Perhaps a small error will be forgiven tomorrow or on one of the other ninety-nine days still to come.

But not today. Today everything must go without a hitch, it must be perfection.

I press the tablet against my knees to stop the shaking. We have planned and rehearsed everything, but today, we can do nothing but watch.

Marcus is on the opposite side of the arena to me. I give a nod and he nods back, then turns his head towards the musicians, who are playing. The music is loud, bold, cheerful. It promises spectacle and grandeur, a day of entertainment.

Marcus raises his hand and the music stops, mid trumpet. The crowd murmurs, confused. The floor of the arena begins to move. What seemed to be thick sand, awaiting the blood of the battles to come, is revealed to be sand-coloured linen scatted over with a tiny amount of sand. The cloth is being pulled away by unseen hands, to reveal…

Black. A silent arena of black. And lying in the very centre, having appeared from nowhere, a golden egg in a nest of golden twigs. A vast egg the size of a laden ox cart. It lies, motionless. The Gate of Triumph opens, and a woman enters, all alone, robed in white, dwarfed by the arena. A Vestal Virgin. A murmur again from the fascinated crowd and all eyes turn to the box where the Vestal Virgins sit, to count them. Four are seated, one is absent, guarding the flame of Vesta in the temple close by. This is no actor. This is a true Vestal Virgin, the most senior of them all, and she is making her way towards the giant nest. In her hands is a brazier and on it are heaped burning coals. The crowd murmurs again. Surely these are coals from the temple of Vesta itself, from the sacred flame that ensures Rome's unending glory and safety.

She reaches the nest and kneels, tips the contents of the brazier onto the golden twigs and at once a flame licks the air.

The Vestal Virgin stands, steps away from the nest and moves back through the gate she came from, her bearing always upright, her face solemn.

As the flames lick the golden twigs, Marcus raises a hand again. A slow, strange vibration begins, before the drums grow louder and faster and suddenly the egg breaks open and from the now-raging flames rises, higher and higher, atop a golden pole, a bird. Its head and wings are tucked close to its body but then its head rises and turns to one side, the wings unfold to a mighty span and this golden phoenix that has arisen from a fire set by a Vestal Virgin is revealed as the Eagle of Rome, the Emperor's own standard. The awestruck crowd breaks into rapturous applause, quietening only when a herald makes an announcement.

"Today we are blessed to witness the inauguration of the greatest amphitheatre the world has ever seen, the Flavian Amphitheatre, commissioned by Emperor Vespasian and dedicated today in his name by his son, Emperor Titus. Roma Resurgens!"

Titus rises in his seat and the trumpets sound. The crowd waits in anticipation. "My father commissioned this glorious amphitheatre as part of his commitment to rebuild Rome from the ashes of the fire and civil war," he begins. "It stands on the ground once claimed as the lake and gardens of a tyrant, used for his pleasure alone. Now it is given as a gift to the people of Rome. My father's motto, Rome Rises Again, is exemplified today in its inauguration. There will be one hundred consecutive days of Games held, such as have never been seen before. May Jupiter and all the gods look upon my father's gift and be pleased with it."

The crowd breaks into applause again and then all watch, enthralled, as the Praetorian Guard march into the arena, lift down the standard and present it to the Emperor, who accepts it, two aides arranged by Marcus taking it and fixing it onto the front of the imperial box, completing its decoration. As soon as the arena is clear once again the black floor is revealed as cloth, again pulled away, the still-burning nest disappearing below. Now the true arena floor can be seen, layered thickly with green sand. Trap door after trap door opens as a forest grows before our eyes, trees and even a hill rising from the green, some complete with birds who flutter into the air and fly away or resettle. Antelope, zebras, camels and deer, scatter across the arena, some taking shelter amongst the grove of trees. Most are drawn by piles of fresh-cut grass and buckets of grain. They have been kept hungry for days and rush to eat, giving the impression of a peaceful scene of foraging animals, grazing throughout the arena, accompanied by gentle music from the lyres and singers softly crooning shepherding songs. The audience are delighted, exclaiming over the zebras, a rarity most have not seen. The Gate of Triumph opens again and the crowd gasps as giraffes enter the arena, their height meaning they can look down on the first ranks of seating. The trees that have grown from nothing are indeed edible and they begin to eat, taking hungry mouthfuls of leaves. There is another round of applause.

Marcus is not looking at the arena at all but is watching the crowd. They lean forward, murmur at the animals, chattering to one another. The gentle lyres continue their melodies. But now people begin to sit back in their seats. The scene is delightful, it is unique, but it is not a hunt. They expected a hunt. They turn their heads from side to side, expecting one of the gates or trapdoors to disburse men in armour, the beast hunters who will put on a show.

Marcus senses the time has come and his hand moves again.

Six trapdoors slide open, more quietly, more subtly than the others. At first nothing happens and then…

The crowd sees movement and everyone leans forward. They expect men but it is lions that emerge from the trapdoors, one from each of the six. The lyres stop strumming, there is silence and the crowd keeps quiet, watching the lions to see what they will do.

Unlike the previous animals who rushed to eat, the lions group together first. They nuzzle one another briefly. We have kept them apart for days; they reacquaint themselves with one another, re-establish their pride. But their timing is even better than Marcus'. The crowd has no time to grow restless. The lions fan out, crouching low and now Marcus moves his hand and the music begins, a slow drumbeat, the flutes over the beat building suspense.

The lions take their time, even though they must be hungry. They don't rush for the closest animal, but stalk the arena, their bodies low, using our scenery as camouflage, creeping from tree to tree. The herd animals shuffle, turn their heads, move a little further away. They smell something they should fear but they are so hungry they must take one more mouthful of the fresh grass we have cut for them, just one more…

The lions leap. They have identified a zebra and the beast lets out a whinny of terror, fleeing as best it can, but there is no vast grassland here to outrun its predators. It comes up against the walls of the arena and turns desperately to one side, running as fast as it can along the wall as the drums speed up the beat and the flutes rise higher, giving the illusion of cries. The other animals, panicked by the hunt going on around them, fearful of being caught up in it, also begin to run, causing confusion as they career about the arena floor, the vast giraffes with their long legs unable to build speed in the confined space, turning and turning on themselves as smaller animals dart past. But the lions are not distracted. They have identified their victim and it does not matter what else goes on around them, their eyes never leave the zebra. The other animals are only in their way. At last the closest lion leaps forward and the zebra screams as its throat is bitten, blood spurting, its legs still trying to run even as it falls to the arena floor. The other lions join the victor, ripping and tearing at the still-living animal, its last sight the hungry jaws of the six lions surrounding it.

The crowd are on their feet screaming, the trumpets sound again, and an armed troop enters. They stay well clear of the lions who are still feasting on their warm meal as the men round up the other animals. Some make a half-hearted attempt at escape, but most, well aware of the fate of the zebra, try to avoid the lions and are swiftly caged and taken below, the trapdoors closing one by one until only the two closest to the lions remain open.

Three of the men approach the lions with long hooked poles. They catch at the zebra's neck and torn-open flanks and slowly pull the body towards the trapdoor, the giant cats snarling and following their loose-limbed prey back down the lift shafts, into their pens. One swipes at a man but is pushed back by two others using their pronged poles. Having been fed, the lion decides that the men and their weapons are to be avoided after all; it follows the bleeding carcass it finds more interesting back to a sudden re-imprisonment. It roars but it is too late now, and the danger is over, each lion is locked in with a piece of meat to tear apart. The crowd sees none of this, only the lions disappearing into the arena floor. The hill opens upwards to reveal, hidden within and now streaming outwards, more than two hundred dancing girls in costumes which leave little to the imagination, swathes of coloured ribbons trailing behind them and rippling with every movement. Music fills the arena, the girls sway and glide in bare feet across the bloodied sand. Each of our normal dancing troupe leads ten girls of her own, having learnt the steps so that the others can copy her movements.

Titus stands in his box and begins to throw little wooden balls into the crowd, swiftly assisted and augmented by his strategically placed attendants located around the amphitheatre, who can throw a great deal further than he can. Shouts go up from the crowd as they catch and examine the balls, finding them marked with the names of gifts.

"A female slave!"

"A gold ring!"

"Fish!"

"A pack horse!"

"Bread!"

People leap into the air to catch the falling balls, there are scuffles and even one or two fistfights, swiftly broken up.

"An ox!"

"A silver cup!"

Besides the wooden balls there's the glint of bronze coins falling through the air. The bronze sestertius we saw being minted bearing the image of the Flavian Amphitheatre. Those lucky and well-off enough to be here today may well keep them as a memento of the day.

Titus waves and smiles at the growing applause and now people begin to chant his name, "Ti-tus, Ti-tus, Ti-tus."

Officials stand waiting as the balls are brought to them and they dispense items or hand over scrolls which confirm the more handsome or large gifts. The dancing girls twirl and whirl while the gift-balls continue to be thrown out, until a final blast of trumpets signals the end and the girls make their way out of the arena as Titus acknowledges once more the ongoing chanting of his name and settles back down in benevolent comfort.

THE CROWD ARE HAPPY NOW. They have seen great things and we have barely started the day's events. When the Gate of Triumph opens again and the procession they expected arrives they jump to their feet at once, cheering and calling out the names of local favourite gladiators. The procession is thoroughly impressive. Every gladiator in Rome has been collected together today, whether they are fighting or not. All are dressed in the very finest ceremonial armour, nothing like the dull dented pieces they use for practise or wore in previous fights. There are hundreds of them in gleaming armour, helmets with mask-like features of men or animals, weapons glinting in the sunlight, the music at full volume. The procession makes its way round the whole arena before assembling in front of the imperial box. Within the crowd of fighters, a trapdoor opens and the men part to show two gladiators all recognise. The audience goes wild. The two men are Priscus and Verus, famous gladiators, of equal standing. They will be the last fight of the day, the headline battle. I can already see bets being laid in the crowd, both between friends and larger bets being placed with professional bookies. By the time the gladiators have bowed to Titus and the procession has left the arena, there are smiles on all the faces I can see.

NOW IS THE TIME FOR a little rest from the excitement we have had had so far. Vendors of food and drink begin to walk the tiers, peddling their wares. Meanwhile the arena must be kept busy at all times.

There's a comedy show by the actors, lots of bawdy romping and cheeky references to rumoured affairs and liaisons, some of which may be true. None of them dare reference Titus' own romance with the Jewish Queen Berenice, of course; that would be a step too far right in front of him and besides the senators were too relieved that he took their advice and sent her home rather than flaunt her round Rome like some minor Cleopatra, as they'd feared. Titus is in everyone's good graces today; he has been generous in the aftermath of Vesuvius and no doubt will be similarly so after the fire. He sent Berenice away without fuss and today he is inaugurating the greatest amphitheatre of the empire. It would be ungracious to make fun of him, so the actors stick to low-level nudges and winks. Their appearance is the signal that we are drawing close to lunchtime, and the execution of criminals. Those with weaker stomachs and little inclination to watch brutal slaughter can remove themselves now, if they wish. They can go and eat, chat with their friends with no hurry and still return in time for the main event of the day, the gladiators.

There's a shifting in the upper seats as most of the women leave. They don't much care for the executions as a whole, although the Vestal Virgins remain in their seats. Clearly, they have strong stomachs. Their slaves arrive with trays of food, the five Virgins picking through delicacies. The same thing is happening in the imperial box, where Titus is receiving one guest after another from the patrician classes. Men arrive, sometimes accompanied by their wives. There is a lot of bowing and perhaps the offer of a glass of wine or some dainty morsel before they are excused and another guest is received into the imperial presence. Little or no attention is paid to the actors except by the few plebians allowed in today. They are buying food from the many sellers wandering the tiers. There is wine, bread, cheese, fruits, olives, nuts and small cakes. One can even buy little cups of garum sauce in which to dip bread. Some of the dancing girls also offer refreshments. The water fountains and toilets get crowded but settle down again. Now that the grand women of Rome have made themselves scarce and will not return until the gladiatorial combats of the afternoon, the execution of the criminals can begin.

I shuffle in my seat, wishing that I could sit far enough away from the action to believe it only a play, a pretence. But I have no choice. For these inaugural Games, Marcus has chosen to make a real show of the public executions, drawing on the mythology of the founding of Rome, beginning with the Trojan war. And so we see Agamemnon sacrifice his own daughter Iphigenia to bring luck to the Greeks as they set sail for Troy. This, at least, is a quick execution for the hapless female criminal. Her throat is cut on an altar, splashing the characters around her with blood. Most of the other actors in this scene are trained gladiators, wearing shining armour and clothing befitting the Greek kings for the occasion. Sacrifice made, a fleet of over 100 wooden toy boats skim across the arena, before the entry of a shining, glorious Achilles in a magnificent chariot borrowed from the racing stables. Behind him should be the corpse of Hector, dragged around the city of Troy by Achilles in retribution, but this is no corpse, it is a criminal who will lose their life by being dragged to death. His screams have me gritting my teeth and digging my hands into my thighs. I keep my eyes fixed on Marcus, who will give the signal to stop, but of course he does not give the signal until the man has died; to do so would be to risk the Emperor and the crowd's displeasure. The man's screaming can be heard even above the roar of the crowd and I shut my eyes, rocking in place, willing it to stop. The crowd cheers on each death, revelling in what? In justice being served? In relief at not finding themselves in the arena? In the lavish spectacle we have created, with costumes, chariots and music accompanying each execution? I do not know. I would prefer not to be here and yet I must stay, and not only for the executions today, but for the ninety-nine days to follow and who knows beyond then? I brace myself for what is still to come.

Achilles stands alone in the arena, but this is not the same man who drove the chariot, but another criminal, dressed in shining armour and pushed through the gates to meet his end. The armour reveals his leg and ankle, the weak spot of the demigod Achilles. He knows what will happen to him and tries to turn about on himself so that he cannot be easily shot. But there is not one archer but several, so that wherever he turns he is still a target. Marcus nods and the marksman's arrow flies across the arena striking the man in his calf. It is a flesh wound, nothing more, but just as in the myth, the arrowhead has been dipped in poison and the crowd leans forward, interested to watch someone die of poisoning. The man staggers before blood pours from his mouth and he falls to his knees. His body convulses in silence while the arena holds its breath and then lets it out in a cheer when the convulsions end.

Now comes the showpiece. It's elaborate for executions, but today is a special day. The Gate of Triumph opens yet again, and a vast wooden horse is rolled into the arena. The crowd whoops and stamps their feet, ready for a re-enactment on a greater scale than they had expected. Out of the horse come hundreds of Greek men, ready to do battle with the Trojans who have mistakenly let them into their city, believing the horse a gift from the defeated and disheartened Greeks rather than the trick it really is. The arena fills with fighting men, swords clashing, armour glinting. From here, it appears to be a magnificent battle, with high quality swordplay and real deaths, blood spouting across the sand and dismembered limbs accompanied by dying screams. It seems unrehearsed, just like a real battle. It is only if you look closely, if you know, that what you are really seeing is more than two hundred trained gladiators, working both sides of the story, shedding a little blood here and there but nothing dangerous. The deaths and dismemberments are coming from the hundred criminals who have been saved up for today. They look the same as the gladiators, wearing good quality armour, helmets, shields, but their swords are blunt. They have no chance against trained fighters. One after another goes down, the gladiators identifying them by the dot of red paint touched to each criminal's forehead before they spilled into the arena. Troy falls, the Greeks are victorious, the applause is deafening.

I stand up. I will not watch this next part. A wailing woman is pushed into the arena, dressed as a Trojan princess. This criminal has been given the part of Cassandra, warning against the trickery of Greeks. I step into the cool of the arches, making my way down the corridor as quickly as I can, hoping that from this distance I will not hear her screams as she is raped on scenery designed as Athena's altar before being mercifully stabbed to death offstage. Cassandra lived beyond her dishonour but a criminal cannot be permitted to survive. One more woman makes her entry, some other poor wretch dressed in cheap jewels and lavishly decorated clothes, another Trojan princess, Polyxena, sacrificed on the grave of Achilles. I hear their screams from a distance, but the roar of the crowd makes it clear that the re-enactment of this founding myth has been well received, combining mythology with justice towards the enemies of Rome.

Leaning against the cool stone in the shadowy corridor, I listen to the final touch Marcus has put on this vicious scene. I close my eyes and remember the rehearsals, a man representing Aeneas, brave survivor of Troy, leading a little group including an elderly man, Aeneas' father, carried on his pious son's back. Having reached the imperial box, Aeneas will be lifted into it by a prearranged signal; the actor portraying him will drop to his knees and crawl out of sight, leaving Titus to stand, replacing him. I hear applause break out and step back through the arch to see the response. Titus is all smiles, the crowd is delighted. Aeneas, founder of Rome, is now embodied in our latest Emperor, emphasising the continued glory and permanence of Rome. Marcus, as ever a true showman, has put a final flourish on proceedings. The executions are over. The women will return soon and then the gladiators will begin their bouts. I drink from one of the fountains and try not to think about what I have heard and seen.

THERE ARE A FEW BOUTS leading up to the main event, seasoned, high-quality gladiators who would normally be headliners, but for once only the hardened gamblers care about them, feverishly placing bets on each outcome, but they are not the main spectacle. What the crowd is waiting for is the big showdown between Priscus and Verus. These two gladiators have fought for years, each claiming life after life of less experienced gladiators, always victorious, wounded but never defeated. Their names and faces are known throughout the Empire, they are heroes in Rome. They have never faced one another though; this is a showdown years in the making, both of them now close to retirement, one last chance to see them at their best. The bets being placed have reached epic proportions for the two are closely matched and it's hard to know where to place one's money. Keen followers of Games in the audience swap notes on the many years they have been watching these two fighters. They comment on everything in their lives, from the women in their beds and how many children they've sired, to whether the heat favours or harms the chances of either. It's all speculation, nobody knows for sure, but that only makes the gambling more interesting.

Nothing has been left to chance. The men enter the arena in spectacular armour, ceremonial helmets depicting mythological creatures, armour which has never seen a fight in its life, polished to perfection. Each comes with his own entourage, his own music, while the crowd shouts a strange combination of encouragement and disparagement. Marcus lets the tension build. There's a lot of swaggering as the two men face up to one another, swapping ceremonial armour for something more battered and believable, leather soaked in blood and sweat, metal dented and scratched.

I don't generally find fights that interesting, but when watching two fighters who know their trade, it's hard not to be drawn in. The moves they make are large, exaggerated for the benefit of the upper tiers, but they are not without aggression or cunning tactics. The blades whip through the air and the sounds they make when they touch on metal leave your skin cold. A slicing sound as one sword comes round in an arc and a patch of red appears on an upper arm, the crowd screaming bloodlust and grief over gambling choices already made. But a cut to an upper arm is nothing to a gladiator. The battle continues despite drops of blood sputtering through the air, each man receiving more than one wound.

There is a referee to keep order and, knowing how to put on a good show, he calls for breaks here and there, allowing the entourages of the gladiators to rush forward and attend to their wounds, set cups to their lips and whisper tactics in their ears. The fight continues longer than one would have thought possible, neither man giving way. Titus, meanwhile, is gaining the crowd's approval by sending lavish gifts to both men, yet neither seem swayed by this, continuing to fight with vigour in their arms and bloodlust in their eyes.

I make my way to where Marcus is seated, leaning forward on his thighs, watching the fight intently.

"It's lasted twice as long as all the other bouts," I say. "Won't the crowd get bored?"

He glances at me with amusement. "Do you see them getting bored?"

He's right, the crowd is watching intently, still swapping bets which will cause those who have to pay out severe difficulties. "How will it end?"

"We will have to see, won't we?"

"You look like you know something."

"Shhh. Trying to make history."

"How?"

"You'll see."

"Are you hoping they'll kill each other?"

"Better than that."

"Which is?"

"Watch the Emperor."

"What do you expect him to do?"

Marcus sits back in his seat as though he hasn't a care in the world. "Free them."

"What, both of them?"

"Yes."

"But the Emperor always rewards the victor! Titus can't reward both. No emperor has ever done that."

"But if he did," says Marcus with a grin, "you'd remember it forever, wouldn't you?"

"How do you persuade the Emperor to do what you want?"

"Carefully," says Marcus, his eyes back on the fighters. "And part of it is down to the fighters," he adds.

"Are they trying for a draw?"

"No, it would be too obvious."

"So?"

"They both know it's in their interests to keep fighting and not get wounded too badly. They've already accumulated a nice set of gifts. Neither of them wants to die now."

"And Titus?"

"I sent a message up after the fourth round, reminding him that no emperor has ever set both fighters free."

"Did you say he should?"

"Of course not. You can't tell the Emperor what to do. But I think our Titus is not without astuteness when it comes to pleasing the plebs. He makes sure to be generous when it counts and when it's most visible."

I think of Titus' response to the disaster of Vesuvius, how visibly and generously he responded, including his own funds towards rebuilding damaged cities or those where refugees had moved to. And his most recent pronouncement about the fire. "I hope you're right."

"We'll see."

"I wish Fausta was here," I say. "She'd have loved it."

He is silent for a moment and I'm not sure he's heard me over the cheering and stamping of the crowd, who are sensing a finale as both men, bleeding and gasping, attack one another again on the referee's nod. "She'd have finished the pair of them off single-handed," he says and I should laugh at his joke, but

271

instead two tears slip down my face and Marcus takes my hand in his briefly, a quick warm squeeze before he looks away. "She'd be proud of you. She'd say there was no need for her anymore, you're as good a right-hand woman as she was."

My hand is cool now his touch has gone but my cheeks are hot at his words, a sudden welling up of pride mixed with the grief of losing Fausta. I look round the arena again, trying to believe that I have had a hand in all of this, that it is my work that has helped Marcus create a spectacle the like of which has never been seen before.

THE FIGHT EXCEEDS ALL RECORDS for duration, when suddenly Titus stands and declares a draw. The crowd, most with money on the line, groans, Titus declares both men victors, and sets them both free, sending down two wooden swords and laurel wreaths, symbols of their freedom. The two bleeding men wrap their arms around each other, before kneeling in front of the imperial box, holding their wooden swords to their chests in a display of loyalty and gratitude. The crowd is delighted, they have never seen anything like it. It is an unheard-of event, one which they will tell their grandchildren. Today has been everything it should have been and more, it has exceeded everyone's expectations. Marcus watches the rapturous applause with me, leaning against a column in one of the corridors, nodding to himself, a small smile on his face.

Karbo's face peers round the column. "You're sent for."

"By whom?"

"Titus."

Marcus nods to me. "Come on."

"He didn't ask for me," I say.

"He'll remember you," he says.

272

We make our way out of the darkness and up through the staircase, along the corridors to the imperial box. The Praetorian Guards are blocking the corridor, standing guard. They seem to know who we are though; they nod.

"No weapons allowed in the imperial box."

Marcus spreads his hands wide. "No weapons."

They nod again and pull back the heavy silk curtain over the doorway.

The box feels crowded. I think of all the times Marcus and I have sat in here, looking out over the arena, leaning over the edge to give orders or pass on comments about how something works. Guards surround Titus and his brother Domitian, who is sitting to his side but a little further back. A woman with a preposterously elaborate hairstyle dressed in flowing silks must be Domitia, Domitian's wife. There are a few other grandly dressed people, presumably family or friends of the Emperor, although I can't identify them.

Marcus focuses on Titus. "You sent for me, Imperator."

"A most elegant show," says Titus.

Marcus bows.

"And you have many more delights planned, I am sure?"

"More than I could name, Imperator. Many designed specifically for your presence, should you continue to grace us with it."

"You can count on it. I understand the arena can be flooded for naval battles?"

I try not to laugh, thinking of the architect's outrage when Marcus asked the same thing.

Marcus keeps an entirely straight face. "Of course, Imperator."

"I would like to see a naval battle. Augustus used to hold them, I believe."

"He did, Imperator. We will outdo whatever has gone before. Perhaps for the closing ceremony at the end of the inaugural Games?"

"That is an excellent idea," says Titus. "Finish in style, something memorable."

I can't help but admire Marcus' swift thinking. Titus could have asked for a naval battle in a few days' time and we would have had no choice but to obey. Marcus' offer has given us three months' time to prepare.

Titus' gaze swivels to me. "Ah," he says. "The scribe who beat the Emperor at shorthand. Still as fast?"

I bow my head. "I hope so, Imperator."

"Very good," says Titus. He looks at Marcus again. "You have been well remunerated, I hope?"

"Generously, Imperator."

"Then take this as a small token of my appreciation." A gesture has an aide hurrying forward with a large leather pouch, which Titus takes and passes to Marcus. "Your opening scene was very appropriate, in the light of all that has gone on this year. Rome shall indeed rise again from the ashes."

"Your father's name shall live eternally," says Marcus.

Titus nods and Marcus withdraws, I follow him from the shadows as we make our way back down the corridors. Marcus pulls open the pouch and nods at what is inside. I catch a quick glimpse of large gold coins, before he puts the pouch away. "Not long to go now," he says. "Final procession and music, release the birds, then we're done. Let's get it over with."

THE FIVE HUNDRED WHITE DOVES have had their feathers stained every possible colour. As the procession of gladiators, dancing girls, actors and the tamer animals wind their way round the arena, the trapdoors open one more time and the birds take to the sky, drawing final chatter and applause from the audience, who take their flight as a good omen, no matter how stage-managed. The few blue-painted ones almost disappear once in the sky, proving Marcus right, but those of scarlet, green, yellow, pink and violet look magnificent. As they disappear, the crowds begin to disperse. Titus and all the other members of the imperial box were escorted outside while the procession drew everyone's attention elsewhere. He will already be safely on his way back to the imperial palace.

THE CROWDS ARE ALL GONE, their seats empty. I stand in the imperial box. The silk awning has been carefully rolled up and packed away, the Praetorian Guards have disappeared with the Emperor. The space feels large again. All I can hear is the swish-swish of brooms and the gurgling of water. The cleaners have finished sweeping all the tiers, and are being followed downwards towards the arena by buckets of water swilled over the stone, sluicing away the stickiness of dried wine, the grease of dropped food. On the arena floor itself the bloodied sand has been scraped up, the last parts swept away. The wooden boards are stained with blood, the stains will only grow darker over the years to come. The trapdoors have all been thrown open, allowing more light below where the disposals are of a more serious kind. I rest a hand on the cool marble, then make my way down under the arena floor to find Marcus.

The staff are gathered in one corner, pouring drinks from several large flagons and munching on sweet cakes piled high on several platters. It looks as though Marcus has allowed them a celebration for having got through today.

I catch Karbo and pull a cup of wine away from him. "Enough of that, you drunkard. Stick to the cakes, will you?"

He gives me a sticky smile. "We did it!"

I smile at his enthusiasm. "We did," I agree. "And tomorrow it has to be done all over again."

He takes a huge bite of cake. "Bigger and better," he manages to get out through the mouthful.

"Bigger and better," I say with a sigh, walking towards the other end of the space, where the animals are being kept. I pause by the lions, who are happily gnawing on the remains of their zebra. One growls when I come too close to the cage.

Marcus and Bestia the beast-hunter are walking past the pens, noting which animals are left to us before the new consignment arrives.

"How many animals still usable for tomorrow?" Marcus asks.

"None of the lions," the beast-hunter says. "You'll not get a damn thing out of them for six days at least. Unless you want them to fight men, of course."

"Got bears tomorrow," says Marcus. "Don't need the lions for a few days. They put on a good show."

"Good quality," agrees Bestia. "You should have paid double for them, you tight bastard. Just water, then. Don't feed them before they're needed again."

Marcus nods.

"Might be worth feeding the two tigers a little. Just enough to keep them interested, don't sodding overdo it. Not a whole body."

Marcus gives him a sideways glance. "Body?"

"Cack, they need to get a taste for men, if you want them to really go for them. Say, an arm each?"

Marcus gestures to Strabo, who has joined the discussion.

"Do it." He glances at me and catches my shudder. "They're dead now," he says. "The dying was the worst part."

I nod. The smell of blood is heavy in the air, despite the shafts of light from the open trapdoors above us which should bring fresh air. The tigers pace and growl in their pens, smelling prey nearby, hungry. The newly delivered animals for tomorrow, a combination of African goats and antelopes, tremble, backed into the tightest corners of their pens, sensing their imminent deaths.

"Tomorrow's criminals arrived yet?"

I nod, point behind me at the chained men being led down the other side of the space, into their own pens. No women in this batch, I'm relieved to see. "Are they fighting tomorrow?"

"Yes," says Marcus. "Much chance they have against the Amazons. We've got an all-female troupe from Labeo tomorrow."

"Are they good?"

"Yes. And they have real weapons. That lot will have blunt swords, as today. Their best chance is to be fast on their feet and as brave as possible. You never know, the crowd may feel sorry for them."

"I doubt it." My voice cracks, my eyes filling up.

Marcus steps closer to me. "It's a hard life, Althea," he says simply. "I never told you any different. Now you see what it is. It isn't trumpets and the Emperor being magnanimous, handing out gifts and gold. It isn't rehearsals and costumes to make myths come to life. All of that's the show, the spectacle. But we're the ones left with blood and guts, the smell of fear and a pile of dead bodies to dispose of at the end of every Games."

I nod. "I just…" Just the screaming for mercy that went on and on and on during the executions. A tear rolls down my cheek, then another.

"I know," he says, and touches my shoulder. "I know. Why do you think I wanted to live on a farm instead?"

I nod and try to smile.

He's silent for a moment. "You can leave," he says at last. "I won't hold you back. You're a freedwoman, you may do as you wish. You could be a scribe in the imperial household, Titus likes you, he'd snap you up. You'd be back in the fancy villas with very little to do except look pretty and do a bit of writing here and there. You wouldn't have to mingle with the likes of gladiators and whores or watch the executions every day. You'd be paid well. You could… marry, have children."

I meet his gaze. "Would you manage on your own?"

He gives a half smile. "I've managed for many years," he says, "though it's a lot easier with a good woman at your side."

I don't know if he's comparing me to Livia or Fausta, but either way I'm touched. I look down at the floor. He's right, I could easily find a better position, one which would take me away from the dark life beneath the arena, the grim spectacles above it. It's tempting. But I think of what we've gone through together and more importantly, how he has treated me. He has never laid a finger on me. He set me free. He has treated me almost as a man, his right hand in this strange life. And he is so recently returned from the darkness I thought would swallow him up. I think of Julia and Maria who watch over me every day and how Fausta guided me, how she made me a woman who could stand up to an emperor. I take a deep breath and let it out in a rush. "You wouldn't last an hour without me," I say.

His grin is all the reward I needed for my decision. "I wouldn't," he agrees. "I'd be in the arena within a week."

"A lot quicker than that," I say.

"You're right."

We stand there for a moment, grinning at each other like two idiots.

"Boss! We're leaving. You need anything else?"

Marcus raises one hand. "Check on the elephant on your way home, will you?"

"Will do, boss."

I look up through the trapdoors. The sky is turning a pale pink, with gold and purple streaks. We need to get back to the insula before nightfall. I follow Marcus up through one of the trapdoor ladders onto the arena floor, the two of us standing alone in the vast empty space. I clear my throat and unroll the scroll in my hand, nod to Marcus to begin.

"Animals?"

"Yes," I say, holding my pen against the list. "Woodlands tomorrow. Bears. In the pens. Half trained, half wild."

"Criminals?"

"Yes."

"Gladiators?"

"Ready. The Amazon costumes have been delivered directly to Labeo's barracks."

Marcus nods. "I frightened off two of the worst ticket touts this morning. We might get a few days' peace before they start up again."

"The cleaners have nearly finished. All the tiers have been swept and washed."

"Corridors and toilets?"

"Yes."

"Arena floor?"

I look around me. It's been swept clean, the bloodied sand disposed of. "Yes."

"Fresh green sand for the morning hunt?"

279

I nod and point. "Sackfuls left at each quarter of the arena, ready for spreading when the wood has dried." I can't bear to say that it's the blood which has to dry.

"I think we're done," Marcus says. "And if not, we'll sort it out tomorrow first thing. The Emperor won't be here tomorrow. He'll only attend some of the shows, so we have a little breathing space. The crowd tomorrow will be less fancy, not so many airs and graces to take care of. Let's get back before dark, I don't care to walk around with this kind of money on me."

WE WALK THROUGH THE FORUM in silence, too tired for talk. My mind is whirring at all the sights and smells of the day, the sounds of beasts and trumpets still echoing in my ears. Here and there we pass groups of men still discussing the day's events.

"When Priscus struck Verus on the neck, I thought he was a goner, but did you see how swift he came back?"

"Verus has always been swift. There's a man who fights on his toes, I tell you. But you can't argue with Priscus' wits: swifter than his feet. And both given their freedom! Never seen such a thing, screamed myself hoarse!"

"Then you need more wine, here, pass your cup. To Verus and Priscus."

"Verus and Priscus!"

I glance at Marcus, who gives a weary smile. "You were right," I say. "They'll never forget."

"It could have gone either way."

"It went the way you planned it," I say.

"One can never tell with emperors," he says.

WE PASS THROUGH A BURNT landscape to reach the insula. It seems empty, the tight streets opened up into gaping holes, the odd building still left, as ours is, the rest gone, smoking ruins and ashes everywhere. The courtyard feels like a refuge from it all. Marcus heads towards Julia, who is coordinating the women, setting up a small cooking area.

Balbus is standing behind me, holding a large bundle wrapped in a cloth. "I m-made what you asked for. We grabbed it when we took our valuables."

"Thank you," I say. I sigh and wipe my hand across my face, bone weariness sweeping over me. "I am not sure he will accept it."

"All homes m-must have a L-Lararium," says Balbus with certainty.

I nod and hold out my arms, taking the bundle with reverence. Balbus gives a jerky nod back and steps away.

I hesitate. Will Marcus be angry with what I have done? Will we even stay here? The building is so damaged, I am not sure it can be repaired. But I asked Balbus for it before the fire and here it is. I use my elbow to open the door of the first-floor apartment we will be sleeping in for the foreseeable future. We have one room of it, sharing the rest with the baker's family, who have warmly offered us the space. The smell of smoke is still heavy in here, unable to escape. I rest the bundle on the bedding mats, clear a shelf of a few odd items, leaving it empty. Then I squat down and undo the bundle. Inside is a wooden shrine, painted beautifully with two spirit ancestors, as well as a bearded snake in the centre as is the custom. This one has been exquisitely coloured. The tail is black and white and grey, but slowly colour emerges, ending with a gloriously bright head and beard in many colours. Balbus has done a beautiful job. I lift the shrine up onto the shelf, where it just fits. As I do so, a collection of tiny figures drops from the bundle. I stoop to collect them, then stand clutching them, tears falling onto their tiny woollen clothes. I take a deep breath and place each one on the ledge of the shrine. A delicate woman, her hair the bright brown of a freshly plucked hazelnut, a child in her arms. Livia and Amantius as I recall them. Another woman, tall and broad, with tumbling black hair. Fausta. And finally, two figures that I did not ask Balbus for, a tall man holding a wax tablet, a woman clasped to his side, her hair dressed in the Greek fashion. My parents, as he has imagined them.

It takes me three fumbling attempts to light one of the two candles I had already bought and kept for this shrine. My tears flow so heavily I can barely see what I am doing. I almost set fire to the curls of the tiny Fausta and have to take a breath to steady myself.

"What is this?"

I turn to Marcus and watch his face as he takes in the Lararium, the candle I have finally lit flickering wildly in the draught from the open door. He steps forward and I move out of his way so that he can reach the shrine. He stands for a few moments, staring at the tiny figures. At last he lifts a hand and reaches out to touch the figure of his wife and son, one finger following the loose hair of Livia, before coming to rest on the head of Amantius. There is something so terrible in his tenderness that I turn away and step out onto the landing, pulling the door shut behind me. Only then do I hear him cry.

I take a few deep breaths, then make my way downstairs to the courtyard. People are milling about, the men pulling down the last small charred parts of the wooden stairs, adding them to a brazier.

"Where is Adah?"

No-one seems to know. I have to use the interior stairs again.

They smell so strongly of smoke I am coughing by the time I reach the roof.

She is where I expected her to be, squatting by the ruins of her little hut, poking through the remains. When she sees me coming, she stands, gripping a candlestick with many arms. The candles have long since melted of course, but the metal has withstood the fire, though it is dirty with soot and ashes.

"The Almighty has not forgotten what Titus did to us," she says, and there is a bitter joy in her voice. "He has burned Rome's empire three times over for the burning of the Holy Temple of Jerusalem. First Vesuvius, then the fever burning people up inside so they could feel the pain of the fire and now this, a fire burning up the great places of Rome." She spits. "The Almighty has shown His greatness over your mish-mash of gods, He has burnt the very temple dedicated to all of them together, a crowd of false idols."

I feel a chill of fear at her words. These things may all be coincidences, but still... Titus came to the throne and in just one year these three disasters have occurred, all of them linked to fire and burning... I think of the Pantheon, blackened and still smoking. A shiver passes over me. "Do you think your god has been appeased?" I ask. "If it was all done at his hand, as you say, do you think he has finished punishing Titus now?"

Adah looks away, across the rooftops, at the smoking haze still staining the pink evening sky. "He may have finished punishing Rome," she says. "He will not rest till Titus dies."

I swallow.

Adah is using a piece of her wrap to try and clean the candlestick, rubbing at the dirty metal. "What did you want?"

"Everyone is gathering downstairs to eat together."

"I won't celebrate that place being inaugurated."

283

"We are celebrating being alive more than anything, I think." She hesitates.

"Please, Adah," I say. "We will all be together. I do not want to think of you being alone up here."

She shakes her head. "A good child," she says at last. "I will join because you asked. Only because you asked."

I smile, although I am so tired tears spring to my eyes again at everything that has happened: the fire, the inauguration, the Lararium, now Adah. "Thank you," I manage, a little sob escaping me.

Adah comes closer, reaches up to my cheek and wipes the tears away as they fall. "Come," she says, more gently than I have heard her speak before, and it is she who leads me by the hand, as though I were a child, down the smoky stairs and into the courtyard, where tables are being taken from every household and workshop and laid together. Every family and person has brought lamps and whatever food they have to share, little dishes of olives, radishes, a few large pots of bean stew and savoury porridge, cheese, roasted chickpeas, dipping cups of garum sauce, dates, figs and melons, plums, nuts. The baker's family are busy stacking loaves and little fruit buns in a huge pile, Cassia is pouring wine. The brazier has been piled high with logs, and is burning brightly, illuminating our gathering. I gaze at it for a moment. Contained, the flickering flames are cheerful, giving of warmth and comfort.

"Adah is joining us? You're more persuasive than I gave you credit for." Marcus is red-eyed but smiling.

"I must have worn her down," I say.

He nods. We stand in silence for a moment. "Thank you," he says at last.

"It was nothing," I say quickly. I am afraid he will cry, and I don't know what to do if he does.

"You remembered the colour of her hair," he says and his voice cracks.

AT FIRST, I WORRY THAT the amphitheatre will be toasted, that the excitement and spectacle of the day will be rehashed despite what I told Adah, that she will retreat back up the stairs to sit alone. But I was right. Exhausted and relieved, people embrace one another quietly and eat, sitting shoulder to shoulder, glad for the comfort of our little community, for the mercy shown them. Later there is some music and dancing, the children chase the dogs about the courtyard, there are a few stolen kisses in the shadows between couples or those who would like to be so. There are no noisy toasts, instead one person after another comes up to Marcus and quietly raises their cup, embraces him, speaks softly with him and then makes their way back to the gathering. He nods, smiles, embraces them back, listens to what they have to say.

The children are growing sleepy and even the dogs lie panting under the table, tired of games. Marcus nods to me to join him. I make my way across the courtyard to him. He is sitting with Julia, the two of them a little apart from the others.

"We had a deal, you and I," he says. "That when I was rewarded, I would leave Rome and go to buy my family farm. And I would set you free."

I nod.

"You are free already, but I had intended to give you money to start a new life." He pulls out the pouch Titus gave him, heavy with gold. "Enough to buy the farm already. Plus enough to give you that new start."

I wait.

"I find myself without the heart to go, just yet. The farm would feel without purpose. Perhaps in a year or two I will feel differently. For now, my share will go to Julia, to rebuild the insula."

Julia is shaking her head, her hand raised to stop him, but he pushes it gently away. "I need a family about me and this –" he waves at the gathering "– is all I have for now. Let me help, Julia."

She looks away but nods, then turns and gives him a fierce embrace. "You are a good man, Marcus," she says. "May Vesta bless you."

Marcus is still holding the pouch. "Your share is here, Althea," he says.

"No," I say. "Give it to Julia with yours." I look round the courtyard. "This is my family too. I have no other," I add to Julia. "Use my share to get running water put in and build us a fountain in the courtyard. I'm sick of carrying water from the street."

We laugh.

"I will have a large apartment set aside for the two of you when we rebuild," she says.

"No," Marcus and I say together. He gestures to me to finish, smiling.

"I – prefer the roof hut," I say, and he nods.

Marcus passes Julia the pouch and she shakes her head at it, smiling at us both. "Then I shall build you the finest roof hut Rome has ever seen," she says and we all laugh.

"Don't tell the others it came from us," says Marcus. "Just say there was insurance after all."

"The gods will know your deeds and bless you," she says.

SLOWLY, IN TWOS AND THREES, people begin to leave, some carrying sleeping children, a few leaning on one another to steady their tipsy gaits. They make their way into the half-charred building, their voices fading.

"I will wish you a good night," says Julia, when there is no-one else left. She stands and stretches her back before looking down at Marcus and me, sitting opposite one another, Marcus staring into the flames as though about to speak an oracle, my own face tilted up to look at Julia, catching myself mid-yawn. "Today was a triumph brought forth from the ashes of what went before."

I nod and she looks at Marcus, but he doesn't reply, only continues staring into the last flickers amongst the embers. She smiles at me and places her hand lightly on my head in what feels like a blessing, then walks away, her feet quiet as ever, the darkness of the building swallowing her up within a few paces. I watch her go, then look back to realise Marcus has lifted his head and is watching me. I meet his gaze. I wonder if I should say something about how proud his wife and Fausta would have been of him drawing back from the darkness that he was heading for, of what he has managed to accomplish, the triumph of the inauguration. But then I think of the grey fields of Hades we scrambled over, his little son lost beneath them, and close my mouth. We have come a long way together. But not far enough for words of hope. Not yet.

The last flickers of flames have gone out, now there are only dark embers left, a sullen red beneath their ashen coatings.

"Only ninety-nine days to go, then," says Marcus, raising his cup towards me. I am not sure if there is a glimmer of humour in his weary words, but I lift my own cup to him and nod.

"Ninety-nine days."

I hope you have enjoyed this first book in the Colosseum series. If you have, I would really appreciate it if you would leave a brief review, so that new readers can find *From the Ashes*. I read all reviews and am always grateful for your time in writing them and touched by your kind words.

AFTER FIRE, COMES WATER.

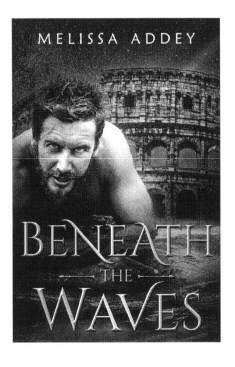

Rome, 80AD. The Emperor orders that the Colosseum be flooded. There must be vast battles, spectacular props and epic storytelling. While Marcus, manager of the amphitheatre, must face the dangers, mistakes and emotions of the watery depths, his scribe Althea must move beyond survival and name her desires. As the backstage team takes on new challenges, change is coming. Second in the Colosseum series.

Watch the trailer at:
www.melissaaddey.com/books/beneath-the-waves

Have you read the Forbidden City series? Pick up the first in series FREE on your local Amazon website.

China, 1750s. Lady Qing has spent the past seven years languishing inside the high red walls of the Forbidden City. Classed as an Honoured Lady, a lowly-ranked concubine, Qing is neglected by the Emperor and passed over for more ambitious women. But when a new concubine, Lady Ying, arrives, Qing's world is turned upside down. As the highest position at court becomes available and every woman fights for status, Qing might have found love for the first time in her life… if Lady Ula Nara, the most ambitious woman at court, will allow her a taste of happiness.

Author's Note on History

T HIS IS THE FIRST BOOK in a series that started as the simple question I asked myself: who were the people who made up the 'backstage team' for the Colosseum? There is hardly any mention whatsoever of them and yet Games on such an immense scale could not possibly have been put on without a very large and permanent team in place. Who were the stage managers, the makers of costumes and scenery, the technicians? I did a lot of research, but the team were still invisible, so I have had to construct them from a combination of historical evidence and common sense. For example, there are mentions of large-scale painted scenery (so someone had to make it, store it, hoist and remove it), of mythological re-enactments (there must have been rehearsals and costumes), beast-hunts (someone had to provide/store/release at the right moment a variety of animals), trainers for the gladiators as well as their remains which show that physicians patched them up, etc.

It has been fascinating. At the heart of the team is Marcus, because there had to have been someone in overall control, and his scribe Althea, because you can't run a show on that scale with nothing written down.

This first book focuses on fire, from the burning of the

Temple of Jerusalem to Vesuvius erupting, fever and fire breaking out in Rome, to the sacred flame cared for by the Vestal Virgins. The next three books in this series focus on the same team through the themes of water (*Beneath the Waves*), earth (*On Bloodied Ground*) and air (*The Flight of Birds*).

79 AD was the year in which Vesuvius erupted and wiped out Pompeii. Traditionally the date of the eruption was accepted as the 24th August, but in fact more recent discoveries including autumnal fruits, heating braziers and an inscription (as well as the fact that the original date in a letter was transcribed multiple times with varying dates between August and November) convincingly set the date as the 24th October instead, so I have gone with this more recent historical record. Fausta's description of events is closely modelled on that given by Pliny the Younger, the only person to have fully recorded a personal description of what happened; he was based in Misenum as a teenager. His uncle, the admiral and scientist Pliny the Elder, died of a heart attack while trying to save people in Pompeii with his fleet. Pompeii was buried under 5 metres of ashes, Herculaneum under 20 metres. We know very little about the days and weeks after the disaster, except that an imperial messenger could get to Rome in one day by changing horses every 12 miles and that refugees with Pompeiian names begin to show up afterwards in Cuma (near Puteoli) and Naples (Neapolis), tending to marry one another, suggesting they stuck together in their own communities. The Emperor Titus was considered to have handled the disaster well; he visited the area twice, put a lot of money including his own personal funds into building up the cities that were not damaged (presumably so refugees could settle there) and appointed two senators to look after the area and get it back on its feet. Looting

started very quickly, with looters tunnelling into the houses beneath the ashes. It still goes on to this day.

There are a lot of erotic paintings on the walls of Pompeiian villas, but not all of them can have been brothels. My thanks to Steven Cockings, who suggested there might have been very fast painters at events, for example painting your favourite gladiator as an item of merchandise, which I developed further as an idea for fancy dinners.

80 AD saw both 'pestilence' and a three day fire break out in Rome in the spring/summer and although there is not a lot of detail available, it seems possible that the former was malaria, which was rife during this time period. Up to 10,000 people died during this outbreak. Some people believed that the ashes from Vesuvius had created the illness. Jewish people believed that the three disasters (Vesuvius, pestilence and fire), taking place shortly after Titus became Emperor, were a punishment on him for his troops looting and burning the Temple of Jerusalem. This looting partly funded the building of the Colosseum and it is also possible that the prisoners of war were put to work on its building site. It is not clear when exactly the fire was, so I have used a little poetic licence to have it very close to the inauguration of the amphitheatre.

The Colosseum was formally inaugurated by Titus in 80AD, with one hundred consecutive days of Games. We can't be sure of the date but looking at the Roman calendar of events and celebrations, I have chosen what seems a likely starting point. No-one knows who the architect was. No mention is made of the members of the backstage team.

Some of the specific Games I have written about actually happened. Those that I have invented were based on very similar approaches, such as the regular use of re-enacting myths and legends of the Greeks and Romans.

There is a wonderful vase in the British Museum which shows 'the dwarf assistant to a physician, showing in patients.' I loved this so much I immediately created the physician Fabius and his daughter Fabia.

The area in which Marcus and Althea live in Julia's insula is an in-joke on my part. It is approximately where my mother and I lived in Rome when I was a small child. The main road outside our block of apartments was called Via Arenula and when I looked it up it meant Sand Street (arena means sand, because of the sand scattered across arena floors). I wanted to base my characters here but thought that I might need to move them elsewhere as I didn't know in which region the fire of 80AD would have been. In one of those magical coincidences that happens when you write, when I did the research it turned out they were in exactly the right place. My mother worked in an office by the Colosseum and saw it every day on her way to work. Virgin's Street is a made-up name, many small streets had no formal name and would just have had a local name based on whatever landmarks existed. Few Vestal Virgins married after their thirty years' service and it was considered bad luck to do so as a rather large number of their husbands died.

THANKS

THANK YOU TO STREETLIGHT GRAPHICS, you give me so much more time to write! And to Debi Alper for your chameleon-like ability to shape your excellent editing skills to my style, it is mightily impressive.

Thank you to my beta readers for this book: Helen, Etain, Martin. I am always grateful for your insights.

A particular thank you to Steven Cockings for your extraordinary dedication to Roman times and enormous kindness in agreeing to read this manuscript and act as my historical consultant for the series. I am so grateful for your expertise.

Thank you to my children Seth and Izzy, who studied the Romans alongside me. Between them they made a shield, toga, honey biscuits, ate 'dormice', played Gladiators & Beasts in the ruined Roman theatres of Ostia and Gubbio and won their laurel wreaths (and ice-cream, of course) at the Colosseum itself. You made great research assistants.

Many scholars and historians were very helpful during my research period. My thanks for all their fascinating work and especially to:

The Legio Secunda Augusta re-enactment group, including the great gladiators Alisa Vanlint and James Reah, for a warm welcome and sharing their huge enthusiasm for, and knowledge of, the era. You've no idea how wonderful it is for a writer to see living breathing Romans up close, not just in books or behind glass! Also to expert in Roman clothing, Ratna Drost, for explaining the changes in fashion over time which were causing me confusion.

Professor Kathleen Coleman of Harvard University for her fascinating research on gladiators and naval shows and great kindness in helping me access her articles.

Martina Santangelo was my guide when visiting the hypogeum (the area under the arena floor where the backstage team would have worked) of the Colosseum and also gave me lots of documents on the work that went on there.

Professor Kyle Harper at the University of Oklahoma who suggested that the 'pestilence' of 80AD could have been malaria, amongst other options.

Richard Bale at the Colchester Archaeological Trust for a very enjoyable series of talks on aspects of Roman life and his kindness in answering my specific questions in great detail.

David Corfield at 422 South for the CGI reconstruction clip of the lifts/slides used to bring scenery up into the Colosseum and to Professor Michael Scott, his assistant Claire and Will at ScanLab for helping me track it down so I could watch it in slow motion!

Boxing manager Steve Goodwin who very generously spent time talking to me about the boxing industry when I was thinking about gladiators.

My respect and thanks to Caroline Lawrence, who writes wonderful books for children set in the same time period and locations. I learnt a lot from her research and ideas, loved the stories and am grateful for her kind help along the way.

All errors and fictional choices are of course mine.

CURRENT AND FORTHCOMING BOOKS INCLUDE:

Historical Fiction
China
The Consorts (novella, free on Amazon)
The Fragrant Concubine
The Garden of Perfect Brightness
The Cold Palace

Morocco
The Cup (novella, free on my website)
A String of Silver Beads
None Such as She
Do Not Awaken Love

Rome
From the Ashes
Beneath the Waves
On Bloodied Ground
The Flight of Birds

Picture Books for Children
Kameko and the Monkey-King

Non-Fiction
The Storytelling Entrepreneur
Merchandise for Authors
The Happy Commuter
100 Things to Do while Breastfeeding

BIOGRAPHY

I MAINLY WRITE HISTORICAL FICTION AND have completed two series: The Moroccan Empire, set in 11th century Morocco and Spain, and The Forbidden City, set in 18th century China. My current series focuses on the 'backstage team' of the Colosseum (Flavian Amphitheatre) set in 80AD in Ancient Rome.

I have a PhD in Creative Writing from the University of Surrey, run regular workshops at the British Library and speak at various writing festivals during the year. I was the Leverhulme Trust Writer in Residence at the British Library and won the 2019 Novel London and Page to Podcast awards. I live in London with my husband and two children. For more information on me and my books, visit my website www.MelissaAddey.com

Printed in Great Britain
by Amazon